I0546002

CONSPIRACY OF INNOCENCE

#4 in the Peter Sharp Legal Mystery Series

By Gene Grossman

From Magic Lamp Press
Venice, California

Magic Lamp

Press ™

This is a work of fiction. Names, characters, places, and incidents are either the product of the author's imagination and are used fictitiously. Resemblances to actual persons, living or dead, is coincidental.

CONSPIRACY OF INNOCENCE
Peter Sharp Legal Mystery #4

The Magic Lamp Press website address for Peter Sharp's Legal Adventures is
http://www.petersharpbooks.com
ISBN: 1-882629-09-4

The Complete Peter Sharp Legal Mystery Series

www.legalmystery.com

Single Jeopardy

…By Reason of Sanity

A Class Action

Conspiracy of Innocence

…Until Proven Innocent

The Common Law

The Magician's Legacy

The Reluctant Jurist

The Final Case

An Element of Peril

A Good Alibi

Legally Dead

"If any one bring an accusation against a man, and the accused goes to the river and leaps into the river, if he sinks in the river, his accuser shall take possession of his house. But if the river proves that the accused is not guilty, and he escapes unhurt, then he who had brought the accusation shall be put to death, while he who leaped into the river shall take possession of the house that had belonged to his accuser."
From Hammurabi's Code of 282 Laws (law #2)

Some time around 3.800 years ago, someone must have said: "there oughta be a law," and a Priest King named Hammurabi heard him. During his forty-three year reign of Mesopotamia (1792 – 1750 BC), he wrote a set of laws that covered everything from murder, to eye surgery, to gardening. Some of his rules were quite harsh, but back in those days they seem to have gotten the job done.

1

I'm an Internet shopper, so I just couldn't resist ordering a matching yellow *Hummer Shake Flashlight* from the Sharper Image just before they filed for bankruptcy. I also buy my shirts, underwear, socks, and accessories online. The only things I won't purchase online or through a catalog without first trying them on are shoes, because I firmly believe that they are one of the two things that you must try out for size and comfort first before making a commitment.

Stuart disagrees. He's both a good friend and a client, and last week he went to Thailand to spend some time with his new fiancée. They met as a result of her appearing in a mail-order bride catalog on the Internet. I tried to explain my shoe philosophy to him, but it was too late. He's in love, which means his brain has now been replaced with another part of his body, as the thought control center.

Getting a bride through an internet catalog is a very difficult concept for me to understand, so I Google 'mail order bride' and to my surprise, there are almost ten million sites listed. Included are lovely ladies from the Ukraine, Russia, Thailand, China, the Philippines, the UK, Colombia, Korea, Ethiopia, and from countries that the UN probably hasn't even heard of yet. They're all looking to make an American a very happy husband, and if you order now, they'll probably throw in their country's disease du jour at no extra cost.

The phone is ringing, but the caller ID is having a problem; it can't seem to fit the caller's number in the display, so it starts blinking, in distress. I answer anyway, and to my surprise, it's Stuart. "Stu, welcome home, how was the trip. Hey, I hear there's a club in downtown Bangkok that's named 'Lewinsky's,' and their big neon sign outside depicts a moving..." he cuts me off mid-sentence with a note of urgency.

"Pete, I'm not back in the states, I'm still in Thailand, and I've got a problem that needs taking care of." I can tell by the tone of his voice that he's worried. I just hope he's not in jail, because I don't know if they have bail bond places over there. As urgent as the problem sounds though, he doesn't seem in a panic mode like most people in jail do, so I guess it must be just a business problem. He continues, and I find out that my suspicions are correct.

"Peter, I want you to do me a favor."

"If I can, Stu. What do you need?"

"I know you're probably relaxing on your new boat in the Marina now, but I need for you to be in La Verne during the next hour. Can you do it?"

This is the most amazing request I've ever had. Stuart is one of my closest friends, and he's calling me from Thailand, to ask me to have sex with my neighbor, a lady named Laverne who lives on her houseboat, a few slips down the dock from my boat. This must be a bad phone connection, because I can't believe he's asking me that.

"Excuse me? Did I hear you correctly Stu? You want me to be in Laverne in the next hour?

"That's right, Peter, and I'm willing to pay you well for this service. Is there a problem with that?"

"I would say so, Stuart. First of all, Laverne is not home at this time of day. And second, my personal love life is none of your business, and certainly not the type of thing you should try to meddle in and insult me by offering money. What have you turned into, some sort of phone sex guy? You better get out of Thailand while you can, because I think you've crossed the line, so I'm going to do you a favor and forget you even asked me that question. Maybe it's the water that you're drinking over there, but you're certainly not acting like the gentleman I always thought you were."

7

"Peter, wait a minute. Oh, I see what… oh no, I didn't mean Laverne your neighbor. Heck no, I meant the City of La Verne. It's a town off the San Bernardino Freeway, next to Pomona, by the California Fairplex. I've got a customer of mine there, and the police are holding him for grand theft auto. He bought one of my used Camry's and I guess there was a glitch in the paperwork. If I don't get someone out there in the next hour with the original documentation, they're going to book my customer for grand theft auto, and I'll get sued for everything I'm worth."

Boy is my face red. Who knew there was town out there named La Verne? I apologize to Stuart for misunderstanding him, and tell him that I'll do what I can for his customer.

I knew this would happen. Not too long ago Stuart made what he considered to be a fantastic connection with a Tony Soprano-type of character in New 'Joisy' named Billy 'Z,' who offered to sell Stuart some like-new Toyota Camrys for much less than wholesale Blue Book. After doing some investigation, we found out that they were all either stolen cars that had been recovered by the insurance company, or 'lemons' that were re-purchased by the factory. For the first several months everything was going fine, but I knew it would only be a matter of time before someone's paperwork mistake back there might catch up with one of Stuart's customers out here, and it looks like it finally did.

"Calm down, Stu, if the paperwork you've got in the office is all in order, then we should have no problem. All you have to do is send Vinnie over to

8

the police station with the file and everything will be okay."

"I asked him, but you know Vinnie. He's deathly afraid of police stations, it's like a phobia of some sort."

I'm quite familiar with Vinnie's fear. It was especially exacerbated not too long ago when his fiancée Olive crashed into a police car while Vinnie was giving her a driving lesson.

"Okay, then what about Olive? She's not afraid of cops. Olive's not afraid of anything."

"Yeah, I know she's fearless, but I'm afraid she'd never find the police station. It's out in La Verne, on the way to Palm Springs off the 10 Freeway. Peter, you've gotta help me out on this one."

If there's anything I don't feel like doing, it's getting on the freeway before Noon. Besides, I'm supposed to attend the monthly luncheon meeting of the Venice Criminal Courts Bar Association, and if I get there on time, I can sit at the same table as my ex-wife Myra, who's the recently elected District Attorney of our county. If that doesn't work out, maybe I'll bump into Deputy City Attorney Patty Seymour. We seemed to hit it off not too long ago, and if it wasn't for the fact that Myra told me Patty was a lesbian, we might have gotten something going. She invited me to be her guest at a luncheon her club holds each month. While there, I didn't think much about the 'L.L.B.' banner hanging on the speaker's lectern, because that's the abbreviation for the degree that most of us got when graduating law school. Later that day, Myra took pleasure in letting

9

me know that it really stands for 'Lesbian Legal Branch.'

Myra and I still disagree about Patty. Just because she attends those luncheons doesn't necessarily mean that she's a lesbian. After all, I was there too wasn't I? And I'm certainly not a lesbian. Although I must admit that I share a common interest with them because I'm also strongly attracted to good-looking women. Somewhere in the back of my mind I keep thinking that given the opportunity, I can get Patty to switch over to our side. Stuart suddenly brings me back to reality. He's still on the other end of the line, calling from an extremely long distance.

"C'mon, Pete, whatta say? I'll pay you your regular rate of a hundred fifty an hour to take care of it."

He finally gets my attention. This problem should be a no-brainer. I shouldn't have to drive to La Verne, because if I get the paperwork in time, all I have to do is hand it to Myra at the luncheon and ask her to use her cell phone to call the D.A. in La Verne and have the guy released. The whole thing should take less than five minutes, and the extra one-fifty will cover my picking up the lunch tab for everyone at our table. I can act like Diamond Jim, and Stuart will pay for it all.

"Okay, Stu, send Vinnie over here as quick as you can. The meter will start running right now, because I'm going to be forced to just sit and wait for him to get here."

Stuart agrees. Ordinarily, I wouldn't be that aggressive with my fee when it comes to helping out a friend, but taking into consideration that in the last

10

year I was responsible for collecting around two million for him in settlements for his faith healer's diagnosis of the non- mesothelioma, being sued by a weight-loss client for negligent nymphomania, and for the death of his uncle in a plane crash in Thailand, I know that he's one of the richest people on the block, so there's no guilt on my part.

Vinnie will probably be here in twenty minutes, so I've still got time to call Myra and get this mess taken care of. Maybe she'll even take my word for it and have the guy released from the La Verne Police Department. I call Myra on her private line. My direct access has nothing to do with the fact that we were once married; it was a political debt she repaid for my helping to get her opponent to withdraw from the election. Unfortunately, knowing her private line number only gives me the access. Most of the time she's impossible to budge and I don't know what a favor from her office looks like.

She hasn't left for lunch yet. "Hello, this is District Attorney Scot speaking."

"Hey, it's me. Are you going to the luncheon?"

"Yes, Peter, I'm just on my way out of the door. What can I do for you? Please make it snappy, my driver is waiting downstairs in the garage."

"I've got some paperwork to give you, but I'd like you to take my word for it and call La Verne to have someone released."

"What's this about Peter?"

"One of Stuart's car customers. The paperwork wasn't processed in time and he was picked up for GTA. I've got the original paperwork

11

here, and if you make the call and have the guy released, I'll bring the paperwork to the luncheon and lunch will be on me for you and everyone at our table today."

"Sorry, sunshine, I can't second guess one of my deputies. One of my dividend checks came in today, so I can handle my own ten-dollar lunch. Have a nice trip."

So much for access. I'd better make a call to La Verne and make sure they know I'm on the way. Myra's Deputy District Attorney out there was in and said she'll be waiting for me at the police station. No doubt she's curious about what kind of guy could actually have bedded her boss. I've never been to La Verne before, but thanks to the wonders of Mapquest.com, I know that it's 50.27 miles from the Marina and should take me fifty-four minutes of freeway driving. I press 'Ctrl-P' for a copy of that Internet page so our office manager can include it with Stuart's invoice.

There's a knock on the hull, probably Vinnie with the paperwork. I'm glad he's finally got himself a steady job working for Stuart. When I first represented him he was directing porno movies, but now he's driving an armored vehicle for Stuart. It's one of two old converted Brinks trucks that Stuart had re-painted to read *He's taking it with him.* Stuart rents the trucks out for funeral processions and gets hired by disgruntled heirs for three hundred fifty a day. Vinnie and his fiancée Olive both now drive the armored vans for Stuart when they're not helping him out at his warehouse, which is full of Camrys and weight control stuff that he sells. Vinnie comes up

12

the boarding ladder onto the fifty-foot Grand Banks trawler yacht that I live on here in the Marina.

"Mister Sharp. I've got that paperwork for you. You know that Olive and I are getting married soon, don'tcha? I mean, you think it's too soon for us?"

"Vinnie, in all the years I've been giving legal advice to people, I've always refrained from telling anyone my opinion about whether or not they should get married or get divorced. That's a personal decision that you have to make on your own, and when I hear someone asking me my opinion or advice on whether or not they should take that step, it always seems like it's not me that they're asking. They're really asking themselves, and just letting me listen in on the question.

"So here's my advice. First of all, would you like to see her right now? I mean, do you spend a lot of time thinking about her and wish you could be with her? If the answer to that is yes, then you must ask yourself what you really want to do about it. If the answer is 'get married,' then don't listen to what anyone tells you. Just do it. But if the answer is that you don't think you're ready yet, then don't hurt her feelings by stringing her along and try to let her down as tactfully as possible."

'Cold feet' is an ailment that affects most men. I had it once, and now Vinnie does. Every guy in the world probably has it at least once in his life. There's no cure for it. Not even time can heal this sickness.

The drive to La Verne is completely uneventful and lacking scenery. From the 405

13

Freeway down the 10 and all the way past Covina, the only thing to see is traffic and industrial parks. At one point you can see Forest Lawn Cemetery, but I wouldn't exactly put that place on the tourist map. I must have made this trip hundreds of times over the past twenty years while going to Palm Springs or Las Vegas, but I've never stopped in La Verne. A friend of mine's father-in-law teaches history at the nearby university, so being a college town, I'm sure there are plenty of educated people there. Looking at some of the townspeople, I guess that La Verne hasn't passed the same ordinance we have in Marina del Rey, making it a crime for any woman weighing more than two hundred pounds to wear shorts in public.

I pull into the center of town and circle around a few times looking for a parking space. Driving a Hummer has both advantages and disadvantages, and finding a parking space to fit in is definitely one of the downsides. The Police Department offers a few 'guest' spots, but I'd have to park on top of a squad car's fender to get into the only space available, and that wouldn't be a good move in a town where you're trying to make a nice impression.

Another couple of times around the block convinces me that the only place I can conveniently get in and out of without causing any collateral damage to other cars is a passenger loading zone. The green curb is a nice contrast to my yellow Hummer, so I rationalize that the space was designed for me to park in it. Lettering on the curb states that there's a twenty-minute parking limit, but that should be no problem. I figure it'll take me less than ten minutes to completely convince them to release Stuart's customer, so I can get back here with plenty of time to spare.

I get directed to the Chief's office, where I have the pleasure of meeting with Wendy, the Deputy District Attorney, and Stan Olshansky, La Verne's Chief of Police.

As I enter the office, I notice that they're both glancing down at their wristwatches. This is not a good sign. It could mean that they're both in a hurry to get somewhere else, or that they're pissed that they had to wait so long for me to get there. After the introductions are made and the paperwork is shown to be satisfactory, the Chief picks up the phone, and acting upon an affirmative nod from Wendy, orders the jailer to cut Stuart's customer loose – with an apology.

That takes care of Stuart, but I can tell by the expressions on their faces that they're still not happy. "Hey, I've got an idea. It's almost two in the afternoon, and from the lean and hungry looks on your faces, I'd say that you haven't eaten lunch yet, so since I'm on an unlimited expense account this afternoon I'd be honored if the two of you would be my guests for lunch at the best place in town."

This suggestion gets their attention. They look at their wristwatches again and both agree that the public government owes them some time to eat, so it's a done deal. Now all I have to do is get my Hummer out of that loading zone.

"Great, I'll go get my car, and we can go to lunch in style. I'll be right back." The Chief stops me.

"Mister Sharp, that isn't necessary. One of the best places in town is a little Italian café just a block

15

or so down Third Street. We can go out the parking lot exit of the station and walk over there in just a few minutes. They've always got my regular table reserved, so we can sit right down when we get there."

So much for obeying the law today. This puts me in an awkward situation because in order to get out of that loading zone and avoid a ticket, I'll have to use the violation as an excuse to get my car. The ethics computer in my head quickly balances both the good and bad results of an admission like that and the Fifth Amendment wins. I decide not to incriminate myself and we go to lunch. Actually, I shouldn't have to worry about it, because I know the kid will add the amount of that parking ticket onto Stuart's invoice.

Per the Chief's suggestion, we go out the back door and walk about two blocks to the Italian Café in the center of town. Sure enough, there's an outdoor table reserved for us under the canopy, and we sit down to start our lunch with some hot Italian onion buns that get immediately dipped into a small container of garlic and oil.

This lunch is much more enjoyable than I thought it would be. The Chief is in his thirtieth year of service and will be retiring next year. He's got plenty of stories to tell, most of them about his experiences on the job in some much larger cities. Other than a car backfiring a few blocks away, it's a quiet, pleasant afternoon lunch. The quality of this place is confirmed when I'm brought the special chopped salad I designed and ordered, which includes the usual greens and tomato plus extra chopped onions, garbanzo beans, anchovies, chopped garlic and mushrooms. As a courtesy to anyone within a ten-foot radius, I keep an extra tin of breath mints with me whenever I order my special salad. The Chief orders one of the house specialties, an angel-hair pasta dish covered with large pieces of salmon.

Wendy, the Deputy D.A. was transferred out here a few years ago from Pasadena. She's married to a court clerk and is rather dull as far as stories about experiences go, but she's friendly. When the check comes, I pick it up and walk over to the cashier's counter. While paying the bill, the cashier looks past me.

"Hey, Chief. Did you hear the gunshots?"

The Chief looks at her with a puzzled expression. "Shots? What shots?"

"Oh, about twenty minutes ago, you know, when I brought your lasagna over, there were some gunshots over on the other end of town."

She must be talking about what we thought was a car backfiring. I sign the credit card receipt and we all start walking back to the station. The Chief is using his walky-talky, bawling out someone on the other end for not notifying him about the incident. I hear the poor employee on the other end apologizing. "Gee, Chief, you've told me a million times that you didn't want to be disturbed while you were at lunch."

The Chief is anxious to get back to his office, so we're walking at a pretty brisk pace when a California Highway Patrol squad car pulls up and cuts us off just as we're about to cross the street. We stop dead in our tracks, not knowing what's going on as the two CHP officers jump out of the car with their guns drawn. One of the State troopers shouts out some orders.

"Step aside, Chief. You too, lady."

The Chief and Wendy quickly follow their instructions. There are only three of us walking together, so with those two ordered to step aside, that leaves only me. I haven't felt like this since kindergarten, when I lost out in a game of musical chairs. Both cops are now pointing their guns directly at me.

"Peter Sharp, you're under arrest for the murder of Michael Luskin. Please turn around and lock your hands behind your neck." At least they said please.

2

In another two minutes I'm handcuffed and seated in the back seat of their CHP car. The Chief sits down next to me as we ride back to the Police Station. On the way, we pass by the loading zone where I parked my car. The brightly painted green curb is there, but my car isn't. "Chief, sorry for the inconvenience, but as soon as they take these cuffs off of me, I'd like to fill out a stolen car report."

One of the CHP officers turns around from the front seat. "Let me guess… it's a yellow Hummer."

By the time we drive that remaining block to the police station, the press has arrived. I'll never know how they manage to appear so magically, like buzzards around a fresh kill. I know that they have

18

radio scanners in their cars to listen in on police communications, but that still doesn't explain how they can slice through traffic like it's warm butter.

I'm being held firmly by both of my arms and being led into the front door of the police station. This is what's called the 'perp walk.' There are only about three reporters with cameramen there, all shouting questions at the Chief, who ignores them as we charge into the station.

Once inside, the Chief looks at both CHP officers. "Okay, boys, what've we got here?"

"Chief, while you were at lunch, there was a drive-by shooting on the other side of town, close to the freeway ramp. We were passing by, heard the shots, and saw a yellow Hummer speeding down the street. By the time we got off the freeway and made it through traffic in the direction of where the Hummer went, we were too late. Whoever was driving dumped it. They must have made a switch back to their stand-by vehicle and disappeared.

"We found about six shell casings inside the Hummer. It's a good thing we were close, because it didn't give them time to police their brass. At that point we didn't know if they were still in town, or had made it onto the freeway.

"Our onboard DMV computer showed that the Hummer is registered to Mister Sharp here, so we had the station send his driver's license picture to our portable computer screen. We were on our way to your office when we saw him walking down the street. We had no way of knowing that you were all together, so we had to follow proper procedure."

The Chief explains to them that we were all having lunch together when the shooting took place. Everyone there seems to now understand that the killers came into town, borrowed my Hummer, and did their job. The Chief theorizes that the reason they decided to use a yellow Hummer is because they were trying to send prospective business associates a message that probably says 'we're here, we're killing someone for a reason, and we're not afraid to be seen, so you'd better not mess with us.' Notwithstanding the fact that the victim was an upstanding citizen, we all can't help but feel that this was a drug-related hit. The Chief also tells us all how much Michael Luskin will be missed, and that for a guy who was orphaned as a child and raised in foster homes, he made a success out of his life and was well respected by the entire community.

The luncheon goes well. Myra is the most popular one there, being the first female elected to the office of Los Angeles District Attorney. The only small hitch happens just after lunch as the speaker is concluding his droning on. "A note was just handed to me about the arrest of one of our own for a drive-by shooting in La Verne, California a little while ago. We certainly hope that he's vindicated for this murder."

At the sound of the word 'La Verne,' Myra's head goes down into her hands. She knows in her heart that if a murder took place in a small town being visited for the first time by her screw-up ex-husband, he's involved somehow. Several of Myra's employees are sitting at her table, and they remember hearing her mention that Peter wouldn't be joining them because he had some pressing business to take care of in La Verne.

Myra uses her cell phone to call Wendy's office in La Verne and hears the whole story, including the fact that Peter wasn't involved in the shooting, but it was his car that was stolen and used by the killers.

As she steps out into the street outside the restaurant, Myra is ambushed by a group of reporters who obviously haven't yet heard that Peter was cleared of any wrongdoing out there in La Verne. They shout questions at her, and the main thrust of their inquiries is whether or not she would recuse herself from the prosecution of her ex-husband, to avoid giving any impression of giving him special treatment. She only has one thing to say to them.

"If anyone should worry about special treatment, it should be the killer who guns down someone in cold blood on the street in broad daylight, because in every case we prosecute like that, I guarantee that there will be something special added, but it won't be treatment, it will be circumstances. And as you should all know, special circumstances in a murder case can justify our asking for the death penalty.

"And as for the prosecution of my ex-husband, attorney Peter Sharp, it would be my pleasure to personally stick the needle in his arm if he kills someone, but I'm afraid that I won't get the chance to do it this time, because he wasn't involved in any way in this drive-by shooting. I've just spoken to our chief deputy in La Verne and learned that my ex-husband's car was stolen and used in the shooting, which took place at the exact same time that he was on the other side of town, having lunch with the local police chief and a deputy from my office, so I guess I'll have to find some other way to needle him. Thank you." Her statement having been made, Myra is whisked away by her waiting driver.

Thanks to some successful case outcomes in the past year, Peter was able to purchase the boat of his dreams… a beautiful fifty-foot Grand Banks trawler yacht – and that's where Suzi, an adorable little Chinese pre-teen girl who is also Peter's legal ward, is watching the local news. As usual, her assistant Bernie is by her side. Hearing about Peter's arrest and subsequent release and then watching her idol Myra on the news, she makes a remark to Bernie. "I really shouldn't let him leave the boat too often. He just doesn't know how to keep out of trouble. I wish he'd grow up." Bernie probably agrees with her but doesn't say much in response, because he's the silent type – which is understandable, because he's also a huge Saint Bernard.

The Chief tells me that he's going to visit with the murdered man's widow. She's already been notified of her husband's death, but he wants to offer his condolences in person. He tells me that she's community minded and volunteers her time at a local suicide prevention hot line and that he's met her on several occasions. He asks if I'd like to come along with him. I accept his invitation, maybe to apologize

22

to her because it was my car that was used by her husband's killers. I don't really know why I accepted, but it doesn't make any difference, because now we're in the back seat of the Chief's car, being driven to the Luskin residence.

I remark to him that this must be one of the nicest homes in the area. He agrees, telling me that her husband had done quite well. In addition to this big house, they own several industrial building on the outskirts of town that are rented out to various commercial companies.

The widow Luskin is an attractive woman in her mid thirties. She greets us at the door and invites us in. It's a terrible thought, but I can't help feel that she'll have no problem finding someone to replace her deceased husband. Even after experiencing what she went through today, she's still a looker. We express our deep sympathies for her loss and the Chief explains who I am. She graciously lets me know that it wasn't my fault that the killers decided to take my car instead of someone else's. Her maid serves us some coffee and cake. As we're leaving, I let her know that I'm an attorney and hand her my business card, telling her that if there's anything I can ever do for her, not to hesitate calling.

She tells me that the only thing she's concerned about is the insurance company and her bills. As the Chief and I are leaving, we both assure her that everything will turn out okay.

It's been a long day during the past two hours and I know that if I don't hit the road now I'll be sitting in bumper-to-bumper rush hour traffic all the way back to Los Angeles. I thank the Chief for his hospitality and apologize for not taking the opportunity to avail myself of his booking procedure. He tells me that he's already heard from Deputy D.A. Wendy and that she's spoken to her boss about the matter, explaining that I've been cleared.

"Chief, being cleared legally and being cleared with a woman are two completely different things."

"I know, Mister Sharp. I've been married for over thirty years now."

We exchange a few chauvinistic remarks about women and I then ask him if one of his people could drive me to the Hummer.

"Oh, we'll be glad to give you a lift, but it won't be to the Hummer. We'll be keeping that for a while until our crime scene people finish going through it. Instead, we'll be giving you a ride over to Budget Rent-a-Car." Damn. It didn't occur to me, but the Chief is right. The car is evidence, so he has to hold on to it for while. No sense arguing with him about it, because he's one hundred percent right.

One of Chief Olshansky's officers drops me off at the local rent-a-car place and as I'm exiting his vehicle he hands me an envelope. "This is from the Chief. He wanted to make sure I gave it to you before you left town."

I'm in no mood to read at the moment, so I put the envelope in my jacket pocket, thank him for the ride, and head into the rental car office.

The Budget office in La Verne doesn't have any Hummers to rent. In fact, they don't have any luxury cars at all to rent. I am now driving back to Los Angeles in a like-new Ford Focus, which has neither air-conditioning nor electric windows.

Over the noise of rush hour freeway traffic I hear my cell phone ringing. The caller display show's Stuart's office number at his Van Nuys warehouse. I answer. It's Vinnie calling.

"Mister Sharp, I spoke to Stuart and told him that it's all straightened out in La Verne. He thanks you very much. I told him about the other little problem there, too."

"You mean the drive-by murder in broad daylight, using my Hummer, which was stolen and is now impounded? The murder I was arrested for? You mean that little problem, Vinnie?"

"Er, yeah, Mister Sharp, I told him about that too. He says he's sorry to hear about it and that he wants you to use one of his Camrys until your car is released, and that he'll personally drive you back to La Verne to get it."

"Okay Vinnie. Here's what you do. I'm bringing this little toy car I'm now driving over to the Rent-a-car's Van Nuys office and turning it back in. You meet me there and we'll go back to your warehouse for me to pick up a grown-up's car to drive."

It took a little over an hour and I'm now exiting the Northbound 405 Freeway at Burbank Boulevard. As I make a left turn onto Sepulveda I spot Vinnie parked and waiting for me in front of the Budget Rent-a-Car lot. After turning in the Ford Focus I get into the Camry with Vinnie for the ride to Stuart's warehouse. During the drive I mention that Stuart must be spending a bundle making all those calls from Thailand to here. Vinnie explains that

Stuart has learned some way to use the computer to make international calls for only two cents a minute, over the Internet. Leave it to Stuart, the most entrepreneurial guy I know.

When we get the warehouse, Vinnie shows me the row of Camry's and lets me know that Stuart says I can take whatever car I want. I know about the key box on the warehouse wall, so I go over there, remove a set of keys and to Vinnie's surprise I walk past the Camry's, unlock Stuart's personal Lincoln Town Car and drive it out of the garage.

On the way out, Vinnie is waiting for me at the raised garage door. I wave at a smiling Vinnie. "You're a class act, Mister Sharp."

This is a definite improvement. It's hard to believe that the same company manufactures both cars I've driven this afternoon: The Ford Focus and the Lincoln Town Car.

The 405 Freeway is usually packed this time of day, so I take a leisurely ride South on Sepulveda, up through the tunnel near Mulholland and then down through Brentwood. I take Sunset Boulevard West to Barrington, and then south to Venice Boulevard, which I take west to the Marina.

Back at the boat, I see the kid and her beast going from the galley to her forward stateroom. The look she gives me is the same one usually reserved for the dog when he accidentally steps in his water bowl and spills it all over the floor.

She must think I'm a big dummy who only serves two useful purposes in her life - dragging heavy sacks of dog food up from the cart and onto the boat, and driving her downtown every quarter where she takes some examinations at the school board. Her grades on the home schooling tests were so high, that they now insist she take her tests in an officially supervised setting. Her IQ is probably off the charts, and it never ceases to amaze me how she runs our law practice from her computer.

When her stepfather died in a plane crash with Stuart's uncle, I took over as her legal guardian, and I keep wondering who's the guardian and who's the ward.

Once the two of them are out of the room, I sit down for a moment to relax. My jacket is hanging on the back of a nearby chair and I see something white sticking out of the inside breast pocket. It's the envelope that the Chief wanted me to have. I reach for the envelope and sit back to read it, thinking it's probably a nice note from him inviting me back to La Verne soon.

I was partly right. It is an invitation to come back and visit his building. It's a parking ticket for unauthorized use of a loading zone.

3

I call Chief Olshansky to thank him for his generous going-away gift. He beats me to it. "Mister Sharp, I issued you that ticket for two reasons. First, you voluntarily confessed to having

27

parked there, and second, I wanted to make sure you'd be coming back to our little town so that I could return the courtesy and buy you lunch."

"Chief, I guarantee that I'll be back in your little town to get that free lunch, and warn you that I'm going to demand a jury trial on my ticket. I'm entitled to have a little fun every once in a while too."

He chuckles and we agree to be friendly enemies until my case is over.

"By the way, Chief, did they find anything of use in my car?"

"Other than the shell casings, they didn't leave much. We dusted the casings, door handles, seat adjustment levers, shift knob, steering wheel, and back of the rear-view mirror. Our techie says he got some good results, probably because the Chippies got there before they had a chance to wipe things down. The return date on your ticket is next week, so when you get here, you can drive your Hummer home." 'Chippies' is an affectionate nickname we use here to describe the State Troopers, members of the CHP - our California Highway Patrol.

"Thanks, Chief, I appreciate that. What about the victim's body? Did you or the D.A. request an autopsy?"

"Naah. We all know what the cause of death was. All we were interested in was recovering the lead from his body to make sure it matches the casings we found in your car and see if it gives us a positive hit on any others in the database. Mrs. Luskin called and pleaded with us to release the body as soon as possible, so after we remove the bullets and finish with some photos, we're going to let the funeral parlor pick him up."

I'll let him worry about solving the murder case. I'm too busy trying to figure out how to beat the ticket he gave me.

Several days have passed by with nothing exciting going on, so I'm pleased when the phone rings and my caller ID display shows that it's Stuart's home phone number.

"Hey, Stuart, I know this is a local call, so now I can righteously welcome you back home. You still single?"

"Oh yeah, I'm still single, but not for long. That's what I'd like to talk to you about. I want to bring my girlfriend over here, but it requires a special kind of passport, and I want to see if you can help me get through the paperwork."

"Okay Stu, I've got to go back to La Verne in a couple of days to make a court appearance and pick up my Hummer, so if it's okay with you, I'll hang onto your Town Car. When it's time to go out there, I'll pick you up and we can talk about Thailand all the way to La Verne."

Stuart agrees, so I've got a car to use until next week, and a ride to La Verne to pick up the Hummer and for my arraignment in traffic court. It's a funny thing about criminal charges when they happen to an attorney. For some reason you stop thinking like an attorney and start sounding like a client, with thoughts like 'they can't really do this to me, can they?' That's probably why people should never try to represent themselves in court; they'll be guaranteed to have the fool that they turn into as a client.

I find out that I'm not the only attorney who is having trouble with the law. Over the past few months I've been fortunate enough to earn some pretty big fees on cases assigned to me by Charles Indovine, the senior partner of a huge insurance defense firm. His main client is Uniman Insurance, and for having been successful in saving them from paying out on some pretty big policies, I've been rewarded quite nicely.

I hear the pitter-patter of huge paws. On our boat, whenever the animal comes into my private area it's because he's the bearer of tidings. We call it dog-mail and it takes the form of a note tucked into his collar. I finally convinced the kid to stop letting him deliver my mail in his mouth because inkjet printing has a tendency to smear when it gets drooled on.

The message is removed and the messenger receives the tip he waits for: a pat on the head and a 'good boy' compliment. He turns and makes a not-so-graceful exit, knocking things off of the table with his tail. The note is a personal message from Charles Indovine. He wants to talk to me, but not on the telephone. He wants to meet in person.

Indovine and I exchange some e-mails under the heading of 'policy discussion.' He obviously doesn't want his office to know anything about this. We agree to meet for dinner near my boat at the Charthouse Restaurant. It's a pricy place to eat, but I'm sure that he'll be picking up the tab.

My Charthouse barstool near the window gives me a clear view of Charles Indovine's limo pulling into the parking lot. A real gentleman, he gets out of the car himself without demanding that the driver open his door. The limo driver parks down the street and Charles joins me for a drink while we wait for our table. Charles leans over to me and speaks in a hushed tone. I have no idea why he's talking like this, because there's we're the only two people sitting here at the bar. This is obviously something he considers extremely confidential.

"Peter, I've got a slight legal problem and wonder if you could possibly help me out with it. Of course, you'll be given a nice retainer, and I'd appreciate it if on this matter alone, you send invoices to our firm for a special consulting service, instead of the real reason I need your assistance."

He usually calls me 'Sharp,' but this time I'm 'Peter.' Boy, he must really be in trouble to get on a first name basis with someone like me, who went to a non-accredited evening law school. As long as we're using first names tonight, I might as well go along with the program.

"Sure, Charles I'll be glad to help you out. What's the problem?"

His answer is a real shocker, because I'd never expect a guy like him to be in this situation.

"Peter, I was arrested last night. The police were nice enough to let me out on my own recognizance, so no bail bondsman was required, but I've got to fight this thing and keep it as quiet as possible."

Boy, he caught me off guard with that one. Years of experience as a trial lawyer kick in and I manage to keep a straight face with no emotion.

"That's unfortunate, Charles, why don't you tell me all about it and let's see what can be done."

The waiter shows us to our table, but because it's completely surrounded by others, we request a more secluded spot further from the windows, facing the water and closer to the bar. It's a slow middle of the week so there's are several empty tables we can sit at back in the corner, away from anyone else who might come into that section of the restaurant. Once seated, Charles tells me the story, but it doesn't seem as bad to me as he feels it is.

After his divorce he began seeing one of his secretaries on a social basis. He drove himself to her apartment on the evenings they got together because he didn't want his driver to know about the affair.

Because she lives in a neighborhood that isn't as nice as the one where Charles lives, he decided that it would be nice to have some protection with him, so he started carrying a small .38 caliber snub-nosed revolver with a 2-inch barrel, just like the police detectives used before they switched over to Glock and Baretta automatics. It was originally purchased by him and duly registered in his name.

The problem is that he's not licensed to carry a concealed weapon. Several years ago he did have a valid Carry Permit, but that was a favor from some past assistant police chief that he helped get promoted. He lost track of the time and was under the impression that the permit was either still in force or had been renewed automatically, like some real property leases.

He had a few drinks at his secretary's house and later that evening as he was leaving, he stumbled down her front stairs. Just at that time, a police squad car was passing by, and seeing a well-dressed gentleman having some difficulty walking, especially in this neighborhood where he obviously didn't reside, they stopped to assist him. Everything would have been okay if the revolver hadn't fallen out of his coat pocket and landed on the foot of one of the cops.

"I've gotta tell you Charles, this doesn't sound as serious as you make it. With a copy of your original permit, I can probably make a good argument to the judge that you were confused about the expiration date. He's probably one of the many judges on your election campaign list, and you'll get off with a slap on the wrist and a warning not to do it again."

"That's not good enough."

"What do you mean that's not good enough? Didn't you hear me? I told you I could probably make this whole thing go away with no conviction, no publicity, no probation, no nothing. What could possibly be better? You want me to do it for free too?"

"Peter, I hear you perfectly. It's not the results you offer that I have a problem with, it's how you intend to go about it. I don't merely want this thing to go away because of your ability to make a good argument on my behalf to a judge I've contributed to, I want this thing to go away on a constitutional ground."

33

This guy amazes me. In my twenty plus years of practicing criminal law, I've never once heard a client turn down a promise of acquittal. That's all that any criminal client wants. But is that good enough for Mister Indovine? No. He wants me to make a Second Amendment argument.

"Now it's my hearing that must be defective Charles. Am I correct in assuming that you want to make this a federal case? You want me to argue that you've got a constitutional right to carry a concealed weapon, a right you claim is guaranteed by the Second Amendment?"

"That's correct Peter. You heard me right. And I don't care how much it costs. I don't even care if we lose. I just want the argument made."

"There's something you're not telling me Charles. I know you're an intelligent man who watches his finances. I can't believe that all of a sudden you want to push this rock up a mountain just to make a fool out of both of us, spend a lot of money, and ultimately lose. Not you, Charles. There's got to be another reason, so let's have it. Why?" He hesitates and takes another sip of his drink while he thinks over whether or not to let me in on the secret agenda or not. His decision is made, and I now find out what's really going on.

"Peter, our firm bills several million dollars a year to companies like Uniman Insurance and some other large carriers. We make a very nice living off of our practice, but that's nothing compared to what we're going to make if we can land a certain big client we're now talking to. He's a multi-billionaire who wants to retain our firm on a yearly basis. If he

34

does, that will mean another couple of million dollars annually for us. In order for him to make his final decision, we want to show him what we stand for."

"Oh, now I get it Charles. You want me to fight this battle for you so he can see 'losing' is what your firm stands for."

"Not quite, Peter. He's an ultra right wing conservative who donates millions a year to the National Rifle Association, and we want him to spend that much with us each year too. We want to show him how strongly we feel about the Second Amendment. It doesn't matter what we really feel like, or even if we win or lose. He'll be impressed by the fact that we stood up and fought for what we he thinks we believed…it's what he believes too."

Charles reaches into his pocket, pulls out an envelope and hands it to me. I open it up and see that it's a check made out to me for fifty thousand dollars.

"That's just an initial retainer, Peter. If you can get this case up to the appellate court level, there'll be another few checks like that waiting for you. And don't worry, if you can't get it any further than the Municipal Court, there's no rebate expected. The check is yours no matter what. Win or lose… but please, no quick making it go away. There must an argument made in court somewhere... an argument that this new prospective client can come and watch being presented."

He can tell that I'm hesitating. I certainly want to keep this check, but don't know if I want to make a spectacle out of myself by arguing a losing case and polarizing an entire universe of prospective clients. I've got a good relationship with the legal community. My ex-wife isn't in love with me, but like the rest of the bench and bar that I'm constantly in contact with, she has a respect for my ability as an attorney and my reputation as a guy who never bullshits. If I say I'm going to try a case, they know it's not just to bully them into a plea - I'm really prepared to take it all the way to a trial. And when I make a representation to the court about one of my clients, the judges know I'm not lying to earn an extra couple of bucks by saying that I know the defendant for years and personally vouch for his intention to honor his release terms and return for further court appearances.

If I sell out and take this check to make an argument merely for the purpose of helping Indovine land a big fish, I'll be jeopardizing the reputation it's taken me over twenty years to build, and I don't know if I can afford to do it, because it might cost more than this in the long run.

"What's the matter Peter, do you have a problem with the Second Amendment?"

"Charles, I know the Second Amendment by heart. It's only one sentence. It says that 'A well-regulated Militia being necessary to the security of a free State, the right of the people to keep and bear Arms shall not be infringed.' When I was in high school I was a card-carrying member of the NRA and competed on our ROTC rifle team. And as for your question about me having a problem about the Second Amendment, my personal feelings or problems have nothing to do with whether or not I accept a case.

"Since we've been doing business together, on two occasions your firm has retained me to represent people charged with murder, and on those occasions you never once asked me if I have a problem with murder. I'm a professional. I represent any client I take on, to the best of my ability with no regard to any personal problem I may have with his or her conduct. You should know that. You're a professional too.

"My only concern here is not about your right to carry a gun; it's about my duty as a sworn officer of the court to not commence spurious or frivolous actions for some other purpose than to serve my client."

"That's admirable, Peter, but do you know how many lawyers I can find, probably in this restaurant, who would love to have that check you've got there in your hand? You don't think that by trying to get this case up to a higher level that you'd be serving your client? Hell, Peter, that'll serve me just fine. I don't care if I go down in flames, as long as those flames are printed in color on the front page of the newspaper that my prospective client's butler delivers to him the next morning.

"I'll tell you what. You take your time and think about it for a few days. My arraignment in Municipal Court isn't scheduled for another week or so. If by the time of my court date you haven't decided to come on board, you can send the check back. But if anything else happens, and I mean anything else, you keep the check. Is it a deal?"

"And you pay for dinner here tonight too?"

37

"Yes, Peter, I'll pay for dinner tonight too. Now, put that check in your pocket and let's head for the salad bar."

Back at the boat after dinner I call Myra and discuss the whole matter with her on a 'hypothetical' basis, on the usual 'no names mentioned' basis. We talk about it for at least an hour and come up with no conclusions. Once in a while I see the kid making trips to the refrigerator, so I know she's probably tuned in to the whole discussion. What she doesn't overhear she'll probably worm out of Myra. I suspect that they talk on the phone every day. The kid is quite talkative to a lot of people, but I never made it onto her list.

I hang up the phone and sit here looking at Indovine's check for a little while. Out of the corner of my eye I spot the kid peeking at me from behind her slightly ajar stateroom door. I know exactly what's going through her mind. This retainer is outside work which has nothing to do with our law firm... the one that she runs... the one that I took over from her deceased stepfather and in which she's an equal partner. If I keep this retainer, the firm gets no portion of it. That's our deal on my outside work. On the other hand, if for any reason the law firm gets involved in it, she gets a portion of the fee for administration costs and other charges she consistently dreams up on a daily basis.

Her little brain is probably spinning at top speed now, trying to figure out how to get her paws on this check.

4

Stuart is out in front of his warehouse waiting for me as I pull up in the Lincoln Town Car. This is the first chance we've had to have a real conversation since his return last week from Thailand, and he can't wait for our long ride to La Verne so he can fill me in on all the details.

It takes him from Van Nuys all the way through downtown Los Angeles just to finish describing his condo there. And in answer to a question I started to ask him during his last phone call to me from Thailand, he tells me that yes, there is an establishment in Bangkok called 'Lewinsky's' and the person that the place is named after probably wouldn't be too happy seeing the neon sign outside the place, complete with it's graphic, simulated motion.

We finally get around to talking about the main thing on his mind. He wants to bring his sweetheart over here so they can get married. I tell him the results of my research and from consulting an attorney friend of mine who specializes in immigration law.

"Stu, if you're really serious about this, you're going to have to apply for a fiancée visa."

"Wow. You mean they really have things like that?"

"Yes. It's really called that, but the official designation 'Fiancée Visa K-1' and it's good for only ninety days. If you don't marry her within that period

39

of time, she must return to Thailand and will never be able to get another fiancée visa to come here. They only give a girl one shot at getting married here, so if you're not serious about this, you'd better not apply."

"Peter, I'm really serious. What should I do first?"

"The requirements aren't that tough. All you have to do is establish that both of you are legally able to get married, with no existing marriages still valid. The other requirement is that you've personally met with her during the past two years."

"No problem, I've got pictures to prove it."

"Spare me the details Stu, I'm just telling you the rules. If you want to start the ball rolling you should contact the local INS office because you'll have to file your petition with them. Your petition will also need two additional forms completely filled out. They'll want your birth certificate, passport photos, a picture of the two of you together, your financial info, and a lot more stuff, so be prepared to go into form hell."

Hey, Pete, I've got an idea. There's a mail order bride place not far from my warehouse. that specializes in girls from the Philippines. I'll bet they have all the forms and everything, and know exactly what to do. Whatta think about me using them?"

"Sure Stu, that might work, but what happens when you bring a bottle of wine into a restaurant and tell the waiter that you'll drink your own instead ordering some from the restaurant?"

"Uh, I think they charge you a corkage fee, which is usually about the same amount their lowest price wine sells for."

"Exactly, my friend. If you go into that place and want them to do the work without ordering from their meat catalog, they'll want a corkage fee."

"No problemo. I'll just drop a grand on the desk and have them do all paperwork."

"Whatever works for you, pal. By the way, have you thought about a pre-nup?"

"Oh, you mean one of those things you make a woman sign before you marry her?"

"Yep, that's what it is. And considering the substantial assets you've accumulated, and your ongoing successful businesses, you should definitely consider having one drawn up."

"Sure Pete, what do you think it should say? Something about her not getting anything of mine if we ever split up?"

"C'mon Stu, you can't do that. It has to be fair. In fact, there's a mnemonic device they use to describe it. It's called F.A.I.R. The 'F' is for Fairness, 'A' is for Assets and Liabilities that must be fully disclosed, 'I' is for Independent counsel, because the same lawyer can't approve the agreement for both of you, and the 'R' is for Reasonable time. You can't shove the agreement under her nose the day of the wedding. She's got to have a reasonable amount of time to have her own lawyer look it over before she signs."

"Really, Pete, they insist that she has time to think it over?"

"Yes Stu, there have been some big cases where the agreement was thrown out because the wife didn't have time to get counsel."

"Oh yeah, name one."

41

"Okay, ever hear of a billionaire named Carl Icahn? He had his lawyer draw up a pre-nup that said his wife would get absolutely nothing in property distribution or alimony if they ever divorced. And to make it even worse, he had her sign it on their wedding day, when she was already pregnant with their first child."

"What happened, did they split up? Did the agreement work?"

"They were married for around twenty years before they split up. I don't know if the matter's been completely settled, but the last time I read about it, she was receiving about thirty thousand a month in support, and she allegedly turned down a fifteen million dollar settlement offer. What I'm trying to say here is that you can't be unreasonable."

"I get it. And thanks a lot, Peter, I really appreciate your taking the time to look into it for me."

The rest of the conversation is all about his fiancée, and our talking all the way really shortens the trip, because before we know it we're pulling up in front of the La Verne Police Station, where my Hummer is parked taking up two spaces. I'll probably be getting another ticket in the mail next week.

I thank Stuart for the ride and use of his car and almost make a clean getaway before he starts to tell me out his new business. It's the first assignment he' gotten for his private investigation company, and it's from Mister Indovine's defense firm. We agree to meet again later during the week to talk about it.

42

Chief Olshansky is in his usual good mood and the release forms for my Hummer are all ready for me to sign. We exchange small talk for a while and then check our calendars to see what would be a good date for me to come back for my traffic ticket trial. Once a date is agreed on, I'm on my way over to the courthouse for my arraignment and trial setting.

"Oh, by the way Chief, how's that murder case coming along. Any leads?"

"Yes, counselor, as a matter of fact we did get lucky on that one. Some of the prints recovered from your car matched up with a couple of very bad boys involved in the drug trade up in Oregon. We can't tell for sure if their prints got into your car before the day of the shooting or not, but because there were several sets that overlapped yours, we ruled you out as a co-conspirator."

"Gee, I'm glad to hear that Chief, because I try to avoid getting arrested more than once a week. What about the victim's wife? How's she doing?"

"About as well as can be expected. After taking some of the deceased's blood for a DNA sample and getting those slugs out of him, we released the body to a local funeral parlor. I think she's going to have the body cremated. I don't really blame her. Funerals are miserable rituals that prolong the healing process."

"If there was no question about Luskin's identity, why did you take that DNA sample?"

"The widow doesn't even know we took it. The insurance company wanted it. I guess they've been having some problems with husbands that they

43

pay death benefits for who magically are found alive on some tropical island sometime in the future."

"What good will DNA from the deceased do unless they have something to compare it to."

"They do. He was one of those ultra conservative types who had some of his own blood stored at the local hospital, just in case he needed a transfusion some time in the future. I guess he wanted to avoid any possibility of getting a disease from some donated blood. It's been known to happen, you know." His answer satisfies my curiosity. I go to the Pomona courthouse, make my impassioned plea of not guilty, and set a trial date.

Before heading back to the Marina I think it would be nice to say hello to the widow Luskin. I've heard that she mentioned my name to the insurance company and it may have helped to get her claim processed a little faster. I call her number and she says it's okay to stop by, so I'm now pulling up to her home and see that she's standing in the open doorway waiting for me. Gee, she looks nice. I know that her husband was recently gunned down, and every-one says they had a loving relationship, but all men are dogs... especially me, and she does look very nice standing there in that open doorway.

"Hi, I hope you don't mind my stopping by. I had to come back here to pick up my car, so I thought I'd see how you were doing."

"Oh, that was so nice of you. Why don't you come in and have a cup of tea before you drive back to Los Angeles?"

This is dangerous. She's beautiful and I'm horny. That makes for a bad combination, but I'm

44

just going to have to control myself, play it by ear, and see how things develop.

She brings out a nice spread that includes cheese, crackers, and some other little things I never saw before. We have our tea, and she tells me that once she mentioned my name to the insurance company, they never called to bother her again with stupid questions. She was really impressed by that.

Chief Olshansky mentioned to me that she volunteered her time on a Suicide Prevention Hotline, so I figure that might start a new conversation and maybe give me another half hour to look at her.

She says that there was quite a bit of training involved, and also mentions the fact that a recent survey shows that every eighteen minutes another life is lost to suicide, for a total of about thirty thousand a year. She also tells me that suicide is now the eleventh cause of death in the United States, and in the last forty years, the rate of adolescent suicides has tripled.

We spend the next hour discussing other interesting statistics and I find out that her local Prevention Center gets calls from all the Western states. Many times a person is reluctant to call their local prevention center for fear of being recognized, as a result of incidents described that may have been publicized.

I tell her how much her work is helping people out, but that it's time to try to beat the traffic back to Los Angeles. She also knows I'll be returning to La Verne for a court appearance in a couple of weeks and insists that after my legal business is done, I call and stop by.

I really don't know what to make of my progress to date. She walks me to the door and gently shakes my hand as I leave. Driving back to the Marina, I'm trying to analyze what the body language meant, if anything. The only thing I can put my finger on is that she didn't completely open the door as she shook my hand. If she did, that might mean that the visit is over with no chance of a hug or kiss goodbye. The door was about half open, which meant that a peck on the cheek might have been in order, but I didn't have the guts. Next time I stop by, I'm going to be very aware of the exact position of the door when I leave. In fact, I think I'll invite her out to lunch, like sort of showing my appreciation for the cheese and crackers tray. Maybe that'll soften her up a little and she'll shake my hand before opening the door when I leave. At least I got to know what her first name is. It's Beverly, a beautiful name for a beautiful girl.

My thoughts, along with listening to Tony Bennett sing, make the trip back a lot shorter. Too bad she's geographically undesirable. My daydreaming of her is interrupted by another CD track that comes on featuring Count Basie's big band. Now I'm sitting on the stage of the Hollywood Bowl, at the piano. Basie is standing up in front leading the band and we're playing an introduction for the singer, who's some skinny guy with blue eyes and wearing a bow tie. He comes walking out with a cordless microphone in his hand. On his way, while still in the wings, he starts singing " The Lady Is A Tramp," and by the time he gets to the center of the stage, the place is going crazy. People are standing up, applauding.

My daydream concert continues with Mel Torme, Joe Williams, Ella Fitzgerald, and then Tony Bennett, and before I know it, reality sets back in and I'm approaching the Marina. I don't think it's necessary to lock my car to protect my CD collection because petty thieves usually aren't over twenty, and just not interested in the music of my generation. Not too long ago I remember reading a news item about some convenience store owner that solved his problem of teenagers loitering outside the front door by playing recordings of Lawrence Welk. It worked. That must have been like holding up a cross in front of a vampire. The kids scattered every time Larry's band started playing that potted palm, society two-beat dance music.

Whenever I hear these classic old songs I'm reminded of the times we used to dance to them at our high school dances and social gatherings. Unfortunately, high school reminds me of my days on the Von Steuben ROTC rifle team and NRA membership, which then brings me back to Charles Indovine and his crusade to get a new client.

I think there's a way to handle this. His arraignment isn't for a while and the judge should have no worries about him being a flight risk, so I'll appear at his arraignment and ask for another month or two before we make a plea. I'm sure we'll get the extension, and then there'll be more time to figure out how to retain both my integrity and his fifty grand.

47

If the problem becomes insurmountable, I can always offer to make the fee a law firm matter and let the kid figure out some way to solve the problem. The combination of her IQ and a little innocent childish greed will no doubt result in an answer. It usually does.

Back at the boat, a new dog-mail message informs me that Mister Uniman called. He's probably Charles Indovine's largest insurance client, so I'm curious about why he'd call me directly instead of going through Charles' office.

I call his company and amazingly, get put right through to him.

"Thanks for getting back to me Peter. How're things going with you?"

"Fine, Mister Uniman. Listen, I appreciate your courtesy, but being the busy guy I know you are, there must be an important business reason why you called me directly, so why don't we save your valuable time by cutting right to the chase."

"Very good Peter. I like your direct approach. The reason for my call is because I understand you were in La Verne that day the shooting took place. I also saw on the news that it was your car they used. Now I know you had nothing to do with the shooting, but since you're peripherally connected to the players out there, I'd like you to look into the matter for us. With the combination of Mrs. Luskin's claims for life and mortgage insurance policies, we're looking at an exposure of over three million dollars. When our investigator called the widow she referred us to you. Said that you gave her your card and offered to help."

48

"That's right, I did. I was with the Chief of Police when he went to pay his condolences and I felt a little guilty because it was my car the shots were fired from, so I promised to do what I could for her."

"Well, that's fine. As long as you're already into the matter, maybe you could find out if anything's fishy there."

"Mister Uniman, I appreciate your position, but I can't serve two masters at the same time. If I find out that there's some out-and-out fraud, I'll be sure to let you know about it and I'm sure you'll be as generous as you've been in the past, but absent some obvious hanky panky, I think I'd rather not work for you on this one. Nothing personal, you understand, it's just that I really want to see this poor woman get the benefits she's entitled to."

"Okay, Peter. I respect your integrity in this matter, but please, if you sense anything wrong, please don't hesitate to call us. I'm sure you know that your usual ten percent bonus is still on the table."

Very strange. Does he know something I don't know about in this matter, or is he just being the normal insurance company who doesn't enjoy paying claims?

The phone rings. It's a call from Van Nuys but I don't recognize the number. I answer and hear an hysterical Olive.

"Mister Sharp, you've got to help me. Vinnie doesn't trust me. He thinks I'm after his money."

"Okay, okay, calm down Olive. First of all, I don't believe that Vinnie doesn't trust you. I'm sure that you've misinterpreted something he said. Secondly, I know for a fact that neither he nor I think

49

that you're after his money, because he doesn't have any. Now what's caused all this distress you're suffering?"

"He wants me to sign a pari-mutuel agreement of some sort that says I won't take anything from him if we ever get divorced."

They say that the most dangerous types of people in our society are first year law students. They take courses in Contracts, Torts and Criminal Law, and then think that they know everything. Olive's pari-mutuel agreement is no doubt a prenuptial that Vinnie wants her to sign, and since Vinnie hadn't the slightest idea of what that was a few days ago, it's too coincidental that he should know all about the subject so soon in time after my discussion about the same topic with first year law student Stuart.

I try to calm her down by letting her know that this type of agreement is quite common nowadays, and that it can be a two-way street. Both parties want to trust and protect themselves and each other from the greedy lawyers who get involved when relationships go sour.

This gives her some temporary relief. We both agree that since they haven't even set a date for the wedding yet, there'll be plenty of time for us all to work things out smoothly. Unlike the last time they tried it, when Olive got spooked and ran off, this time the wedding will go on without a hitch and they'll live happily ever after. I'd better warn Stuart that by playing lawyer with Vinnie or anyone else now, he may be endangering his chance to practice law in the future. All it takes is one complaint to the State Bar about his being an overly ambitious law student, and he'll find himself tossed out of law school and prevented from ever taking a Bar exam.

Unfortunately, the pre-nup cat is already out of the bag and there's no ignoring it, so I'll have to meet with them both and send each one to Los Angeles County Bar Association's referral service to get some independent counsel before signing anything. I'll do the initial paperwork for both of them, so their legal fees should be kept to a minimum. Other than a few bucks that Vinnie received from a personal injury case I settled for him last year, he really doesn't have any assets to speak of and I'm sure that Olive doesn't either.

The phone rings again. It's Indovine calling.

"Hello Charles, what can I do for you today?"

"I was wondering if you've made any decision on whether or not to jump on board with us on this one?"

"I think we can get some more time here. I'll be appearing at your arraignment and asking for another couple of months to make a plea. I'm sure I'll get that continuance, and that'll give you a reason to tell your prospective client that this extra time will be spent in preparing the constitutional arguments. That way, there's a possibility that you can land him on that annual retainer without us being forced to go to Federal Court."

"I don't know, Peter. If we do that, he may feel cheated."

"He's not getting cheated, Charles. If he retains your law firm he'll be getting the finest legal representation that money can buy. You guys are top-

51

notch and he couldn't find a better law firm if he tried, so let me do my job and stretch this thing out as long as possible, and you do your job by showing him the fine work your law firm can do for him."

It worked. Indovine accepted both my flattery and the argument. He couldn't break my logic into pieces, so accepted both parts.

Another dog-mail has just arrived. It's a note telling me that Stuart will be here soon. I tip the delivery animal and take this brief opportunity to lie down and relax.

The quick nap helped. Stuart's now aboard and filling me in on his investigative assignment. Vinnie and Olive must have agreed to a truce, because they came along with Stuart and are now interested only in how the investigation plan will unfold.

The subject of this investigation is an automobile whiplash claimant, Loren Sherwood, who is supposed to have been injured in a questionable rear end collision that took place just days after the defendant driver became insured by Uniman's company. There were no witnesses to the accident and the damage to both cars didn't look too recent, so this accident was suspicious from the beginning.

The insurance company's computer database shows that neither party involved has made any auto accident injury claims before, but that doesn't necessarily mean that they're both legit. The defendant had stopped making premium payments and his policy was cancelled, but he definitely was covered at the time of the accident.

How convenient for the defendant. He's been driving in Southern California without insurance for more than five years since moving here from Arizona, but coincidentally took out an auto insurance policy just three days before the accident.

The plaintiff claimant was riding in the rear seat of his cousin's car, which was uninsured at the time. In addition to the claimant, the car was packed with three other adults and a small child. Other than the claimant, all the injuries were minor. They were all treated by the same chiropractor and all four of the adults now wear the most important and fashionable part of their wardrobes, a whiplash neck brace.

Because Sherwood was the most injured claimant, the chiropractor referred him out for an orthopedic consult with an M.D. specialist. The result was a diagnosis about some disc injury, so Sherwood was ordered to spend the next two months in a wheelchair, due to his alleged inability to walk for more than a few feet without great pain.

Stuart's assignment, if he chooses to accept, is to get videotape footage of the claimant in the act of normal mobility. I'm sure that Stuart would have appreciated receiving his assignment on a tape-recorded message that would have self-destructed in five seconds, but it came by fax instead.

I've handled quite a few personal injury cases over the past twenty years and from what I hear about this one, it's a classic 'set-up,' complete with a cooperative chiropractor and an extremely willing patient. The insurance company's file indicates that the claimant's medical bills already are more than eight thousand dollars, and the ambulance-chasing attorney handling all of the injured people in the car has made a settlement demand of over one-hundred thousand dollars for the most injured, the one that Stuart has been asked to get the goods on.

Members of a jury don't have the same background as attorneys like me, so they sympathize with the poor plaintiff and try to act like Robin Hood by taking large sums from the insurance companies and giving it to the poor injured plaintiffs.

The courts don't allow the fact that a defendant is insured to be mentioned in a trial, but any jury who takes a look at the defendant driver and sees his well-dressed Anglo-Saxon, White, Protestant legal team marching in step into the courtroom, usually can put two and two together and figure out that the defendant's attorneys aren't from the local Free Legal Aid office. Those free volunteer lawyers usually wear jeans and corduroy jackets with elbow patches when they come to court.

I explain to Stuart that merely getting some footage of the claimant walking normally or dragging out his garbage won't be enough, because at trial, his lawyer will simply argue that the guy was 'having a good day,' without the normal amount of pain. He might even bring in his own videotape to show how stressful the claimant usually is on those days that aren't so 'good.'

If Stuart's going to catch this guy, he's got to be caught on tape doing something that's so obviously indicative of a healthy normal person, that it will be impossible for even the slimiest plaintiff's lawyer to rebut the evidence.

Insurance companies nickname this type of assignment a 'rope job,' because it gives a claimant enough rope to hang himself and destroy his claim.

We all brainstorm the situation for a while and finally settle on a plan that also involves Olive and Vinnie, and if we're right about the claimant, it should get him out of his wheelchair very nicely.

Previous surveillance has established that the Mister Sherwood comes out of his first floor apartment each day in the wheelchair, using the 'handicapped' ramp that the insurance company paid to have installed over the steps at his front door. He usually wheels himself down the ramp at about one in the afternoon and goes down the street a half block or so to the liquor store, where he buys a six pack, and then has someone push his wheelchair back up the slight incline on his street and all the way up through the ramp to his front door.

Stuart takes one of his armored trucks and goes to Home Depot to purchase a four-foot by eight-foot sheet of plywood that will be carried by Vinnie. The planned action will coincide with the time that the claimant wheels himself down the ramp for his daily beer trip.

The sheet of plywood that Vinnie will be carrying has some hooks screwed into one side. Olive will be walking down the street in a skimpy two-piece sun suit, and I must admit that she looks really nice in it.

Stuart has covered up the company slogan with a magnetic sign that identifies his 'he's taking it with him' truck as one belonging to a plumber, and will park the armored truck across the street of the claimant's place with a video camera peeking out of one of the gun-ports. We spend the next hour or so going over the details until everyone knows exactly what to do and when to do it. They all agree that tomorrow afternoon will be a good time, because that's the day of the week that Sherwood's disability check comes in the mail and he'll surely want to take it to cash down at the liquor store. His mailman gets there just before one each afternoon, so plans are made to get everyone in place at least an hour in advance.

If this plan works, Uniman's company will save almost a hundred thousand dollars in claim payments and legal fees, and he's being very generous with Stuart. Overtime is no problem, so the planning is meticulous. They all appreciate my expert advice in making the plan and insist that I come along and direct the action from inside the truck. Stuart bought some inexpensive walky-talky devices and both Olive and Vinnie will be wearing ear-pieces to receive direction as to the split-second timing required for success in this operation. My curiosity gets the best of me and I agree to go along with them.

The next day, right on schedule, we're parked across the street from Sherwood's apartment building in Stuart's 'plumbing' truck. Olive is standing by the curb in front of Sherwood's place, leaning on a mailbox. She's chewing gum and keeps looking at her wristwatch, like she's waiting for someone to come and pick her up.

Vinnie is stationed further up the block and he's slowly walking down the street carrying the sheet of plywood. He's stalling, waiting for the mailman to reach Sherwood's apartment building.

The mailman gets to Sherwood's door and slides a few envelopes through the mail slot. Seeing that, I cue Vinnie to start walking down the street a little faster.

Our plan is working. Sherwood's door opens and his wheelchair comes rolling down the ramp towards the sidewalk. I instruct Olive. "Okay kid, start looking at your watch, like you're getting sick of waiting for whoever it is that's supposed to be coming to pick you up. Vinnie, it's your turn, so start moving. The mark has almost reached Olive, so you've only got another twenty or thirty seconds to get there with the plywood. Okay Olive, you see him wheeling up to you. Start your act."

Olive starts her routine for Sherwood's benefit. "Damn. Where the hell is she?" Olive slams her hand down on the mailbox in anger. Sherwood sees her, hears her complain, and can't resist speaking.

"What's wrong miss - got a problem?"

She looks down at him. "Hey what's a good lookin' guy like you doin' in a chair like that?"

Just as their conversation starts to get rolling, Vinnie comes walking by and turns toward the apartment building, making sure that he walks in between Olive and Sherwood. He looks at Olive. "Excuse me miss, is this building 15293 Gault Street?"

Olive answers him with the exact words we prepared for her. "How should I know? I'm just waiting for my sister to pick me up." She points down towards Sherwood. "Ask him, he lives here, not me."

Sherwood looks up at Vinnie. "Yeah, this is 15293, you here to repair something?"

Vinnie has an answer for him. "No, I always walk around with a four by eight sheet of plywood." After giving this answer, Vinnie slowly starts to walk towards the apartment building. As instructed, Olive hangs one of her brassiere straps onto a hook that's screwed into the plywood sheet. She screams out to Vinnie. "Hey, hold it asshole, one of your damned hooks has my bra."

Vinnie pretends that he doesn't hear her and continues carrying the plywood slowly toward the building, while Olive is shouting at him to stop and appearing to be dragged along with him.

Suddenly, her top flies off and over the top of the plywood sheet, leaving her standing there bare-breasted, with her hands covering herself up. Vinnie stops. Sherwood knows that a bare breasted babe is standing on the other side of the plywood, so using his arms, he pushes down on the chair, straining to see over the top of the plywood.

Olive looks at Sherwood and uncovers one of her breasts to point at Vinnie and shouts to Sherwood. "Hey pal, would you please get my top back from his hook and help me on with it?"

Sherwood can't resist this request. He jumps up out of the wheelchair, grabs the loose top and walks around to Olive's side of the plywood sheet. I direct Vinnie. "Okay Vin, he's out of the chair and looking at Olive, so gently nudge it along."

Vinnie follows my direction and with his foot, gives the wheelchair a little push, so that it turns and starts to roll down the slightly inclined street. While Sherwood is still helping Olive put her top back on, Vinnie walks toward the apartment building carrying the plywood sheet that had been blocking Sherwood's line of vision. He can now see in the direction of the wheelchair, which is now picking up speed as it rolls down the street. Olive waits another few seconds and then alerts him. "Hey mister, your chair's rolling away."

Sherwood looks in astonishment at the chair rolling away and as he starts running down the street he shouts to Olive. "Wait a minute, beautiful, I'll be right back."

Sherwood then proceeds to run at top speed down the street. He grabs the wheelchair and starts to drag it back up the street to where Olive is standing. Olive looks at him and exclaims. "Oh my God, it's a miracle. You're cured. Does that mean you can make love to a woman now?"

Sherwood smiles and speaks a line for our tape recorder that's better than anything we could have written for him. "Honey, my lovemaking was never in trouble. This whole wheelchair act is my crooked lawyer's idea."

At this point, a Toyota Camry pulls up, driven by Stuart's secretary. Olive hops in and tells Sherwood "sorry honey, gotta go. Maybe I'll be back this time tomorrow, so watch for me." The Camry pulls away.

By now Vinnie has deposited the plywood sheet up against Sherwood's apartment door and walked across the street to our armored truck. We wait for another minute until Sherwood sees the plywood against his door. He walks over, picks up the heavy plywood sheet and tosses it out onto the lawn. The whole event has been videotaped for posterity. Our work is done here. That's a wrap.

5

Our Mission Impossible team meets at Mi Ranchito for a victory celebration, to be paid for by Mister Uniman's company, whether he knows it or not. The Margaritas are flowing and some chocolate statuette awards are presented to Vinnie and Olive for 'outstanding performances in the line of deviousness.'

Vinnie isn't happy the way that Olive let Sherwood help her put the top back on. He was under the impression that she had a back-up bra underneath that sundress top, but Olive insists that she's a 'method' actor and wanted to go for reality.

Stuart's deal with Uniman will probably result in a reward of as much as ten thousand, and he promises to distribute two thirds of it among the other team members, so that his secretary gets five hundred for the pick-up, with the remaining surplus of what

60

will be more than six thousand going to Vinnie and Olive for their honeymoon fund. I'm told that I wasn't a true member of the team, so I'll have to settle for an extra Margarita.

Vinnie informs everyone that on future assignments, he'd be much happier if Olive switches roles with Stuart's secretary.

Olive is their designated driver, so she's wisely not drinking. While the others are getting plastered Olive lets me know that she's deeply into astrology and wants to do my chart. The only information she needs from me is the date of my birth and the hour.

I give her the date and time and she starts a whole discussion about how important date and time are to her calculations. After two minutes of what seems like an hour of her lecture, I ask her if it makes any difference where I was born. This stops her for a second and she asks what I mean.

"Olive, if I tell you I was born at twelve Noon, that doesn't take into consideration whether it was Noon here in Southern California, Chicago, or New York, because when it's Noon here, it's two PM in Chicago and three PM in New York. And if I was born somewhere on the other side of the earth, which I'm sure you'll agree is round, it might even be a completely different date. Doesn't that make any difference to you?"

I don't mean to put her on the spot like that, but it doesn't make any difference because just then, everyone decides it's time to leave. They all want to get home in time for the final episode of some stupid reality show.

61

Olive drives the armored truck and they drop me off at the Marina del Rey Liquor Store, where I purchase a box of Laverne's favorite wine.

There are some interesting boats on our dock. On the end tie is what I've been told, and firmly believe, is George Clooney's mega-yacht. Closer to the gangway ramp that leads up to the sidewalk and parking area are a few boxy houseboats that the Marina rents out to people, and Laverne occupies one of them. She's a mid-forties broad with quite a few miles on her. On many past occasions she's heard the gate slam shut as I walked down the ramp to the boats and this time should be no different. By the time I get to where her houseboat is, I see her at the window holding up two elegant plastic wine glasses, clinking them together and winking at me. I've affectionately nicknamed this act the 'clink and wink,' and tonight I'm ready for it.

Our usual procedure is to make sure that the wine is finished and then we get in bed to watch whatever crap the network has to offer.

By the time I get up the following morning, she's already gone, having been picked up for work by someone, who has taken her to do whatever she docs for a living. My reward for the evening's performance is some greasy French toast left out for me.

I never worry about leaving the kid alone on our boat, because I know she's got my cell phone number on her speed dial, and absolutely no one could get past that dog to do her any harm. Also, whenever she notices that I'm not there for the entire

62

night, she looks for my big yellow Hummer in its parking space. If it's there, she then knows that I'm only a few boats down the dock, with Laverne. I've discovered in the past that if she ever needs me for anything while I'm on the houseboat, dog-mail can be effectively delivered. My life must really be an open book if even the dog knows who I'm sleeping with.

There's a note waiting for me next to the French toast this morning. Laverne wants me to know that her vacation time is coming up soon and she would like me to be her guest on a one-week trip to Cancun, Mexico. She's written down a URL for me to check out that is supposed to have all the vacation details. Returning to my boat, I visit the website she suggested. Hmmm… it sure looks like a nice place to go, but Laverne neglected to mention that the flight from Miami to Cancun is aboard Naked-Air, a new clothing-optional airline that allows passengers to fly in their birthday suits. The trip will be on a Boeing 727-200 that can carry 170 passengers, and the rules state that the undressing doesn't commence until the plane reaches cruising altitude. They do stress hygiene though, so everyone will be provided with a towel to sit on – and no sex is allowed during the flight. Darn. But it doesn't end there. The travel agency that handles these flights has taken over an entire Resort & Spa for the week, so that the Nude Week activities can continue, which will include a 'Toga Night,' body painting, a Karaoke night, completely nude beaches, volleyball, and restaurants. What ever happened to the 'no shoes, no shirt, no service' days? If there's anything that I think would act as an appetite suppressant for me, it's a completely nude restaurant.

I have to admit that the idea looks kind of interesting, but one main thing stops me from doing it... it's insane! I can just picture in my mind the exact scenario that would be sure to play out if I ever allowed myself to be on a flight like that. Somewhere over the United States a situation would suddenly develop that requires all passengers to immediately return to their seats, buckle up, and prepare for an emergency landing. The plane is cleared to land at one of the country's largest airports, and with news camera crews from all over the world waiting and watching, the plane safely touches down, the emergency inflatable exit slides deploy, and I can then join more than one hundred naked passengers sliding out of the plane to safety, all captured for posterity by news crews and cameras. Film at eleven. No thank you.

6

The Luskin murder didn't attract much news attention. With so many drive-by shootings in Southern California, Luskin's murder was just another one of the type that the public is sick and tired of hearing about. The only reason it got a few extra days of coverage was probably because the victim was a successful white guy in a small town, instead of some innocent black bystander, or child in a South Los Angeles drug-infested neighborhood.

What's really surprising isn't the small amount of coverage our local news had about the Luskin murder in La Verne, it's the total lack of coverage on another apparent murder that was supposed to have taken place in Oregon. Local television news programs usually lead off with something bloody, and I can't remember one mention of this one. The fact that it supposedly took place in Oregon shouldn't make a difference, because any murder within a thousand miles or so should still be close enough for a bloodthirsty local news show.

The only reason I know about it is because Mister Uniman called again, asking if I'd look into it. Apparently the body was never found, but the deceased's widow is going to court to have her husband legally declared dead so that she can collect on his Life Insurance policy with Mister Uniman's company.

As much as I appreciate the opportunity to work for him again, digging into insurance claims really isn't my main field of interest, so I suggest that he turn the matter over to Stuart's private investigation firm. Uniman sounded extremely pleased with the way that Stuart handled that phony Sherwood claim, so he agrees with my suggestion and says he'll have his secretary call Stuart. In the meantime, my curiosity gets the best of me and I start to snoop around to find out about this murder. I know it sounds ghoulish, but wherever there's a murder, there's a murderer who needs a lawyer.

Uniman mentioned that the Oregon widow would be going to court in some county up there, so I start out by checking their local papers on the internet, looking for any case involving a person with the name Uniman mentioned. No luck. I also start to call some of the local police stations up there, but can't get any information that way either.

Last year I met a fellow named Jack Bibberman, whose testimony helped me get re-instated to practice law, after being framed by a crooked lawyer and suspended by the State Bar. Since then I've been using Jack B. wherever I can on investigations. Between working for me and doing odd jobs for Stuart, he makes an almost decent living. Jack's been spending most of his time and money flying between here and Chicago, trying to keep a romance going with his girlfriend, a waitress he met there named Phyllis Morse, who works at the Barnum & Brisket Deli. I leave a message on his answering machine to give me a call when he gets a chance. I'm going to ask Stuart to hire Jack as his lead investigator on the Oregon insurance case that Uniman will no doubt assign to him. You never can tell, maybe I'll meet another attractive widow with plenty of insurance money coming in soon.

Right now it looks like I've got another important task that requires my attention. The dog is sitting in front of me with his leash in his mouth. This is another trick he's taught me. Whenever I see him sitting here like this, I'm supposed to hook the leash onto his collar and let him take me for a walk.

I must be one of the smart humans, because it took him just a minute or so to teach me this trick, and I figured it out the first time. He usually doesn't come and fetch me like this unless the kid is busy on the computer either studying for another home-schooling test, or figuring out ways to appropriate money from outside work I conduct for my clients, by turning it into fees that belong to our 'firm.'

Our deal with the Marina provides for us to get the Grand Bank's slip rent free as a partial retainer, to be on call and handle all the landlord-tenant legal work. Unfortunately the economy must be picking up, because our Marina caseload has dropped drastically, which must mean that all the apartment and boat tenants are paying their rent on time. I share my Marina fees with our little law firm, but am allowed to keep fees earned on outside client work. At least that's the way it's supposed to be, but for one reason or another it never works out that way, because the kid always manages to wrangle her way into every case that I work on. It's not the sharing of the fee that bothers me as much as the fact that most of the time she's the one who figures out how to solve the case long before I do.

A call comes in from a number that I haven't heard from for many months: it's the FBI's West Los Angeles office, so it must be Special Agent Bob Snell, a guy who I've bumped into on several cases in the past.

"Hello Special Agent Snell, what can I do for you today?"

"Hello, Sharp, I see your caller ID is working today. And your outgoing lines are working fine too."

"C'mon, agent Snell, you don't have to tap my phones, I'll be glad to come down there and make my calls from your office and let you listen in. Is there anything in particular that you want to discuss other than my telephone activity?"

"Yes. I understand you've been making some inquiries into an incident that took place up in Oregon. Is that correct?"

"That's correct. Why are you so curious about it? It's only an insurance claim I was asked to look into."

"I'm going to do you a favor counselor. Stay away from this case. It has nothing to do with you." End of conversation. He's not the talkative type.

If he really wanted me to stay away from this case, he wouldn't have called me. I'm sure he realized that if I didn't get anywhere with my phone calls to Oregon that I'd probably drop the matter. Anyone with half a brain who knows me will tell you that the best way to get me involved in a case is to tell me to stay away from it. This conversation with Snell leaves me with only two possible conclusions. Either he doesn't have half a brain, or for some reason he wants me to stick my nose into it. Either way, I'm intrigued. The only problem is there's no one around to pay the tab, and I'm certainly not flying up to Oregon on spec.

I think the best thing to do on this case is sit back and let Jack Bibberman do all the preliminary legwork on Mister Uniman's dime. There'll be no problem getting info out of Stuart, because I'm sure that he'll look forward to my expert opinion in analyzing any facts that Jack comes up with on the case.

In the meantime, I've got to start preparing a reasonable explanation for why I need another month or two for Indovine's arraignment. From what Charles told me, he's only been charged with a misdemeanor. My research shows that California's law with respect to carrying a concealed weapon is called a 'wobbler,' which means that it can be charged as either a misdemeanor or a felony. In Charles' case he qualified to have only misdemeanor charges filed because he met the several requirements of having legally purchased and registered the weapon, not being a gang member, and not having any prior record for carrying a gun.

This pleases me because it means that being a member of the State Bar of California, populated with thousands of crooked lawyers, is not considered being a member of a gang. I guess they use arithmetic for classification purposes. My most recent copy of the State Bar Journal lists around two hundred thousand members, so if two thousand of them get convicted of serious crimes, that's still only just one percent. On the other hand, a street gang with only fifty members might have as many as thirty to fifty percent of their membership breaking the law, so it's classified as a true 'gang' for purposes of the wobbler laws pertaining to carrying concealed guns.

As interesting as this math is, I don't think I'll bring any of it up at Charles' arraignment. From what I've seen over the years, Municipal Court judges presiding over arraignments aren't interested in hearing constitutional arguments. All they want to hear is 'guilty,' 'not guilty,' 'nolo contendere,' or 'my client would like a continuance to make a plea, your honor.' I'll be using the latter of these choices and hoping that my client will be given additional time due to his busy trial schedule and past financial contributions to the judge's favorite cause.

The Olive and Vinnie wedding is back on track. Stuart calls to let me know that they've decided against using a pre-nuptial agreement. Due to the fact that their assets are next to nil, anything they might accumulate would be as a result of both of their efforts. They both work for Stuart and make the same amount of money. If they decide they need something in writing later on, they can always make an ante-nuptial agreement, which can say the exact same things and be signed after the marriage.

I think that's a sensible idea. The main problem with pre-nuptial agreements is that no matter how much an attorney might know about the law, there's usually a complete lack of knowledge as to how to go about getting one of those pesky little contracts brought up in conversation or suggested, let alone getting one signed.

No matter how gently it's mentioned, the spouse being asked to enter into a pre-nuptial agreement always feels as if he or she isn't being trusted, or that the person requesting the agreement thinks that the relationship is on a shaky footing. The subject is almost as touchy as when a person goes into a hospital for some minor elective surgery and the surgeon wants the patient to sign some form that provides for disposal of the body, should something go wrong in surgery.

Past experience has shown that it shouldn't be the requesting person's job to bring it up to his or her prospective spouse. The best scenario would be for the more asset-heavy of the two to say something like "Honey, I think that my lawyer wants to go over some things with you about my businesses before we get married, so why don't you make an appointment to see him?"

This way the burden falls on the client's attorney. When the fiancée comes in, the attorney can go over some of the client's holdings, mention that there are some formalities that will make the business more secure, and then try to maneuver the conversation into the subject of the pre-nuptial, starting out by making it appear to be only an arrangement for smooth continuity of business management, should anything drastic happen – and that's part of the arrangements put in place by the business several years ago. This isn't exactly what you might call a truthful approach, but sometimes you have to do what you have to do to keep your client happy and not break up a relationship.

71

Once the subject has been broached, the next step is to pull out a standard pre-nuptial form and make it appear like "I didn't draw this thing up, it's just the regular form that everyone uses."

If the prospective spouse has any level of maturity, it shouldn't be too difficult for the suggestion to be understood with no animosity. The presentation should be sort of like when a professional killer has to execute a 'contract' on someone he knows, and says "nothin' personal, this is just business." In similar past situations like this, I've known attorneys to say something like "Your future spouse doesn't know that I'm getting into this area of the business, but since you are going to be married, I'm sure it's okay for me to divulge some information." This gives the prospective spouse a feeling of being included into the inside private business aspects of his or her fiancée, and they rarely balk at this approach.

The bottom line is that you never bring up the subject of a pre-nup in a public place like a restaurant or anywhere else where other people might be around, like friends or family. This is a personal matter and if your client would rather handle it without getting a lawyer involved, a suggested approach might be something like "I hate to get into this crummy business stuff, but my family's lawyer wants us to have an agreement signed in which I promise to help you with the household chores and some other little items. Do you mind if we set down some ground rules in writing before the marriage?" If the fiancée has half a brain, he or she will know what's coming and possibly appreciate the tender approach. Maybe.

Fortunately, none of this is needed for the Olive-Vinnie marriage, and I'm glad I won't have to step in the middle. One of these days someone will establish an agency that does nothing but counsel people who have been asked to sign pre-nuptial agreements. They can act like suicide prevention or other types of grief counselors, who know how to talk a person down and explain the reality of things.

Maybe I'll suggest this idea to Stuart. I can just see his advertisement now: "Want your prospective spouse to sign a pre-nup? Call us! We'll explain it to her or him, and you won't have to bring up the subject at all."

In Southern California, every wealthy female movie star can send her 'boy-toy' over for an explanation before purchasing the wedding vows. I'm sure that Donald Trump, Joan Collins, Cher, and Elizabeth Taylor, and many others would all liked to have had that service on their speed-dials.

I hope that Olive and Vinnie succeed in this latest wedding attempt. Vinnie asks me for some suggestions as to where they should honeymoon, and the only two suggestions I have are either Maui, where I can arrange to have them as my guests for dinner at the Lahaina Yacht Club, or Petra, in Jordan.

Maui is a no-brainer. Several airlines fly directly from LAX here in Los Angeles to OGG, the Kahului Airport on Maui, just twenty-seven miles from Lahaina. It's only about a five-hour flight, and with a good book and a couple of drinks, you're there before you know it.

On the other hand, Petra is in the southern region of Jordan, and if you're not really interested in ancient history, then it's not for you. But if you do decide to go there, then you'll never forget that mile-long walk through the 'cold alley,' a fifteen-foot wide path that the sun never shines into because of the surrounding four hundred foot high rock cliffs. At the end of this alley, which is really called the 'Siq,' you make one last turn and then right before your eyes is a sight you'll never forget. Carved out of a solid rock face is the Khazneh, commonly referred to as the 'Treasury,' a ten-story high temple-looking edifice. If you've seen the motion picture 'Indiana Jones and the Temple of Doom,' then you've seen the 'Treasury,' because it's the building that Jones and his father run out of at the end of the movie.

I don't think that Vinnie and Olive will choose Petra over Maui, so I don't go into much more detail about the place, other than to mention that if they ever decide to go ahead with a pre-nuptial agreement, an ancient Priest King named Hammurabi started the whole subject with his own version of a property settlement. Of his 282 laws, the 137th states that

"If a man wish to separate from a woman who has borne him children, or from his wife who has borne him children, then he shall give that wife her dowry, and a part of the usufruct [easement] *of field, garden, and property, so that she can rear her children. When she has brought up her children, a portion of all that is given to the children, equal as*

74

that of one son, shall be given to her. She may then marry the man of her heart."

As expected, Vinnie prefers Maui, so I call the club, buy the honeymooners a 15-day guest membership, and arrange for them to eat on my tab their first night on the Island.

The phone rings again, and this time my caller ID display shows a number with the La Verne area code. At first I think it might be Chief Olshansky calling about some new info on the Luskin murder, but I'm pleasantly surprised to find out that I'm wrong. It's Beverly Luskin, and she sounds friendly.

"Hello, Mister Sharp? This is Beverly Luskin, you know, I'm the one from La Verne. You were at my house the other day."

Is she kidding? Does a good-looking dame like that think that I could have possibly forgotten who she is in just a day? I hope she doesn't think I'm gay, because I'd love to have the chance to prove her wrong on that one.

"Oh, no, Beverly, I haven't forgotten you. To what do I owe the pleasure of this call? And please, call me Peter." That's a start. At least we're on a first-name basis. I think that every love affair should start with people knowing and using each other's first names.

"Peter, I want you to know that I appreciate what you did for me with the insurance claim, because I've been told that they're now processing it. You must be a wonderful lawyer, and I'm going to need someone to help me with all the matters left

75

behind by my husband's passing. I was wondering if it would it be possible for me to retain you?"

Wow. What a combination. Brains, beauty, money, and wants me to help her. And to top it off, she thinks I actually did something for her already. Little does she know that Mister Uniman wanted me to try to find a way for him to wriggle out of paying off on her husband's life insurance policy. I think that information should remain untold forever.

"Why certainly I'm available. Do you have any pressing needs now, or are you just looking for general counsel?"

"Nothing pressing at this moment, but there are quite a few things that will require attending to, so why don't you send me a retainer agreement with your hourly rate and we can get started."

This is easier than I thought it would be. No sense in making the rate too high, because spending time with this client will really be pleasurable and I don't want to queer the deal by pricing myself out of the market, so I call up my standard retainer on the computer, fill in some blanks with her info, insert an hourly rate of one-hundred dollars, which probably fits in with the going rate in her neck of the woods, and email the whole thing to her.

Less than an hour later, I get a dog-mail that says a confirming message has come in on the firm's inbox, and that PayPal.com informed us that we have money waiting for us.

One of the internet's most popular websites is a person-to-person auction site called eBay, where private parties buy and sell merchandise between each other. Because private parties don't usually accept credit cards and people are understandably reluctant to give their credit card number out to a complete stranger, the PayPal service was created to facilitate payment between buyers and sellers. To use PayPal for sending money, all you do is go to the PayPal website, sign up by providing bank and credit card information, and then fill out a payment form authorizing payment of any sum you want. You give them the payee's email address, and they do the rest.

PayPal notifies the payee that money is waiting. If you're already signed up with PayPal, then it's easy to have them either direct-deposit the sum to your bank account, or send you a check. If you're not yet signed up with them, it's an easy procedure.

I'm personally not signed up with PayPal, but guess who is? Right. Some time ago, the kid had our law firm signed up to receive money that way, so she has succeeded in glomming on to my retainer, and Beverly Luskin has just become a 'house account.' She did it to me again.

That's the bad news. The good news is that Beverly sent an initial retainer of five grand, so she just bought fifty hours of my time, and I'm looking forward to it being the most enjoyable fifty hours of my career.

Jack B. is calling from Oregon and he sounds disappointed. He tried to interview some people up there, but can't get any information out of anyone, especially the local cops. No crime report, no suspects, no details, no nothing. He gets the feeling that no one there wants to talk about this crime.

The only few facts he has are from the widow, Mrs. Kathy Potter. She told him that their marriage wasn't going too well, and that occasionally her husband Paul would get drunk and slap her around. She wanted to leave him, but had nowhere to go. The story sounds like one that every Special Victims Unit cop has heard hundreds of times: "He's really not that bad of a guy, it's just that when he's been drinking, he gets angry at little things. I still love him, and he always apologizes the next day and promises it'll never happen again."

Jack tells me that there were no kids in the marriage, so at this point neither one of us can figure out what kept her around that jerk. To make matters worse, it looks like he was involved in some drug dealing, which puts another few pieces of the puzzle together.

On the day in question Paul was sober, but he was in a terrible mood because some business deal he was working on wasn't going well. Paul wasn't an executive of some dot-com company, so it must have been some drug transaction. The door to their rental cottage was open and several of the neighbors heard what was going on. He was bawling her out for some little thing like not having one of his favorite foods that he was expecting for breakfast.

After about fifteen minutes of loudly berating her he stormed out of the house. She went running after him, but when she grabbed his arm as he got into his car, he turned around and slapped her in the face so hard that it knocked her on her ass. He didn't even stop to help her up, and instead got into his pick-up truck and burned rubber as he angrily drove away, leaving her on the ground, holding her scratched face.

One of the neighbors came over to help Kathy up and then brought her over to their cottage, where they cleansed the facial scar and tried to calm her down. Kathy stayed at that neighbor's house for the rest of the afternoon, finally falling asleep on their couch. They gave her some booze to ease the pain, so it must have knocked her out.

Her husband didn't come home that evening and no one had an idea where he was, until a few days had passed and the local sheriff called. They had reports that a truck matching the one Paul drove away in was seen going off the road. By late that evening the cops had recovered it from a nearby lake. His body wasn't in the truck, but his shirt was found nearby in the bushes. It was bloody and riddled with bullet holes. The cops formed the conclusion that he was shot and then his vehicle was pushed into the lake. They also think that his body was removed so that it could be disposed of somewhere else, probably in small pieces.

The only other detail Jack learned was that the shirt they found near the truck accident matched the description of what Kathy and the neighbors said Paul was wearing when he left the house that day.

Kathy hired some local lawyer who no one around here was familiar with. He got a court order that forced the police to compare DNA from the bloody shirt with the DNA sample that her husband Paul was forced to give to the police not too long ago when he was arrested for felony drug possession. Oregon has a statute that requires taking DNA samples from people arrested for any felony, so it was available for the testing. It was a perfect match with the blood on the shirt.

Mrs. Potter's next move was to have her lawyer petition the court to have Paul declared legally dead so that she could put in a claim on his life insurance policy. The benefits were only two hundred thousand dollars, but that was enough for her to buy a car, get a nice new trailer to live in, finish beauticians' school and start her life over again somewhere else.

I don't know what more Jack can do up there, so my only suggestion is that he get her telephone number in the cottage, plus any past phone bills she may have laying around. If her husband was dealing drugs, he probably also used a cell phone, so I tell Jack to also ask the widow for any of those bills too, and then to come back to town first thing tomorrow.

Stuart calls to request a brainstorming session at our boat, so after he picks Jack B. up at the airport this morning, they're coming by to talk about the case. If he can find any reason for Uniman to get out of paying the policy benefit to Kathy Potter, his fee will be in the neighborhood of twenty thousand dollars, so he's very much interested in any advice he can get from me or Jack.

I can't help notice that Stuart is wearing a gold Rolex Submariner wristwatch with a two-tone gold bracelet and a blue watch face. I've seen several like that around the Marina, usually worn by guys with boats almost as big as George Clooney's. I don't remember ever seeing him wear that thing before, and I'm sure I would have noticed, because it's a real eye-opener. I've always wanted one of those, but in addition to not being able to justify the ten thousand dollar expense, I'm a little afraid of getting mugged for a flashy piece of jewelry like that. I've read about one incident where a guy pretended to be a customer at the local Mercedes Benz dealership. He just sat around in the service area's waiting room until some unsuspecting customer might come in wearing a beautiful gold Rolex like Stuart's. The crook didn't have to wait too long before some well-healed Mercedes owner strolled in wearing the wristwatch of choice. Needless to say, the mugging took place then and there.

"Stuart, aren't you afraid to wear a fancy watch like that? I mean, it sort of makes you a target for a mugging."

"You really like it, Peter?"

"Sure, Stu, what's not to like? It's a great looking piece of jewelry."

His next move almost knocks me cold. He unfastens the wristwatch clasp, removes the watch from his wrist, and hands it to me. "Here, Peter, this is a gift from me to you."

I'm stunned. Is he kidding? While I'm still sitting there speechless with my mouth open, he surprises me again. "Don't worry about it Pete, I've got a whole case of 'em back at the warehouse. Looks real, doesn't it? I'll be distributing them soon."

He really catches me with this one. I've heard of some counterfeit merchandise before, because there's a news item every once in a while about people getting busted at some flea market for selling fake fashion purses. I never thought that a phony watch could look this good.

Stuart explains that there are several types of phony Rolex watches being sold on the 'street.' Other than the quality of workmanship in the case and band, the main thing about keeping customers happy with their purchases is how the watches keep time. The cheapest ones and easiest to spot as phonies have quartz movements. You can tell they're fake because the sweep second hand jumps from second-to-second, instead of moving in a slow, smooth path around the dial. Rolex doesn't put quartz movements in their watches, so when you see that second-hand jump, you know it ain't real.

When you go up a step up from a quartz movement to the self-winding models, there are two main types of 'insides,' or 'movements:' cheap ones from India and the better ones from Japan. Stuart says that the Japanese movements are the best. Why am I not surprised?

"Stuart, before we get into the legality of what you're planning, please tell me that you haven't advertised these things to anyone yet. I don't want to hear that you've already built internet websites telling everyone that you've got phony Rolex watches for sale."

"Not to worry counselor, being a student of the law myself, I know better than to do that. And as for your concerns about me getting into trouble for selling these things, that will never happen."

"Gee, Stu, I'm glad to see you're so confident that you'll be staying out of trouble with your counterfeit merchandise. Would you please be so kind as to tell this poor ignorant officer of the court exactly how you intend to sell this stuff legally?"

"No problemo, senor obligato, I won't be selling them... I'll be giving them away as premiums."

On paper, he might be right. If all you do is give them away, then logic dictates that you can't be accused of 'selling' them, but he's only partly correct.

"I don't know about that, Stu. There's no such thing as 'free.' I'm sure you're not going to be standing on some street corner passing them out to strangers who walk by. If you give the watch away as a premium, it's because someone has bought something else from you, so when you lead them to believe you're giving it to them as a free gift, it only that means you've already factored its cost into the price of whatever they bought from you... and that means technically, you are selling it to them."

"So what's the big deal? I can buy these things by the case in Thailand for less than ten bucks each. I never give one away unless I've tested it out and made sure that it runs for at least a week without stopping. To be certain that the buying public isn't being deceived at all, whoever gets one of these replicas from me signs a receipt for it acknowledging that they know it's not real, and its value may be as little as one tenth of a percent of the genuine article. Do you think that Rolex is worried I'm taking business away from them? That someone who really wants to spend ten thousand for a genuine Rolex will change his mind and instead decide to accept one of my ten dollar fakes? I think not. In fact, I've heard people tell me that they would rather keep the genuine one in their drawer at home and only wear it on special occasions, wearing one of my phonies for everyday use."

"Okay, Stuart, I concede the fact that you've solved the problem of not causing any confusion in the public's mind as to authenticity, and that you won't be taking any money out of the Rolex factory's pocket, but you still seem to be missing the real issue here, and as a student of the law, I expect more from you. Every one of these phonies has a trademarked name and logo attached to it. This isn't like making a copy of a dollar bill, because the watch isn't legal tender that can be spent, but you're still participating in a conspiracy to unlawfully use someone else's stolen trademarked logos on counterfeit merchandise.

"Secondly, because the United States has a high respect for trademarks and our Customs Department does not legally allow counterfeit merchandise like this to enter this country. If they knew about it coming in they would seize it on the spot, at its point of entry.

"It may not be a crime, like smuggling, to bring it in to the U.S., but don't ever try to get this stuff into France, because they have criminalized it there. Here, all they do is seize it. You might not be subject to any criminal prosecution, but companies like Rolex maintain an aggressive policy of civil prosecution, so don't be surprised if you get served with a lawsuit from them. They guard their name and logo as strongly as Disney does, so my suggestion to you, my friend, is don't fool with Mickey Mouse and don't give away Rolex watches.

"And here's the clincher… If the lawyer that represents Rolex is as sharp as I think he would probably is, he'll argue that you've actually sold the phony Rolex as a real one, charged eleven thousand for it, and threw in a free Camry as the premium!"

There's a lot of silence in the room. My last salvo really shot Stuart down, but his ability to bounce back amazes me. If he ever gets to be a lawyer, I think he'll be a force to reckon with in any courtroom, because he can really think on his feet.

"Okay Peter, for the sake of conversation, let's assume that everything you say is one hundred percent true. Here's my 'plan B:' I'll get in touch with my distributor in Thailand and have them make a slight change when they silkscreen the watch faces on these things. Instead of it saying '*Rolex*,' it'll say '*Phony*.' This way, I won't be violating anyone's trademark. I'll even prepare a brochure for prospective customers, letting them know that if anyone asks them if their watch is real or a phony, they should hold up their arm and proudly declare that they're wearing a genuine *Phony*. How's that for marketing? I'll bet that in no time at all my genuine *Phony* watches are the craze. In fact, I'll bet they'll be a big hit with wealthy people who can actually afford or may even own the real thing, and would rather wear one of my genuine Phonies instead."

I like it. Not only is his new idea a clever one, I think it'll be successful. In fact, I'd like to be his first customer for one of those ten-dollar genuine phonies.

85

Having settled the counterfeit wristwatch problem, our thoughts are now back to the case at hand. I tell them Special Agent Snell called and warned me to stay away from this matter, and that's the only reason I'm so interested in it. If the FBI is involved, then for sure there's something fishy going on.

I don't know anything about the alleged murder, but I do see a pattern emerging. First of all, Potter's body hasn't been found. Second, the local police no longer seem to have an active investigation going on this case. Third, no one will talk to us. I'm starting to get the strange feeling that this entire matter may be as phony as the watch that Stuart just gave me, and if it is, I want to know why, because I don't like getting my chain pulled by Snell and his gang.

Jack B. brought back Kathy Potter's home telephone bills for the past couple of months, so I tell him to start calling every one of them to see who she and her husband Paul were talking to.

"What about cell phones Jack? Did Kathy or Paul have one? And if so, are there any bills to be had?"

"She couldn't find them while I was there. When I landed here at LAX there was a voice-mail waiting for me. She found them."

"Bad move Jack. You should've gotten right back on a plane and gone to get them. Why was staying here in town more important than going back there for those cell phone bills?"

Stuart intercedes for Jack. "Peter, Jack's girlfriend Phyllis is in town from Chicago.

86

Remember? He met her when he was back there investigating the Joe Morgan case a couple of months ago."

"Okay Jack, your girlfriend's in town and I'm happy for you. I'm sure that Stuart will drive you to the airport now so that you can fly back up to wherever Kathy Potter is and pick up those cell phone records of hers."

"Mister Sharp, are you kidding? I just got back from there this morning. What's the big hurry?"

"The big hurry, my good friend, is that there's a murderer on the loose and we don't want to wait until something happens to Kathy Potter." Jack looks disappointed. I realize he wants to spend some time with Phyllis, so I cut him some slack.

"Okay Jack, go see your girlfriend... but I want you on the first flight out tomorrow morning. I really want those cell phone bills the widow Potter has for you.

An appreciative Jack calls Phyllis and then leaves with Stuart.

They've been gone about five minutes and my phone rings. The caller ID display shows a La Verne area prefix. It's Beverly Luskin calling from her cell phone.

"Peter, I hope you don't mind such short notice, but I'll be in Los Angeles this evening to look at a commercial property that we were planning on putting an offer in on. Would you like to meet me? Maybe we can get an early dinner or have a drink, or something."

This is music to my ears. It was getting to a point where I was hoping that Laverne would return from her vacation already. "That sounds good to me. Where's the property you're looking at? Maybe I can meet you there."

She gives me an address in North Hollywood and we make plans to meet there in at six, a perfect time for me to show off my new wristwatch.

The property is a motel that is now 'closed for remodeling.' I've seen these on many businesses. It really means 'we're gone and not coming back, but don't want you to know about it.' Beverly's car parked in front of what was the office, and as she turns and sees me, she runs over, throws her arms around me and plants a warm wet one on my lips.

"Peter, it's so nice to see you."

"Same to you, kid." I guess the period of mourning must have ended.

I reluctantly release her and we start to walk hand-in-hand around the parking lot, which is surrounded by a U-shaped one-story building with about ten rental units, and an office in the middle. The place reminds me of one of those forts you might see in an old western movie. It looks like it's been closed for a couple of months, but the utilities are still on, so the neon sign works and the small surrounding lawn gets automatically watered. There's no pool, so the place was obviously a low-budget motel similar to the ones you see all along out-of-the-way interstate routes. Like so many other old commercial buildings in the San Fernando Valley, it has a Mexican feel to it, complete with the faded orange semi-circular tiles on the overhanging roof eaves and large walkway arches in front of each door.

She has a set of keys to the place with her, so we decide to check out a room. Once inside, Beverly asks me if I'm a Lakers fan.

"Are you kidding? Who in this town isn't?" She looks at her watch, which I'm sure isn't counterfeit.

"Well mister lawyer, then you should be pleased to learn that your team's next game starts in about five minutes."

"If you'd like to watch it, I'm sure we can find some nearby watering hole with few television sets."

She surprises me even further with her next suggestion, which sounds much better than mine. "Wait a minute; these rooms are all equipped with television sets fed by cable. The utilities are still on, so let's see if we can get the game right here in the room."

She walks over, turns on the TV set, and in less than ten seconds I see the team in their warm-up suits getting ready to start playing. Fortunately, other than the bed, these rooms aren't furnished with anything but a small writing desk and chair set, so there's only one place to get comfortable watch television from. She sits down on the bed and then pats the mattress next to her.

"C'mon, mister lawyer, make yourself comfortable. I don't bite."

I don't know if she planned this or not, but it couldn't be going better. She kicks off her shoes, so I do the same, and then get comfortable on the bed next to her. For some strange reason, I'm not that interested in the game. The sound is on very low, so we start a long conversation, during which she tells me her life story and I pretend to be interested.

When the conversation turns to me, I explain to her that I'm just an ordinary run-of-the-mill lawyer who drives a yellow Hummer and lives on a fifty-foot yacht, with a young Chinese female computer genius, and a Saint Bernard that delivers the mail. She's amused by my description of my old law school classmate, Suzi's late stepfather Melvin Braunstein. She also now understands why our boat is named the 'Suzi B.'

"Peter, it looks like we enjoy each other's company. If I stay over here tonight, can we spend some more time together tomorrow?"

"Oh, gee, I'd love to, but tomorrow I have to go to a Gun Show out in Lancaster. It's only going to be there one day and I have to get something one of the vendors is offering."

"Really? I don't see you as a person with that military mindset."

"You're right. I don't even have one 'camouflage-style' outfit my wardrobe. The reason I'm going there is to meet with a leather holster maker, because I want to surprise Suzi with a special dog harness that Bernie can wear while we're out boating. If that Saint Bernard ever went overboard while we were out at sea I don't think it would be possible to haul him back onto the boat. The harness will tether him to within ten feet of the main cabin. Maybe after it's over, if you're still in town, we can get together for some frozen yogurt or something."

"Thanks for the invite, Peter, but the 'or something' sounds more inviting than the yogurt, because I don't handle lactose that well."

One good thing about being in a closed motel is that there's no worry about some employee knocking on the door to offer you an extra towel. We enjoy having the whole place to ourselves, and spend several hours completely ignoring the Lakers. Laughing leads to touching. Touching leads to kissing, and before the evening is over, my self-winding watch is completely wound up, I've broken another rule of my own personal legal ethics, and someone *from* La Verne may have just replaced someone *named* Laverne.

7

Per my instructions, Jack B. caught the early flight this morning and returned from Oregon later this afternoon with bad news. While there, he went directly to Kathy Potter's cottage to pick up those cell phone records, but he was too late. The cottage was empty. I had a strange feeling this would happen.

"Honest Mister Sharp, the cupboard was bare. The furniture was gone. It was like no one ever lived there before."

91

"Did you talk to the neighbors? Maybe one of them saw her moving, talked to her, got some idea of where she went."

"I tried that. They all had the same story. No story at all. All of a sudden there was an epidemic of amnesia. They seemed to remember someone living there, but don't recall any details. I did get lucky with a small kid who was playing nearby. Before his mother came and grabbed him away, he told me that there were some big trucks there last night. He heard the noise and looked out his window. But that's all I got out of him before he was whisked away.

"On the way back to the airport I stopped at the local post office to see if she put a change of address form in. Nothing there either."

"Okay, Jack, there are some forces at work here definitely designed to keep us and the rest of the world in the dark You've got her regular phone bills, so just keep calling every number on them and see if it leads us anywhere."

"Are you going to help out on these at all, or should I call every one of them myself?"

"No Jack, I've got other things to do today. You keep at it. Maybe we'll get lucky and find she called a relative, or some friend that she'd like to keep in contact with."

Antelope Valley is in the high desert. To get there, you take the 405 Freeway all the way North and then turn east onto another Freeway that takes you up over a pass that's about thirty-two hundred feet above sea level. People tell me that during some winter storms when the snow level drops below four

92

thousand feet, the California Highway Patrol stops cars and requires snow chains before permitting them to continue through the pass.

Once over the pass, it's downhill most of the way until you drive past the city of Palmdale. This is where Edwards Air Force Base is located, and many shuttle trips from outer space have landed here.

The Antelope Valley Gun Show is being held in what formerly was a high school gymnasium, and it's completely packed with people walking around in clothing that makes them look like jungle fighters. There are plenty of crew cuts, polished military boots, a lot of cigarette smoking, macho tattoos, and some bleached-blonde women sporting black eyes. Most of these people look like they just stepped out of a television commercial for either beer, Airstream Trailers, or the magazine 'Soldier of Fortune.'

I feel out of place dressed in my uniform, which consists of a light blue button-down shirt and a pair of khaki pants. At least my trousers look like part of a military outfit, so maybe I partially fit in. I know I'm only about forty miles outside of the San Fernando Valley, but it feels like a completely different world here. Several vendors notice my beautiful phony Rolex and think I'm some rich dude looking for a 'piece' to carry. They're polite about it, but their suggestions are all quite similar. "Say, wearing a piece of jewelry like that, you should have some protection... now here's an item that would be perfect for you. Fits nicely in a shoulder holster, and you can..."

Several of today's attendees saw me pull up in my Hummer, which is the most military-looking

93

vehicle in the parking lot. There's a buzz in the main room, so I guess I'm being pointed at and whispered about as a new type of 'gentleman mercenary.'

While in the army, I was stationed at Camp McCoy, Wisconsin, and shortly after finishing basic training I was assigned to an Ordnance outfit. We didn't do anything exciting like de-fusing unexploded hydrogen bombs; instead our six-man crew was assigned to the rifle range. Our job was to wait all day until the range was no longer in use, pick up all the remaining ammunition, log it in, and return it to the weapons room vault.

My first day on that assignment I found out that ammunition was never turned back in, because too much paperwork was required for that. Instead, the six-man ordnance detail loaded up the various weapons out there and fired off all the unused ammo. It would usually take us less than an hour, which is about half the time it would take to count it and do the paperwork required to turn it back in.

Sitting out there on the rifle range and doing nothing all day long was boring at first, but after a while I became accustomed to the constant gunfire and learned how to nap through it all, until it was time to wake up and fire off a couple of thousand rounds before dinner.

As a result of my Army experience I developed a couple of unique skills. One, I'm one of the few people who doesn't 'jump' when a car backfires. Guns going off just don't startle me. I also know how to handle weapons, having spent so much time in the army taking them apart and repairing them. I don't feel like telling this whole story to

94

every macho vendor there, but they can see they way that I handle each weapon they give me to try out for balance that I'm no stranger to guns.

This apparent know-how, along with my driving a Hummer and wearing a very expensive wristwatch has turned me into sort of a novelty here. Several people have clumsily tried to ask me what I do for a living. I just say "a little of this, and a little of that." The word has probably been spread around that I'm with the CIA, or some Delta Force type of operation.

I reach the booth where the harnesses are, and buy the largest one they've got. It's not designed for dogs, but since Bernie probably weighs about the same as most humans, it should fit nicely and get the job done. No sense telling them it's for a dog, because most of the people at this stand are no doubt buying them for dangerous commando purposes like scaling up a cliff to attack a hostile Boy Scout campsite, or some other paramilitary assignment here in the wild, wild west of Southern California.

Having purchased the harness, I'm now out in the parking lot answering questions about the Hummer. Most of the tire-kickers here want to know how steep an incline it will climb, what the thickness of the metal is for bullet-resistance, and many more inquiries about dangers that not one of these wannabee soldiers of fortune will ever have to worry about in their jobs at gas stations and warehouses. The only uniforms they will ever be paid to wear will have blue collars and company names embroidered on. No Mensa memberships or advanced degrees here.

95

Back at the boat I get a brilliant idea. If Kathy Potter has disappeared into the ether, I have a strong feeling she's not going to leave that couple of hundred thousand dollars of insurance money behind. I call Uniman's office to find out exactly what the procedure is for her to collect on that claim. Mister Uniman refers me to the lady who's in charge of their life claim department and tells her to cooperate fully with me.

"Yes, Mister Sharp, what can I do for you today?"

"I want to know about that claim Mister Uniman mentioned to you... the one for life insurance benefits on Paul Potter. What I want to know is if there is an address where the check is supposed to be sent."

"Yes, Mister Sharp, there is an address. In fact, it's a brand new one. She must have called it in within the past day or so, because it's just in note form on the file and hasn't been entered into our computer yet."

"Great. Why don't you give me that new address so that I can do some more work verifying that claim?"

"Oh, I don't think that'll help you very much. It's to a Post Office Box somewhere in Virginia. When we're finished processing the claim we'll make the check payable to her and mail it to that P.O. Box."

"Listen, I'm doing some special work on that claim for Mister Uniman, so I'd like you to do me a favor. Put a flag on that file, so that the check doesn't

96

get sent to any Post Office box. Instead, Mister Uniman's office will be preparing a special letter to be sent to the claimant, notifying her that she must make a personal appearance at your office to sign a release form and pick up her check in person."

"Well, Mister Sharp, that's a little out of the ordinary, but I guess we can do it."

That claims lady doesn't know it, but she gave me more information than she thinks. I know that in order to get a P.O. Box, you have to apply for it in person to sign forms and pick up the box key. There are only two ways she could have gotten that P.O. box so fast: one was to fly back and forth from Oregon to Virginia, and the other was to have someone with connections do the work for her. Coincidentally, one particular government organization that I know of has their main training in Quantico, Virginia – and it's the same group whose special agent warned me to stay away from the Potter case.

Living in a trailer park cottage doesn't usually give one an opportunity to make the type of connections it would take to get that Virginia P.O. box, so I have a hunch that she did it the same way she got her husband legally declared dead so fast - with the help of my secretive friends at the Federal Building. I doubt if she's a protected witness, but for some reason, she sure is being protected.

A dog-mail comes in reminding me that Indovine and Uniman have invited themselves out to the Marina and will be at the boat tomorrow at three in the afternoon. The Asian boys will be delivering a late lunch for everyone, so I'm being instructed not to ruin my appetite by eating at noon and then be rude by not joining them.

There's a knock on the hull. Looking over the side, I'm pleasantly surprised to see that it's Beverly Luskin.

"Hello, counselor. Hope you don't mind my dropping in un-announced, but I was passing by the Marina on my way back to La Verne and thought I'd see if you were in."

I invite her aboard and notice that the door to the kid's stateroom is open about an inch. There is a small eye visible, peering out. Beverly comes aboard and makes the usual comments that first-time visitors usually make about how nice everything looks. Quite often they'll be surprised to see that we have a full size galley, complete with refrigerator-freezer and garbage disposal unit. I guess that when people hear you live on a boat they automatically think it's some ten-foot rowboat with a canvas cover.

I give her the tour from flybridge above to engine rooms and master stateroom below. When we come back up to the main salon area, the kid is bringing out a tray complete with three kinds of cheeses, crackers, some greenish dip, and small cups for tea.

Beverly starts talking to Suzi, as if she thinks that the kid's IQ is somewhere down around room temperature.

"Oh, my goodness, Peter, how nice. This must be that darling little girl you told me so much about."

The kid sees that Beverly is looking at me, so she takes the opportunity to make her index finger go into her mouth, in a 'regurgitation-inducing' motion. The smart-alec move stops when Beverly looks back in her direction again.

We sit and chat for about thirty minutes before she looks at her watch, letting me know how fast the time has flown by while she's here. She stands up and tells Suzi how nice it was meeting her and that she can't wait to see her again, to get better acquainted. Fat chance. The kid hasn't said one word to her. The dog didn't even think it worthwhile to come out of his stateroom for a sniff of this new stranger.

I walk her to the car and get rewarded with a wet one. When I get back to the boat, all remnants of the platter, dip, cheese and everything else has disappeared back to wherever it came from. It was like no one had visited at all. As the kid heads for her stateroom, she gives me the ultimate summary of her thoughts about Beverly Luskin: a 'thumbs-down' signal.

The phone is ringing. It's Jack B. calling.

"Mister Sharp, you'll never believe what I got today."

"Let's not play games Jack, please, just tell me."

"Kathy Potter's cell phone records just came in the mail."

"Jack, don't touch them. I want you to put whatever you got, envelope and all, into a plastic evidence bag and get it over to Victor's place."

"You mean the autopsy shop?"

99

"You got it. Victor's got a whole team of experts on his staff and I want that mail dusted for prints. Was there a return address on the envelope?"

"Yes, but it was the cottage. She must have tossed into a nearby mailbox before she moved."

This is interesting. It looks like Kathy Potter wants to help us out, but not too much. That might be because she's afraid that her insurance claim could be adversely affected if we learn too much.

Last year I had the good fortune to become associated with a gentleman named Victor Gutierrez, who runs a company out near Pasadena that he appropriately named after his vanity telephone number 1(800)AUTOPSY. Being a former medical examiner, he now performs autopsies for private individuals. The Coroner's office doesn't perform a post-mortem on every cadaver, feeling that they are not necessary if the cause of death is determined by investigation to be suicide, unavoidable accident, or natural causes.

Quite often a bereaved heir, party to a civil accident, or insurance company wants to have a complete autopsy performed, so they retain the services of Victor's company, because he has a complete laboratory set up to do just that. He also retains a group of former CSI people capable of doing all the scientific evidence-gathering tasks. Their services are often in demand by people like myself who have no access to the government's services. Victor's organization has been invaluable on some recent cases, doing fingerprint and DNA comparisons for us.

I call Victor's place and leave a message for him with instructions to make a copy of those cell phone records and fax it over to me. Once I get the fax, I can have Jack start calling those numbers too.

I've still got some research to do on Indovine's weapons charge, so I'd better start cracking the books, because he'll be calling me tomorrow for his weekly update.

I'm taking the Hummer in at seven this morning for routine service and to have the tires rotated. I wish they could tune it up a little to improve the performance, because I'm only getting about nine miles to the gallon in the city. When I bought it they told me it wasn't too good on mileage, and they weren't kidding. I guess that if you can afford a vehicle like this you're not supposed to be concerned with a little thing like the cost of gasoline.

I don't have to be back at the boat until three this afternoon, so maybe it's time to see about a haircut. My barber has suggested adding a little color to my hair because some gray is showing through. It may be worthwhile doing that to see the expression on the kid's face when she notices it.

Yesterday is still on my mind. Suzi's radar is much better than mine. She thought that Beverly deserved a 'thumbs-down,' but this time I think she's missing something. The kid is still only a kid, and IQ only goes so far – it never can take the place of the experience a person gets going through the process of aging between eleven and forty-two. I may not be the most worldly person around, but I've still had contact

101

with more people than the kid has, and I feel pretty good about Beverly.

The money has nothing to do with it. I'd find her attractive and enjoyable to be with even if the insurance claims weren't going to make her a multi millionaire. This lady has class and I think I can trust her with my feelings in spite of the sabotage that I'm sure the kid has in store for our relationship. Suzi and Myra have bonded completely, and if they weren't so far apart in age, they'd probably be having lunch together and shopping every day. Suzi wants to see Myra and I get back together, and any other woman stepping into the picture is a danger to her scheme.

My barber says he can't take me until tomorrow, and it's a good thing, because the kid just called and told me that she has to be downtown at the school board by ten-thirty to take another test.

It's a few minutes before ten, and as I pull back into the Marina I see that Myra and Suzi are out by the dock gate waiting for me.

As usual, the car seating arrangement is with me driving and the dog sitting up next to me in the front passenger seat, with his head sticking out of the open sunroof. Some inventor came up with a novel safety idea for dogs that ride in cars with their faces out in the wind. To avoid injury, he designed some goggles for dogs. They have two sets of adjustable straps to keep them in place, and have been trademarked as 'Doggles.' The kid had to order at least two pairs for Bernie, and he's now sitting up next to me looking like a World War I aviator. Suzi is

102

in the back seat, deep into a serious conversation and holding hands with Myra.

If I remember correctly, today's test is supposed to be an important one, and I think the kid is worried about it. Myra is her moral support, and when we get there, they walk in together. When Myra comes back to the car, the cross-examination begins.

"What's this I hear about some woman named Beverly? Are you getting ready to make a fool out of yourself again?"

"I see you've been talking to detective Suzi. What did she say?"

"That this Beverly is no good. She's as phony as that Rolex you're wearing."

"You know, not everyone has mastered the ability to communicate with children. So she talked down to the kid. That's a normal response to meeting a child for the first time. They got along fine."

"What did Suzi say to her?"

"Well, you know Suzi can be shy with strangers. She doesn't even talk that much to me, and I'm her legal guardian, her business partner, and we've been living together for the better part of a year now."

"Peter, if there's one thing you should know by now, it's that living with a female is no guarantee that you either know or can communicate with her. And your living experience with both Suzi and me is living proof of that."

"I don't think that's it, Myra. The truth of the matter is probably that she desperately wants both a mother and a father to live with. She's finally found a satisfactory couple to fill those parent positions, and

103

we're it. That means anyone I bring to the boat socially is a threat to her master plan, so she'll try to sabotage the relationship. She definitely loves you, and will tolerate me as long as you're part of the package."

This remark brings a brief stop to the conversation as we both think about my statement. Almost an hour has gone by now since we dropped her off, and the kid is coming back to the car. She gets in the back seat with Myra, smiles, and tells her that she thinks she did a good job on the test.

I have no doubt that the kid knew she was going to ace this test, and I have a suspicion that this whole act of hers to have Myra to come along for moral support has obviously been just part of her plan to get us together more often. Truth be told, I also think the idea is a good one, but no way on earth would Myra ever consider it, so that's the end of that thought.

Myra's driver dropped her off at the Marina, so I take her to the Criminal Courts Building where her office is, and then the three of us head back to the Marina. Doggles have been re-fastened, so it's now Peter, Suzi, and air ace Baron von Snoopy, on the road again.

Back at the Marina, I see that the Asian Boys are working hard on our boat. They've completely removed the large full-width swim step, along with its attached ladder, and laid them both on the dock for varnishing. I drop off the dynamic duo, park the car and walk over to pick up the mail. The kid was busy with other things this morning, so the task rests with me because the dog has only been taught how to deliver the mail, but he doesn't know how to pick it up yet. I spend a while shooting the breeze with the clerk at the mail place and then slowly start my walk back to the boat. Indovine and Uniman will be there when I get back, and they're not the kind of guys I'd ordinarily think of going out with for a beer, so I'm taking my time.

Sure enough, the boat is buzzing. I hear a noise that sounds familiar. It's the engines. I don't know why they're on, but I don't stay curious too long, because Mister Uniman greets me with the answer. "Ah, captain Sharp. It's about time you came back to the boat. We're all here anxiously waiting for you to take us out for a harbor cruise."

Is she kidding? Did the kid really plan this? I can't believe it. She knows I don't even know how to turn the engines on. How are we going to pull this off? Entering the boat, I see that both Uniman and Indovine brought their usual group of brown-noses. Each one has an assistant and a personal secretary, and they're all standing around waiting for Captain Incompetent to give them some orders.

In the middle of the main salon, a table has been set with a beautiful buffet lunch, complete with kasha varnishka, lox, cream cheese, bagels, rye bread, an assortment of sliced cheeses, pastrami and corned beef. The Asian boys brought the stuff over from Jerry's Deli. I'm surprised they even knew that place existed. From the looks of their white outfits and caps, they're also going to be today's crew. Two of them are already off the boat loosening up the dock lines in preparation for our harbor cruise, and the kid is getting the dog into his special safety harness.

Uniman is the leader of the guests. "Okay, skipper, where do you want us all?" I look past him and see that the kid has this thing all planned out. She's pointing up in the air, so I guess we'll be doing a repeat of our boat-handling test. I'll be the shill topside, while she works the controls down below. I might as well get used to acting this part until I actually get up the nerve to learn how to drive this big boat on my own... a skill I'm not that interested in learning. I start to take command and issue my first order of the day.

"All right, everyone topside. The salon is off limits 'till we get back. We'll be seeing the harbor from up on the flybridge while our crew cleans up the mess you guys made down here, scarfing down your free lunch.

Uniman can't let that one go by. "Free lunch, huh? I'll bet it shows up on my next invoice." That gets a good laugh out of everyone as they climb up the ladder to the flybridge. I know in my heart that Uniman is correct about his next bill.

Once we're all comfortable up on the flybridge I decide to play the part, so I shout out to the Asian Boys on both sides of the boat down below. "Okay, cast off the dock lines, we're about to get under way." I sure wish I could see the kid's face as she hears me give that order. The boys are following my instructions, probably because the kid nodded at them that it's okay. The dock lines are loosened from their cleats and the loose ends are thrown up to the other Boys on the boat, while the two on the dock

106

jump up onto the boat as it begins to slowly back out of the slip.

Both Uniman and Indovine walk up to where my helm seat is and compliment me on my obvious boat handling skills.

Going along with the act, I keep my hands on the controls, because it would be very embarrassing if anyone saw one of them move while my hand wasn't on it. Once the boat is slowly backed out of the slip and traveling down the basin at almost five miles and hour, I sit back and relax with only one hand on the wheel. The clutch and throttle levers won't be moving again until close maneuvering is required when we go back to the slip. That much I know, if nothing else.

The harbor cruise is enjoyable. We go down C Basin to the main channel, and then turn left to pass by the California and Del Rey Yacht Club facilities. After pointing out those two landmarks, we turn around and head towards the breakwater, giving our passengers a good look at Fisherman's Wharf, the local tourist attraction that's built and decorated like a small East Coast fishing village. Uniman mentions that they were promised a brief spin out past the breakwater, so I guess that Suzi has one planned. This doesn't make me too happy, because it looks like there are some waves out there, and it's probably pretty deep, too.

Once we pass the Harbor Patrol station, the five-mile-an-hour limit is raised to eight, so we pick up a little speed and head toward the breakwater. Out in the distance we see a couple of medium-sized sailboats practicing some racing techniques and tacking around each other. They're about three miles offshore, so I'm not worried about any collision today. This is the middle of the week, so we're one of the only boats out of its slip, and we've got the whole ocean to ourselves.

Going around the breakwater the boat goes up slightly as we encounter the first open ocean wave. Because the water was shallow where we were, there's usually a nice wave waiting to welcome you as you leave the harbor. This Grand Banks is one heck of a boat. It's really heavy and handles the waves like a true ocean-going ship. I can see that Suzi wants us to be at least a half-mile offshore before she turns the boat back to return thru the other side of the breakwater. From the reading I've done in boating magazines, she's doing the correct thing. Too many times I've heard of people who go out one side of the breakwater and then drive its full length to the other side's opening, being only fifty feet away. That's a dangerous way to do it, because if anything should happed to cause a loss of engine power, you'll only have a minute or two to try and drop an anchor before the boat gets dashed onto the rocks, wrecked, and sunk. As an old boater once told me, "the experienced sailor knows that the sea isn't his enemy, it's the hard stuff around the edges."

He probably knew exactly what he was talking about. I even played his part by telling that to our guests. I couldn't resist continuing my act by adding the three main rules of safe boating: keep the people *in* the boat, keep the water *out* of the boat, and don't bump into anything.

108

Now that I've been firmly established as the most knowledgeable boater that they know, I'm looking forward to getting back to the slip before they start to ask me questions about boating and find out what a fraud I am. Here I am entertaining a boat full of people out past the breakwater, and I have no idea what all these levers, switches and gauges in front of me are for.

Just when I'm starting to feel like a success this afternoon, one of our guests shouts out, pointing toward the sailboats. "Hey, look, those boats out there ran into each other. I think one of them is starting to sink, and the other one's mast is down in the water."

I look out using a pair of binoculars from the rack next to our steering wheel. Our guest is correct. One of the boats is definitely sinking and the other one isn't doing that much better. I hear a voice on our VHF radio, which has an extra set of controls up on the flybridge. It's the kid down below, who also knows what's going on out there.

"Mayday, mayday, mayday, this is the Suzi B., whiskey tango four, three, seven, niner, niner. There are two sailboats sinking about three miles due west of the breakwater. People are in the water. We are responding, over."

"Suzi B, this is the Coast Guard, can you assist them? Our cutter is still being serviced and won't be ready to roll for about an hour, over."

"That's a Roger, Coast Guard; we'll do what we can. Suzi B out."

As the emergency radio messages are being exchanged, I feel the large steering wheel being turned to the right, the engines roar louder, and we are now heading out towards where the sailboats are.

I have absolutely no idea what we're doing. I know she's a genius, but if she can pull this off, it'll be unbelievable. We're now heading toward the survivors at full speed, which is probably a little over ten miles an hour. If those people in the water are three miles out, then it should take us at least twenty minutes to get there, so I hope they can hang on for a while. When we get there we've got another problem. With no swim step on the back of the boat, there's no way for the people to get up and into our boat from the water.

I hear some commotion below. It sounds like a Chinese fire drill. People are running around shouting at each other. We're getting close to the sailboats now, so I hope that Suzi has a plan, because I certainly don't. All of our guests are silently sitting on the edges of their seats. They're in awe of this suspenseful event that they think I'm in charge of.

The flybridge deck of our Grand Banks extends all the way to the back of the boat, so there's no way of knowing what's going on directly below on the rear deck, but I know that something's going on down there because I can hear the activity. There's a lot of rapid Chinese chatter being exchanged.

The people in the water are only about five or ten minutes away, and I see that she's steering the boat off to the side. If she keeps on this course all the way, she'll miss them by about twenty feet.

We finally get to where the survivors are. By this time, both sailboats have completely sunk under the water and there must be almost thirty people treading water waiting for us to rescue them. Just as I think that the kid has blown it by missing them completely, I understand what's going on. The Asian Boys have gotten all of the boat's life jackets out of the storage compartments, along with a piece of nautical rope that must be at least two hundred feet long.

They've tied a life jacket onto the rope about every five or six feet, and they're now feeding the line and jackets off of the rear deck of our boat. I watch as the complete line stretches out over a hundred feet behind us and then hear the engines slow down, as the boat make a slight turn to the left. Wow. What a plan this kid cooked up on the spot. She knows that without a swim step we can't get anyone out of the water, so she's tossed out a two-hundred-foot floating rope. Now she's going to circle the swimmers and surround them with the rope until everyone in the water has grabbed onto a lifejacket.

I hear noises above us and looking up, see that there are four helicopters circling. I recognize the wide red stripe on one as being a Coast Guard chopper, another one has a Los Angeles Sheriff's marking on it, and the other two are from local news stations. They must have picked up Suzi's mayday call and came out to see what's going on.

By this time all the people in the water have firmly attached themselves to our lifeline and Suzi, having completed her circle, is now slowly heading back toward the breakwater with the survivors all safely in tow. She's going to tow them in the water all the way back to the Coast Guard Station.

We finally get back inside the breakwater and I see that every one of the survivors has successfully hung on for the whole ride. They're all smiling and giving us the 'thumbs-up.' It's just a little way to the Coast Guard station. As we approach the police docks, I see that there must be at least a half-dozen news camera crews standing by. Added to the curious onlookers, friends and families of the survivors, and emergency support people, there must be more than fifty anxious people lining the dock.

Suzi pulls as close to the dock as she can safely get and then, just as we're about ten feet in front of the Coast Guard station, the Asian Boys cut the lifeline loose, and the survivors all float toward the safety of the dock, with many outstretched hands waiting to pull them up out of the water.

As the first survivor gets pulled out of the water, there is a loud round of applause for us. Suzi keeps going, steering the boat back into the middle of the main channel and back towards our slip. She did it.

As we approach our slip, my perspiring hands go back to the control levers. Suzi is now maneuvering us into the slip, and several news camera crews are covering the heroic return. When our boat is safely back in its slip, the Asian Boys jump off and tie off the dock lines. There's another round of applause for us. A Coast Guard helicopter circles over us and uses its loud speaker. "Nice job, Suzi B. you really got the job done today."

112

For the next two hours our boat is like a madhouse. Indovine and Uniman are both holding their own separate press conferences, mentioning the names of their firms over and over again. Now I can see why Tiger Woods wears that Nike hat all the time. It's fantastic publicity.

No one bothers to ask the Asian Boys anything, because they pretend to not speak English, which is probably not much of a stretch for them. Suzi and the dog have disappeared into the forward stateroom. Each time I'm interviewed on camera, I make sure to let the public know that I couldn't have done it without my young ward and her friends. I tell them that she was down below coordinating the entire rescue operation. All I did was stay up on the flybridge and steer.

The local news changes Suzi's status, reporting the rescue as having been carried out by a boat-owning attorney assisted by his young daughter. I receive an e-mail from Myra, congratulating me on my new role as a parent.

I am now a certified hero. It's a good thing the kid shut down the boat's engines, because I wouldn't know which knob to turn for that task. Everyone in the Marina now knows how great I am. Too bad George isn't around: if he was, I'm sure he'd be over here shaking my hand and trying to be friends with a real celebrity hero.

8

After that strenuous day at sea I'd like to spend some time on land, so I'm now heading out to Palm Desert. A friend of mine has a house there and when he saw me on the evening newscasts, he must have thought that it would be nice to have a hero as a guest for a few days. My decision to leave the boat is also a much easier one to make knowing that Myra felt like spending some time at the Marina, so she'll be hanging out with the kid while I'm gone. I think they enjoy each other's company much more when I'm not around.

First is a stop at the Union station on Maxella, where I helplessly watch a portion of my life's savings spin by on the gas pump. While my money is flowing down into the tank I notice that there's a voice mail waiting for me on my cell phone. I press the correct button and hear Stuart's voice excitingly announcing what he considers to be the best business idea he's ever had. Sorry, Stu, it'll have to wait until I get back in town. Just to make sure I'm not bothered on my trip, I press another button, and the cell phone is now off. The kid knows where I'll be if she needs me.

In the past, I would never have the nerve to disconnect myself from society, worried that the 'big case' might be missed. What if Bill Gates couldn't reach me, to tell me that he was rear-ended by Warren Buffet, who was driving while drunk? What if some Sheik of Brunei couldn't ask me to bail him

114

out of jail after being wrongfully arrested for something?

Well, I've finally reached a point in my life where I realize that the big case just isn't going to come along that way. I'll turn the phone on every couple of hours to see if there are any emergency voice mails, and if it's not a call from the kid who needs me then it'll have to wait. During my last year of law school I had a part time night job covering the telephones for a bail bondsman. All I had to do was let his answering service put emergency calls through to me from guys in jail. If someone needed bailing out, I would qualify him financially over the phone first, and then call my boss to go over there and bail the customer out.

The phone rarely rang more than once each nite, but I never knew when that would happen. Every time I laid my head down for some sleep, I would glance over at the phone and look at it like it was a ticking bomb, ready to go off just as I fell asleep.

Ever since then, I make it a habit to turn off the phone when I go to sleep. I'm not a medical doctor and can't save lives, so I'm not worried that someone will die because they can't reach me while I'm sleeping.

Two days in the Desert is all I needed to remind me why I enjoy living on a boat. Instead of staying the extra day of my invitation, I tell my host as graciously as possible that I'd better be getting back to the boat for some important calls that might be coming in. During the two days my cell phone only had one message on it, but it was a telemarketer, so I didn't miss anything except a wonderful opportunity to buy some swampland in Montana.

Driving back to the Marina I've got one of my favorite CD's playing, with Oscar Peterson and the Count Basie Orchestra. The windows are up, the air conditioning is on, and I'm bouncing around to the music like some kid driving a low-rider with boom-box speakers blaring some rapper's latest hit. People driving near me on the freeway must think I'm an aging hipster. Maybe they're right.

I don't think the kid will mind my coming back a day early, unless she gets mad at me for scaring Myra away. Just to play it safe, I call Myra to let her know I'm on the way back.

"Hey, it's me. Anything exciting going on?"

"Peter, are you in the car?"

"Yeah, I'm coming back a day early. Why?"

"You'll find out when you get here. It's only two in the afternoon, so I'm taking off. Suzi's busy preparing for her lecture tonight."

"Lecture?"

"Yes, lecture. Stuart's coming over this evening, and she's going to teach him some principles of law. I think they're doing the Palsgraf case tonight and re-hashing Cardozo's opinion"

"Okay, I just don't want her left alone too long."

"My, my. Does this mean there's a little bit of fatherly love in that hulk of yours?"

Myra always did have a flair for words, but regardless of what she says, I'm the legal guardian of that kid and I want to make sure that she stays safe

116

from harm until she reaches sixteen. After that it'll probably be Harvard Law School's responsibility.

Driving back from the Palm Springs area is always a drag. About the only good thing about the trip is that Hadley's Date Orchard and store is on the way, so I can stop there and pick up some honey, dates, nuts and granola. This place has become one of the most popular stops for people returning from Palm Springs. Paul and Peggy Hadley started the business in 1931, and in July of 1999, the Morongo Band of Mission Indians bought the Hadley Fruit Orchard stores and mail order operation, so it's still in business.

Between my first and second years of law school I had a job playing piano at one of the Palm Springs hotels. Unfortunately, it was a summer job. I had heard that it gets pretty hot there during the summer, but the drummer who hired me said, "don't worry, pal, even on the hottest summer days the temperature goes down at night and you need a sweater to go outside." Being even more of a gullible jerk in those days, I believed him.

We pulled into town on the afternoon of July 3rd and were scheduled to start playing that evening. The temperature outside was 113 degrees that day, and people told us it was several degrees below normal for that time of year. Our little band started playing at seven-thirty for the dinner crowd, and I purposely stayed inside the air-conditioned place until ten that evening, planning on then going outside and taking a deep breath of cool, fresh, desert air.

True to my plan, we took our ten PM break and I walked outside of the hotel. It was dark, and I

117

took my deep breath. At first I thought that I was probably standing too close to the building and the hot breeze I felt might actually be coming from the hotel's air-conditioning exhaust fan. I was wrong. I wasn't too close to the building and the hot blast of air was the coolest that the evening had to offer. The temperature outdoors had undergone a drastic plunge from 113 down to 93.

After that summer I made a note never to return to the Palm Springs area during the months of May through September. I'm remembering that summer now as I continue my ride back to Los Angeles, snacking from a bag of Hadley's raw, un-roasted, unsalted cashews. Come to think of it though, I did meet a very nice girl that summer and continued dating her all the way into the following year. I would drive back there every Friday afternoon, and stay for the weekend, so by now, my brain goes on autopilot during the drive back and forth. After you do it over fifty times it becomes second nature.

The cashews are a good appetizer, but I know that because I'm coming back a day early there'll be no dinner waiting for me, so I might as well stop for a snack. There's an Indian place not far from the boat, so I go in, relax with a bottle of Indian Beer and order some Tandoori chicken, which is an elegant dish from the state of Punjab, where tandoori murgh is one of their most popular chicken dishes. This particular restaurant bakes it in an authentic tandoor clay oven, so the food really tastes delicious. The good thing is that it's only got 4 grams of fat. The bad thing is that it's got more than 66 mg of cholesterol.

One Indian beer leads to another, and then another. After about an hour of stuffing myself, I'm feeling no pain and the god-awful screeching they're playing on the speakers is starting to sound like music. Unlike our western world, with a twelve-tone musical scale, some of these Eastern civilizations have so many tones in their scale that it can sound more like a siren than music.

Being only a block or so away from the Marina, I think it's best that I walk from here to the boat. Those Indian beers come in the biggest bottles made, so the three that I had before, during, and after dinner, probably are equivalent to a six-pack, and I'm in no condition to drive. I'm not in such great condition to walk either, but it'll be a lot safer.

Just as I'm leaving the restaurant, the delivery boy is getting into his car. Five dollars later, he drops me off at the C-4200 dock gate, and I'm ready to negotiate the gangplank down to the boats. Most people think that when walking on the dock they're still on land, but they're not. The docks all float and the angle of the ramp that leads down to the docks changes as the tide goes up and down. At high tide, it's almost a level walk from land down to the dock, but at low tide, the water level may sink over six feet, so being low tide this evening, I'm holding on securely to the guard rail as I negotiate the steep incline down to the dock.

It's dark now, but a series of lights on our boat work off of a rheostat, so the low-voltage bulbs make an attractive guide for me to safely negotiate the boarding ladder and enter the wheelhouse. No doubt the kid's already in bed, having finished her law symposium and Stuart's nowhere to be seen, so I guess I've got the boat to myself, and I couldn't be happier. I think I'll just flop down on my king-sized bed and drop a little further into unconsciousness. As I approach my stateroom door it sounds like there's a giggling noise coming from in there, but I know that's impossible, so I ignore it and make a mental note to limit my future Indian beer consumption to only two bottles.

I pull off my shirt and loosen my belt. Just as I push open my stateroom door my pants start to fall to the floor. No problem, the bed's just a few feet in front of me and I'm all alone, so all I have to do is fall forward. The door will automatically close behind me and hopefully I'll wake up some time tomorrow afternoon, with no headache.

Part of the plan works. My pants are down at the floor and the door is swinging shut behind me, but as I start to fall forward I see that my bed isn't empty. I try to stop my fall but instead wind up on me knees at the foot of the bed. The giggling I thought I heard before has now reached a high squeal pitch, and in the dim light I see that my bed is occupied by four, not just one, but four young Asian females, all holding the bedspread up to their chins and gawking at me in awe.

9

This is not the usual thing I see when entering my stateroom. Now I'm thinking that maybe I had more than three Indian beers tonight. A lamp is turned on and from my kneeling position at the foot of the bed I see that this isn't a mirage. I am now attempting the impossible physical act of trying to pull my pants up while remaining down on my knees. This isn't working and I eventually fall over onto my side, in which position it becomes possible to pull up my pants, stand up and run out of my own stateroom.

Sitting down upstairs in the salon, I try to regain my composure. Through the closed stateroom door I can still hear the giggling, interspersed with high-pitched conversation in some foreign language. I feel in my heart that what I just saw and now hear is real, and definitely not a result of the Indian beers. As usual, I have absolutely no idea of what's going on, but know one thing for sure: no explanation will be forthcoming from that quartet in my bed.

This is too much to comprehend right now, so I flop down on the couch and am unconscious before my head hits the cushion.

As I slowly come out of my daze I see that the sun is shining into the boat, four giggling Asian girls are sitting around jabbering at each other, and Stuart is sitting on a chair next to the couch apologizing profusely.

At first I thought those four in my bed might be friends of Suzi's, but in the bright light I can now see that these females are definitely not kids. On the contrary, they're all attractive young women in their early twenties.

"Honest to goodness, Pete, I didn't know you were coming home last night. Both Suzi and Myra said you weren't returning from the desert until tonight. By the way, nice job of saving those people out in the water the other day. I saw most of it on television, and I didn't think…"

"Stuart, forget about the rescue. What about those girls? Who are they and what were they doing in my bed last night?"

"Oh, them? They're my new inventory."

"Inventory? Did you say inventory? What the hell are you talking about?"

"Well, if you wouldn't have had your phone turned off for the past couple of days I would've been able to explain it to you. We're having our first IPO in a couple of days."

"IPO? That's an acronym for Initial Public Offering. What're you going to do, take your company public and raffle these girls off? And you never answered my question. Who are they, and where did they come from? No, wait a minute. Please get them out of here for a while. Take 'em out on the aft deck for a few minutes. I need a half hour alone to get out of this sleeping bag, get into my stateroom, shave, and hit the shower. And then, my friend, you've got a lot of explaining to do."

The transformation is complete and I'm now back to being Mister Jekyll, attorney at law. "Okay

Stuart, start talking. What's going on? Where are they?"

"Suzi and the dog are walking them around the Marina so they can see the boats. Honest, I'm really sorry about last night. It's just that I had no other place to put them for the evening, and since you weren't going to be here, Suzi said that it would be okay…."

There's no need for him to apologize any more. Once the kid's name is mentioned, I realize that whatever happened was out of my control. But I still have to interrupt him because there are just too many unanswered questions at this point. "Stuart, instead of babbling on, why don't you just sit back, relax, and let me ask you some questions. First of all, what do you mean by 'IPO?' Please tell me you're not selling these girls."

"Pete, you surprise me. These girls are all high class and from fine families. IPO stands for Introductions Provided by Olive. That's the new business I wanted to explain to you."

It's not going to work my way. If I'm going to have any chance of finding out what's going on it'll be to just let him go on with his usual spiel. This happens every time he starts a new business venture, and since he's does so well financially with every crazy new business that he starts, I'm going to let him ramble on. With a wave of my hand, I indicate that he should continue. I surrender. The floor is his.

"Remember when I went to Thailand to see my fiancée, and when we drove to La Verne you explained all about the K-1 Visa? Well I kept thinking: there are a bunch of those mail order bride

123

places that show you pictures of girls in a catalog, and a prospective customer is supposed to fall in love with a picture and then spend months of his time and thousands of his dollars flying half way around the world to meet some girl that he might not like at all, and who definitely is not interested in him."

"I get the picture, Stu. Keep talking."

"Okay, well my philosophy is the same as it's always been, when it comes to marketing. And that is, 'you can't sell what you don't have.' Why make guys take off of work and endure eighteen-hour flights to Thailand when I can bring the girls here, protect them, act as their chaperone, and let their prospective husbands meet them right here in town."

I'm sitting here silent. I hear everything he's said, but the computer in my brain is failing to sort the information properly. He takes the blank expression on my face as his cue to go on.

"Peter, Peter, I don't think you see it yet. I'm starting the first international marriage brokerage that has an inventory of prospective brides right here in the states. The guys don't have to fly anywhere. And it's all on the up-and-up. There's absolutely no hanky-panky allowed, no sampling of the merchandise. Olive and Vinnie chaperone the meetings, and it all takes place in a fancy restaurant. We rent a small banquet room and hire a DJ to play some slow music. About a dozen guys will come in, six at a time, and sit around and talk to the girls. After a while, they dance, to try each other out for size. When the guys leave, they take pictures of the girls with them, and we have pictures of the guys, for the girls to look at.

124

"We wait until the next day, because by then, all the guys will know which girl they're mainly interested in. Once they tell us their choice, we show the girls the pictures of the guys who are interested, and then arrange for a second get-together, but this time on a couples only basis.

"In the beginning, after the guys get a look at the pictures, we charge them two hundred dollars each for admission to the first get-together. After that, and the pictures are exchanged and some couple are formed, we charge the guys five hundred to come back for a second call. This time there are only four couples, and each one is seated at a separate table for two. Olive and Vinnie are watching at all times, and the guys are not allowed to take the girls out of the place.

"Then, we wait another few days for the guys and the girls to decide if they think there's a possibility of getting serious. The girls are all pretty anxious to get married and move to the States, so if any guy really wants to go to the next level, we charge him another two hundred, and with his permission, a licensed private investigator does a thorough background check to make sure that he doesn't have a criminal record. If our investigation doesn't reveal any charges of abuse, his financial matters all look kosher, he can afford to provide a wife with a nice lifestyle, and that his HIV test comes back negative, then we're happy.

"We really have all the bases covered, so that no girl getting married through our service winds up in bad situation."

125

"That sounds pretty thorough, Stu, but what happens next? If a couple wants to get together, are they supposed to get married the next day?"

"No, no. Each one of the girls is in this country on a tourist visa, so they've only got a couple of months. A regular courtship goes on for a while, and if they get serious, we make plans for the guy to go back to Thailand and meet her family. If they approve of him, then he can arrange to have her come back here on one of those fiancée visas, and then they have another ninety days to either get married or call the whole thing off. So, whatta ya think? Have I got it together, or haven't I?"

I sit and nod for a time while I try to compose my thoughts. Every time Stuart comes up with something, it's usually so unique, that there's no prior experience to compare it to.

"Well, Stu, I've got to hand it to you. You've really put a good package together, and it looks like the girls are being protected quite nicely."

"Oh, yeah. And if they get married, we even have a pre-nuptial agreement that they sign, so that a guy won't lose everything if things don't go as well as planned."

"That's nice, but you know there have been some nasty stories about women who come over here with an agenda that can be destructive."

I can tell by the look on his face that now it's his turn to sit there and not fully grasp what's just been said.

"Stuart, you should do some research into this stuff. When you first told me about your fiancée, I did some checking, and there are a lot of horror

126

stories out there. I don't know if any of them originated with girls from Thailand, but there sure are plenty that have to do with Russian girls, and others from Europe.

"There are some foreign organized crime groups that have gotten into the mail order bride business and from what I hear, it can be more profitable then selling drugs or arms, but with less danger of getting caught or punished.

"Organizations in this country, like the Global Survival Network, have been very interested in protecting girls who come over her to get married, and they really do need protection, because not everyone over here does the background check and is as thorough as you are. As a result, our government has passed a law called the Violence Against Women Act (VAWA) in 1994. They felt it was necessary because there were too many cases of women brought over here and being treated like slaves, abused, forced to work long hours and used for prostitution. They had no legitimate way to complain, because their passports were taken away from them and they were threatened with deportation and jail.

"Under the provisions of the new law, which is a section of the Immigration and Nationality Act, abused spousal immigrants are allowed to petition for permanent legal residency status for themselves, without needing the sponsorship of their abusing spouse.

"Unfortunately, some brides have been taking unfair advantage of and manipulating the law, by making false claims of abuse and false accusations against their spouses. They then get lawyers and proceed against the husband, trying to clean out his assets.

"Now I'm not saying that any of your girls is planning something like that, but if you're going to be so thorough and check out the guys on this end, I think you should at least be as thorough and check out the girls, on the other end."

"What do you mean check them out? I can't ask them to fill out an application form with questions like 'are you connected with organized crime.' I've personally visited with their families, and everything looked kosher."

Stuart has a point. How can you ever know what a person's secret agenda is?

"You're right, Stu. I guess the only way you can protect everyone is by having a strong pre-nup signed. But make sure that the girl gets her own independent legal counsel, and don't refer her to a lawyer. Have her call the L.A. County Bar Referral department, so she can get her own lawyer. You can help her with the legal fees if you want to, but stay out of the advice business if you want the pre-nup to hold up. And one last thing. I've heard that many Thai families demand that a dowry be paid to them before they allow their daughter to marry. You should pre-negotiate that, so none of your customers gets a surprise after the wedding."

I hope that Stuart's girls live happily ever after, but for the life of me can't understand why anyone would want to import a wife from some other country. I checked out some statistics on the web, and found that there are many thousands of women a year

128

coming over here for marriage, and more than five thousand a year actually get married to American men.

From other figures that I've seen in the past, there are more women in this country than men, so why create a female trade surplus by bringing more of them over here? All over this country magazines contain personal ads from men and women wanting to meet that 'special' someone. On the web there are numerous dating services like Match.com, and the 'Personal' section of Yahoo. You can now select a date by zip code, so 'geographically undesirable' is no longer an available excuse. There are so many desperate women looking for husbands that the television networks have created a new category of reality shows where women compete for the affection of some real or alleged 'catch,' who may even be able to support them.

And speaking of long distance romance, my friend Jack B. remains involved with Phyllis Morse, the girl he met in Chicago recently. I sure hope he can still concentrate on his work, because he's got some important unfinished assignments.

I hit Jack's number on my speed-dial.

"Hello, this is Jack's house."

"Hi, this is attorney Peter Sharp, one of Jack's associates. Is he available?"

One thing that never ceases to amaze me is how people can completely ignore the fact that they've got a telephone near their mouth when they decide to yell something out to someone. This is exactly what Jack's classless girlfriend does, as she shouts out as loudly as possible to another room, and also into my ear.

"Jackie, it's that lawyer guy on the phone." Then, in a miraculous change of tone, she quietly speaks to me again. "I just called him to the phone. He'll be right here."

I'm so glad she informed me that she called Jack to the phone. She must think that I'm one of the few people on the west side of Los Angeles who didn't hear her shout out to him. After a few more seconds Jack picks up the phone.

"Hello Mister Sharp, how're you doing today?"

"I'm doing fine, Jack. I was wondering how you're doing, especially with finding out anything about the Kathy Potter matter. Did you have a chance to call any of those numbers on her phone bill?"

"Yes, I did. I haven't called them all yet, but there are a few that appear more than once. I've got a friend at the phone company who's trying to get some names and addresses for me. Mister Potter's cell phone records show plenty of calls made to other cell phones that the company says were stolen phones. I guess he was calling his drug connections: they all use throwaway phones because they're untraceable.

"As for the wife, her calls were mostly to friends and relatives, but from my survey, it sounds like he was really lousy to her. I think he abused her so much, she may have even contemplated suicide."

"Okay, Jack, keep up the good work. Oh yeah, how're things going with Phyllis? Is she going to stay in town for a while?"

"Uh, I gotta go now, Mister Sharp."

"Yeah, I get it Jack; she's sitting right next to you. Call me if you come up with anything."

Well, that's another dead end. It looks like good old Mister Uniman will have to pay out on all these claims, and one of those claimants is the lovely Beverly Luskin, who I really would like to see again. I hope that Uniman never finds out I've been seeing her socially, because that might look like a conflict of interest. Naw, what am I talking about? I never accepted any assignment to defend him against her claim. Uniman asked me to let him know if I saw anything out of the ordinary, that's all.

Having successfully rationalized that it's now okay to get together with her again, I call her number and when she answers the phone, I get a slight buzz.

"Hi Bev, it's Peter Sharp. Remember me?"

"Why certainly, handsome. How are you doing?"

"Fine. I was wondering when we might get together again. Are you planning on checking out that property in North Hollywood again soon?"

"I don't think so Peter, I'm afraid that deal's no longer on the table."

"Okay, I've got a full tank of gas. How about some place in your neck of the woods?"

"Oh, Peter I'd love to, but I've got so many things on my plate just now, I just don't think I'll have the time. And to tell you the truth, I'm starting to feel the weight of what's happened in my life and it's taking a toll on my libido. Pete, I'd love to talk to you for a while but I've got to go over to City Hall

131

and take care of some paperwork. Maybe we can talk again next week."

This doesn't sound good. Did she just dump me? Has she met someone new, who lives out in her area? I wouldn't be surprised if some guy like me swooped in and grabbed her up. Opportunities like that don't come around too often, and I'm sure there were several guys out there who've had their eyes on her for some time. Now that her husband's been gone for a while, I don't blame someone for making a move.

She mentioned that she was going over to her local City Hall, so maybe I can call up a favor out there.

I call the District Attorney's office in La Verne and ask to speak to the deputy D.A. I met out there the day I got arrested.

"Wendy, this is attorney Peter Sharp. Last time we met I got arrested."

"Oh, yes Mister Sharp, I remember you. I rarely forget murder suspects that I've had lunch with who were also once married to my boss."

She's got a nice sense of humor and obviously remembers me, so I ask her to do me a favor, I tell her that Beverly Luskin will be visiting City Hall shortly, and since that's where Wendy's office is, I ask her to try and talk to Beverly. There's supposed to be an ongoing investigation into her late husband's murder, so it wouldn't be out of the ordinary for the D.A. to casually ask how she's doing, and assure her that they're still working on the case.

Wendy agrees, and promises to call me back if her mission succeeds. What I'm mainly interested in is Beverly's demeanor. Wendy's a professional prosecutor, so sizing up a person by their body language should be a skill she's got down pat by now.

I have less than an hour to wait before the phone rings. My caller ID display shows Wendy's number.

"Hi, Wendy. Did you get a chance to see her?"

"Yes I did, Mister Sharp, but I didn't speak to her."

"What's the matter, chicken out?"

"Not really. I was out in the hallway and noticed her from about thirty feet away. She was wearing a pair of dark sunglasses, but I got the feeling that she saw me and probably didn't feel like having a conversation because she ducked into the filing room before I got a chance to wave at her."

"That's strange. I wonder what she was there for."

"Yes, I wondered too, and I was also curious about why she apparently avoided me. The average person in her position, being the widow of a victim, would be curious about how our investigation was going. I waited until she finished with the clerk and then I went into the filing room. I know the clerk in there quite well, so I asked her about Beverly Luskin."

"You trusted the clerk to give you an analysis of Beverly's behavior? I don't know if I'd accept a filing clerk as an expert witness on behavior."

"Neither would I, but this clerk gave me some information about physical evidence. She told me that under those sunglasses, she was able to tell that your friend Beverly had a shiner."

"Excuse me?"

"You heard me counselor, she had a black eye."

10

Who would want to do a thing like that to her? Beverly Luskin is a successful classy lady, not some low class trailer park broad. I can't believe she'd allow someone to get away with conduct like that. If some guy's been punching my intended girlfriend around I certainly want to know who it is, and I'm sure that the authorities would also want that information.

There's no way I can call her and ask how she got that black eye, so I'm going to have to do something that I really don't feel good about: send Jack B. out there. I call his number and pray that Phyllis doesn't want another crack at rupturing my eardrum. Thank goodness, Jack answers the phone.

"Jack, I'd like you to spend a few days in La Verne."

"Isn't that where your new girlfriend, the Luskin widow lives?"

"Yes Jack, but it's not what you're thinking. I just spoke to a friend of mine out there, and was told that Beverly Luskin was seen wearing sunglasses to cover up a black eye."

"You haven't been playing it rough with her, have you Mister Sharp?"

"Don't be ridiculous, Jack, it wasn't me. That's why I want you to go out there. And listen, I'm not interested in pictures of anyone in a compromising position. Her life is her own business, and if she's found someone else and wants to dump me, I can live with it. I just want to find out if she's getting knocked around. She retained our office to handle some matters for her, and I'd like to know who's doing a Punch and Judy routine with one our clients."

In some ways I feel like a dog that chases cars. What would that dog do if he ever caught one? Jack is a good investigator. I'm sure he'll be taking Phyllis with to keep him company, but that's okay, because a woman might be able to spot and interpret something that Jack might miss. I still don't know what to do with whatever information Jack might come up with.

What if she's got a new boyfriend who likes to beat her up? She's no prisoner. She can walk into the police station and make a complaint any time she wants to. She was just there this afternoon and didn't make a report. She even had a chance to talk one-on-one with a Deputy District Attorney, and she didn't take it. There's got to be some reason why she's allowing this behavior to go unpunished, and that reason is what I'd really like to know.

I've got a pretty good imagination, but can only come up with two possible reasons for her to keep quiet about this abuse. Maybe someone who has something on her is controlling her – and that's being used as a lever to force her to keep her mouth shut. The other reason is money. There's going to be a lot of it coming her way from the insurance claims, and maybe revealing the source of her abuse might endanger that expected money. But what skeletons can she possibly have in her closet?

This is an interesting situation. Uniman Insurance has two large claims pending from widows in different parts of the West Coast. Both widows are mysterious, with one having a black eye, and the other having disappeared completely. If I were a conspiracy nut I'd say they're both connected in some way. But I'm not a conspiracy nut, so I think I'll let Jack do his job on both of those cases.

Stuart calls to let me know that he's refined his due diligence procedure for screening prospective husbands in I.P.O., his international marriage brokerage business. He happened to have been on the boat one time when a landlord client called, and he overheard the advice I gave with respect to qualifying a prospective apartment rental customer. My philosophy on that particular subject is that anyone can get a Visa or MasterCard, because they're being offered by so many banks, credit card companies and retail vendors that there's probably no person in the country who can't qualify to get one of them. On the other hand, there's only one company that can give you an American Express card. If you want to play games with your credit, you can max out one Visa or MasterCard after another, and then probably still qualify to get another one from a different vendor. But, if you screw up with American Express, they won't give you another Amex card.

Taking those facts into consideration, I advised the client to only rent his best apartments out to people who can show that they've had an American Express card for a minimum of five years. That's the advice that Stuart heard and now he's calling to let me know that he's using that standard to qualify his I.P.O. customers. He also wants them to bring a copy of their most recent tax return, so he can verify that they've got at least a minimum high five-figure income.

I really have to hand it to him, because he's trying very hard to make sure that any girl coming over here to get married doesn't get stuck with some schlub who'll take advantage of her. He even goes so far as to let the girls know their legal rights, and in the event there's even a hint of abuse, they should call him to complain. He also plans on sending Olive out to make follow-up house calls on married clients to check on how things are going.

As smart as he is, Stuart may be missing out on another real opportunity. He doesn't have to bring girls over here from another country. I bet there are probably a lot of women right here in this country that would like to have him provide his due diligence for them. Quite often I hear about cases where some lothario marries a woman and then either absconds with her money, lures her into phony investments, or has several other wives that she doesn't even know

137

about. Stuart could probably charge a fee of about five hundred dollars and do the husband screening for them. Any guy who's on the up-and-up should have no objection to his future wife checking him out. I've heard of many parents who've done that, and found lots of phonies who were after their daughters' money. The problem with parents doing it is that even if they find out that their daughter's fiancée is no good, more often than not the daughter will so resent them for going behind her back that she'll wind up marrying the louse anyway, just for spite.

On my first date with Beverly she asked me if I would ever like to get married again. That wasn't the first time the question has come up on one of my first dates. I can tell that the woman is obviously qualifying me to find out whether or not I'm going to be a good investment of her time, but I still think it's a little 'forward' to ask it so soon. My usual answer is, "sure, but not on the first date." They accept that, and the rest of the evening can continue on without further cross-examination, but as far as I'm concerned, if I don't think there's ever going to be a possibility of me wanting to spend the rest of my life with that person, then she'll soon be an entry in my history book.

This is also a revelation to me, because thinking it over like this tells me that Beverly might be the one. She asked the question, I joked my way out of it and then we saw each other again and I'm still trying to go back for more.

The last time I got interested in a female it was Patty Seymour, the Deputy City Attorney. When I

138

discussed it with Myra she told me that Patty was a lesbian. I wonder if it might happen again this time. I'm pretty sure that Myra's through with me for good, so it shouldn't make her jealous to hear about my feelings for someone else. If she tells me that Beverly's a lesbian too, then I'll spot the pattern and realize that Myra's still interested. It's worth a try. She's on my speed-dial.

"Hello Peter. I've got caller ID too."

"Ah, it's so nice to hear your voice."

"Cut the crap, Petey, what do you want this time?

"Now that's no way to talk to your number one ex-husband. I just wanted to see if I could get some advice from you. It's about a female."

"I know. It's that widow out in La Verne, isn't it?"

"How could you possibly know that? Oh, I know, it's your resident spy. You've got a mole embedded on the boat that tells you everything."

"This didn't come from my mole on your boat. Her info is better than that. I also know all about you dropping your pants in front of those four young Thai girls. You should be ashamed of yourself."

"Yeah, I know. If I would have dropped my pants like that to surprise you more often, we'd probably still be married now. Seriously, how did you…?"

I get it. This information must have come from Wendy, her Deputy out in La Verne.

"Okay, Wendy told you. I guess I'll have to be out of Los Angeles County to avoid being seen by

139

one of your spies. Anyway, I really like this Beverly."

"I heard that she got a thumbs down from Suzi. Didn't that tell you anything?"

"Yes, it told me that the kid doesn't want me to be with anyone but you. That only means she's not right all the time. Besides, she's only a kid. What can she possible know about adult relationships? I like this Beverly. Not only is she great to look at, but she's smart, classy, successful, and when she settles with the insurance company, that three million will make her almost as rich as you. By the way, are you sure I'm not entitled to some of that money you inherited from your grandfather?"

"Oh please, give me a break. You don't care about her money. Wendy described her to me, and it's her ass you're after. I know you. You're a dog. Anyway, it doesn't matter what I think about her, because you shouldn't be involved with her now. It's a bad idea. Period."

"Why not? She likes me, I like her, we're compatible on a bunch of levels, so why shouldn't I get involved with her."

"Because she's a suspect, dummy."

"What? A suspect? What are you talking about? You mean in the death of her husband? She had nothing to do with that. What about the fact that his killers stole my Hummer? Does that mean I'm a suspect too? It was my car used in the murder."

"No, stupid, you're not a suspect. We know she didn't pull the trigger on her husband, but I really wish that for once you'd start thinking with some part of your body that's above your waist. She's the wife.

She stands to collect millions of dollars in insurance. We don't know if she put out a contract on the guy, so until we get more evidence in this case, we can't rule her out. You know the way it works: everyone involved is a possible suspect until we rule them out. And we always look at the surviving spouse first. It's standard procedure."

She has a point, but there seems to be a pattern emerging in her opinions. According to her, my first interest was an alleged lesbian, and then my next one a murder suspect. Myra is obviously still in love with me, but can't even admit it to herself. I think I'll stop hinting that I want part of her inheritance. Maybe that'll put her in a more receptive state of mind. Or better yet, I'll let the kid know that I'm still interested, and then let her do the job for me. Myra and Suzi are like a sister act now, talking every day on the phone at least once or twice.

This is a great fantasy. I'm smitten with three beautiful women, and they all want me. Unfortunately one of them may be a murderer, another a lesbian, and the third always seems to be looking for some reason to have me arrested, but nobody's perfect.

Since I'm a total failure in putting a successful relationship together for myself, I might as well call Stuart and tell him my ideas about how to put successful relationships together for other people. I'm reminded of the old saying, 'those that can, do: those that can't, teach.' I guess I'm the relationship teacher now.

I call Stuart and wait to see how his phone gets answered. He's got so many businesses going, it would take several minutes if they were all mentioned in a phone greeting. I learn that he's consolidated things.

"Hello, this is StuartCorp. Can I help you?"

"Hi, Olive, it's Peter Sharp. Is the 'Corp' around?"

"Oh, hello Mister Sharp. Yes, just a minute, I'll tell him you're on the line."

"Hello Peter, to what do I owe the honor of this call?"

"Stuart, you're not going to believe this, but for once it's me calling you with a business idea. It has to do with the fine plan you've put together to check out prospective clients for your marriage brokerage service. I think you should package that service and offer it to local women who want to know more about the guys they're engaged to, here in the States. Lady lawyers, doctors and other professionals would form a line around the block to have you do that work for them."

Stuart's not saying anything, but I can hear the wheels spinning in his head.

"Peter, by George, you may have an idea there. How would you suggest we market that service?"

"Gee, I don't know, Stu, I'm not the marketing maven, you are. I suppose you could get the word out…"

I can tell he's not listening to me, because there's a lot of noise suddenly coming from somewhere in his office. In the distance, I can hear Olive shouting at Stuart. He puts the phone down and tries to calm her down.

"Pete, I'm sorry, but I've gotta go. We've had a little emergency come up."

"Yeah, I heard Olive in the background. Is everyone okay?"

"I don't know, Pete, but I think that Vinnie's life is in danger."

"What's going on, Stu? Who wants to kill Vinnie?"

"Olive does. Vinnie just called from jail. He's been arrested on suspicion of solicitation for prostitution."

11

When it comes to Vinnie, there's never a dull moment. He always manages to get arrested for one thing or another, and I get called on to straighten it out. I only hope this matter can be taken care of before Olive gets her hands on him. I've seen her in a temper tantrum before, and it's not a pretty sight. If she thinks that her fiancée has been trying to get a little 'fresh' on the side, he's a lot safer in jail than anywhere near Olive.

Solicitation is only a misdemeanor, and that means there is a scheduled bail amount, so after Stuart gets him sprung we can get to work on the police report and whatever else they may think they have to base their prosecution on.

To make sure that I don't miss out on anything, I take a leisurely drive out to Stuart's warehouse, because I know that's where they'll all wind up after they pick up Vinnie from the Van Nuys jail.

Sure enough, after sitting in my Hummer and doing a crossword puzzle for a while, Stuart's Lincoln Town Car pulls into the parking lot. Olive is sitting in the front seat with Stuart. Vinnie is in the back seat. He doesn't look happy. There's no need for air conditioning in that car today.

They all march into Stuart's office and I can tell by the look on Olive's face that if there were bullets in gun that she wears while driving one of Stuart's armored cars, Vinnie would already be suffering from a severe case of lead poisoning.

I think the best thing for me to do is the same thing the cops do. Divide and interrogate. As politely as possible I explain to both Stuart and Olive that I'd like to have some time alone with Vinnie. Olive doesn't say a word. The expression on her face does all the talking. Stuart has no objection, and is probably glad that I'm taking Vinnie out of Olive's sight for a little while. We go out to the parking lot and get in my Hummer. Both of us are a little dry, so we decide to find some fast food place where we can get a couple of milk shakes. Vinnie starts his explanation.

"Honest, Mister Sharp, I didn't solicit that girl. She solicited me."

"Vinnie, relax. I'm not here to judge you. I just want you to take your time and tell me what happened. Start out about thirty minutes before your encounter with the girl, and let me know every place you were, who you talked to, and to the best of your memory, what was said."

"Okay. I did an early funeral run with the armored truck and they cut me loose from the cemetery about one thirty this afternoon. We were out in Inglewood, so I wanted to take the freeway back to Stuart's garage in the Valley. I took the 405 up to Venice Boulevard, but after that I could see the freeway was a parking lot, so I went off on the Venice exit and then turned left to go north on Sepulveda.

"I took Sepulveda all the way through the pass, because I could see that it was still packed on the freeway. I went up over Mulholland and then down the winding road to Ventura Boulevard. I crossed Ventura and decided to stay on Sepulveda all the way to Saticoy. No sense in getting back on the freeway, just to get off another couple of exits ahead.

"I passed Victory Boulevard, you know, that's where the Lido Pizza place is, and then kept going. Just before Sherman Way, there's a traffic light at Vose Street, so I had to stop for a red. It was a nice day, so I had the windows open. The air conditioning makes me sneeze, so I try to avoid using it whenever it's not too hot out.

"Anyway, I'm sitting there at the red light in the lane closest to the curb, and this young lady with all the makeup on is standing on the corner by the bus stop, and she smiles at me."

145

I can see that Vinnie is getting flustered. He must be getting to the embarrassing part of his story. I try to assure him. "Vinnie, anything you tell me now is protected by the lawyer-client privilege, so I'm honor-bound to keep it confidential. All I ask is that you be one hundred percent truthful here, because if I don't know the facts exactly as they happened, I can't help you. Okay, she smiled at you. What happened next?"

"She said something like, 'I've never been in an armored car before, can I please see the inside?' She wanted to look at the truck, and she asked if I could please drop her off at Saticoy, because that would save her the bus fare."

"Did you let her get in the truck, Vinnie?"

"Well, yeah. I mean, like it's not like I really had money in the truck, it's not a real armored car, I mean it's a real armored car, but, well, you know what I mean."

"Yes, Vinnie, I know what you mean. It's no longer being used to transport large sums of money."

"Yeah, Mister Sharp, that's what I mean. Anyway, she gets in the truck and sits up front with me, and she asks me if there's a lot of money in the truck. I tell her that I'm not carrying any money today. I mean, I never carry any money, but I just tell her that I'm not carrying any money today. You know what I mean?"

"Yes, Vinnie, please go on."

"Then she tells me that it's too bad I don't have any money in the truck, because if I did, she would really show me a good time. And then she asks me if I like to have a good time. I said 'yeah, I guess

146

having a good time is nice.' And then she tells me to pull over and drop her off."

"That's it? That's all that happened? Did you pull over? Did she get out of the truck?"

"No. When I pulled over, a couple of cops rushed over to the truck. The girl pulls out a badge and tells me I'm under arrest, and the cops grab me and take me to the station."

From what Vinnie tells me there's no case here. I have one important question for him. "Vinnie, exactly how much money did you have on you at the time of your arrest?"

"Only about a dollar and fifty cents. Olive needed some money for groceries, so she took it out of my wallet this morning. I only had that buck and a half in change, and my cell phone. I figured that if anything came up, I could always call her and she'd bring me money for whatever I need. Stuart has us carry one of his gas credit cards whenever we take the truck on a job, so I wasn't worried about money for fuel or anything, and Stuart says it's also okay to use the gas credit card at a station's mini mart if we need some refreshments, like a Coke or a Twinkie or something."

"Vinnie, did the police take your money when they brought you into the police station?"

"Sure. That's the second thing they did. First the cops grabbed my gun. That was on the street where they first arrested me. At the station they took my belt, my shoelaces, and everything I had in my pockets, including the four or five quarters, and Stuart's Shell credit card. They even gave me a

147

receipt for the change and the credit card. It's right here."

He reaches in his pocket and hands me the yellow copy of his Police Property Receipt, and sure enough, it shows the buck fifty in quarters along with the Shell Gas Credit Card.

"Okay, Vin, let's go back to the garage. Maybe I can straighten things out with Olive for you."

"Gee, I hope so, Mister Sharp. I'd rather go to jail than have her mad at me."

It only took us about ten minutes to get back to Stuart's warehouse, but with the time we spent having our refreshments and discussing the case, we were gone for the better part of an hour. When we walk into Stuart's office, Olive doesn't look at us. We sit down in front of Stuart's desk. Olive doesn't join us in the office, but I would bet my boat that she's listening to every word we say, so I make sure that Vinnie comes off in the best light when I explain to Stuart. He understands too.

"Stuart, Vinnie is completely innocent. He's been the victim of a police sting that was poorly conducted. The police botched things up. They should never have arrested him."

"You're probably right, Pete, but the fact still remains that they did arrest him. What facts were they going on?"

When I first started practicing law I represented a girl who was charged with stealing five dollars worth of meat from the market. The police charged her with felony burglary. I didn't know what they were basing that big of a charge on, but they then explained to me that she only had two dollars on her person, at the time she stole five dollars worth of meat.

They interpreted the fact that she didn't have enough money in her purse to pay for the meat as an indication of intent to steal. Their premise being that if you only have two dollars, and take five dollars of meat, the only reason you went into that market was to steal a larger amount of meat than you could have afforded to pay for. It therefore was outside the realm of an impulse theft, and falls under the more serious charge, because she planned it before going into the store.

In some ways Vinnie's situation is similar. I think it can be argued that if a guy only has five or six quarters in his pocket, it's impossible for him to purchase services from a prostitute. You can't intend to pay the going rate of from twenty to fifty dollars to a street hooker if you've only got quarters in your pocket at the time.

I've never hired a girl like that, but from what I understand, they don't give credit or take Shell Gas cards. Even if Vinnie did proposition her, they would be in the awkward position of arguing that he was offering her pocket change for sex. I've heard of 'cheap' hookers before, but this case would be pushing the envelope.

Technically speaking, the amount doesn't matter. The mere act of offering money for sex is enough to constitute the crime of solicitation, but you have to take all facts into consideration.

149

Charges like this are always a he-said she-said situation, and it would be very hard for the People to convince a jury that a guy with only quarters in his pocket would actually offer them to a prostitute and expect to receive some sexual favor in exchange.

But that's not the only problem they have here. This is obviously an open and shut case of attempted entrapment. Not only did Vinnie not offer the girl any money, but he may have been entitled to ask her for some because he saved her the bus fare she was going to spend for that ride to Saticoy.

From out of nowhere, I hear a voice. "What's entrapment?" As expected, Olive was listening to every word. Forget about the State of California. As far as Vinnie's concerned, his fiancée Olive is the judge, jury, and executioner. She must be satisfied of his innocence beyond any reasonable doubt, or the explanation won't count. I might as well give them the lecture.

"Entrapment is a defense that's used quite often in cases of soliciting prostitution or purchasing drugs. What it means is that a guy who ordinarily wouldn't commit a particular crime is pressured into doing it by the police, who then arrest him for doing what they talked him into doing."

Olive wants to know more. "Well then, from what you said, we've got the cops cold. They entrapped Vinnie. That's his defense."

"It won't work, Olive."

Now she's adamant. "Why the hell not?"

"Because you can't have it both ways. You can't say to the jury 'I didn't do it, but if I did do it, the police made me do it.' Either you plead not guilty and deny committing the offense, or you plead that the police caused you to either involuntarily participate in a criminal act or otherwise do something that you were not disposed to do prior to being approached by the police.

"It's a lot like the self-defense contention. You can't say that you never shot the guy, while at the same time, saying that you shot him in self-defense. In this case there was never any offer of money. Vinnie was asked if there was money in the truck, and he told her that there wasn't. She never asked him for money and he never offered any. She may have hinted that she would perform sexually for him, but he never asked her to. That's it, period. No solicitation, no nothing. There's no way that they can show that Vinnie was ready and willing to commit the crime whenever the opportunity presented itself. He's never been busted for soliciting before, he only had some quarters on him, and she jumped in the truck under the guise of wanting to see the inside of an armored vehicle and get a free ride down the street to save bus fare."

At this point, all three of them want to know how I'm going to handle this case and prove that the police lady lied.

"I'm going to do nothing."

Almost in unison, they all replied "nothing?"

"That's right, nothing. And the reason I'm going to do nothing is because the most important part of the case has already been taken care of." I can tell by the expressions on their faces that they're sitting on pins and needles waiting for the grand finale to my presentation.

151

"Olive did it for me. She took Vinnie's money this morning to buy some groceries and left him with only a few quarters. Vinnie found that out later, but kept going to work anyway because he had the Shell credit card and knew he could use his cell phone to call you guys if he ran into any trouble. So I ask you. Especially you Olive, would a guy who knows he's only got some quarters in his pocket stop for a hooker, knowing that she'd want advance payment? I think not. Vinnie was framed, and I'm doing nothing, because when the City Attorney goes over the paperwork that the police bring in, they'll ask how much money he had on him. When they're told that he only had the few quarters, they'll know that there's no case there, and none will be filed."

The expression on Olive's face changes from stone to human. Stuart is relieved that he won't have to face big legal fees and possibly lose Vinnie's services as a bonded, licensed driver and wearer of a weapon. Olive is happy that Vinnie didn't try to get a hooker, and I'm happy because Stuart offered to take us all out to dinner at some fancy theme restaurant next to the Van Nuys Airport. I only hope that my predictions come true, because if they file a case against Vinnie I'll have a lot of explaining to do.

Just in case I've misjudged the City Attorney's office, I have my office prepare a document for Vinnie to sign. I want to have a little ammunition if and when I'm called in to their offices to do battle. With a case as weak as the one they have against Vinnie, I feel pretty sure they'll want to talk about it before filing.

12

Jack's been in La Verne for the past few days, and he's now calling in with his first report. I certainly want to hear what he's got to say, but I'm not looking forward to it.

"Yes Jack, how's it going out there?"

"It's sure a lot smoggier than the Marina, and about twenty degrees warmer."

"Any news for me?"

"Well, she's certainly not running around very much. She's only gone out of the house once or twice in the last couple of days, and that was for groceries. And she didn't sneak out at night, because I left a thread on her garage door at night, and it would have fallen off if she opened it while I wasn't there watching."

"How about traffic to the house?"

"Nada. It's like she's a hermit."

"Did you happen to notice what grocery store she went to?"

"Yes, it was a market about a half mile from her house. She went there on the afternoon I got here, and she went yesterday and again today."

"Did you see her bring the groceries out of the store or unload them from her car?"

"She didn't bring them out of the store. A grocery clerk carried the bags out for her. At the house, she unloaded them herself, before closing the garage door."

"Were there a lot of bags?"

"Yeah. Come to think of it, she's a pretty heavy shopper. There were about three of four bags each time."

I usually go shopping once a week, and each time the bag usually has the same things in it: a half-gallon of chocolate soy milk, a box of Hansen's Natural Cereal, a carton of Lactaid non-fat milk, and some protein powder. There's no need for any more, because I don't cook very often. But if I did, the only extra things that would be in that weekly bag would be a few one-pound bags of pasta, some grated cheese, and a couple of cans of things to dump on the top of the cooked pasta.

Beverly lives alone. If she's not stocking up for a big holiday feast, I'd like to know why she needs three or four bags of groceries a day.

"Jack, I hope you brought Phyllis with you, because we need her on this job."

"Yes, Mister Sharp, I didn't think you'd mind if she kept me company."

"No, no, Jack, that's just fine. Here's what I'd like you to do: every time the widow goes to the market, I'd like Phyllis also in there to make a list of what she buys. Phyllis can pretend that she's marking things off on her own shopping list, until the widow leaves the grocery. There's no need for you to follow her when she leaves, because she'll probably just go back home and unload the groceries and you can probably get back there before she's through bringing them into the house. Got it?"

154

"That's a roger, Mister Sharp. We'll have a list or two for you in the next couple of days."

This is getting interesting. If she's only cooking for one, then what's with all the groceries? Somewhere in the back of my mind I have a hunch that she's cooking for more than one person. But who else can be in there with her? Whoever it might be is definitely someone who doesn't want to be seen, because if they weren't hiding out, Jack would already have e-mailed me the photos.

The phone is ringing and it looks like a City number. I answer it and hear a familiar voice. "Hello, Peter, this is Patty Seymour, remember me?"

How could I forget her? She's the City Attorney I thought could be the one, until Myra clued me in about her being a lesbian. I still have hopes of making a conversion over to our side, but never got enough of the right vibes to encourage the effort.

"Sure I remember you Patty. I'm still waiting for you to call and invite me to another one of those law luncheons. And next time, it's on me."

"Well, I'll certainly have to do that, but in the meantime, I've been referred to your office by the District Attorney's filing section. They kicked out a solicitation case and sent it over to our office with a note that you might be representing the defendant."

"Vincent Norman?"

"That's the guy. Is he your client?"

"He might be, if he needs a lawyer. Are you guys considering filing?"

"Yes we are. I mean, my boss is. Could you come to our office for a conference about this case? Any day this week at ten AM is good for us."

155

Once again it's show time. Most of my mental energy is now being directed to Beverly Luskin, so I really don't feel like putting forth too much of an effort on Vinnie's matter, but a promise is a promise. I chat with Patty for another minute or two about trivial things and then make a note in my calendar that they'll be expecting me there the day after tomorrow at ten.

Just as I hang the phone up, the kid passes by and hands me a brochure on some evening course that the U.S. Power Squadron is conducting on Safe Boating. Attached to the brochure is a note informing me that I've been registered in the next course. It starts tomorrow evening and continues one night a week for the next six weeks. After four years of college and another four at night law school, I was thinking that I'd never have to park my rear end in one of those chair-desks again, but I was wrong. The note also mentions that if I pass the course, we'll get a completion certificate and discount on our boat's insurance.

I can't believe that she wants me to take this cockamamey course just for some ten-dollar insurance discount. Either this is some form of punishment for not getting back together with Myra, or the kid actually wants me to learn this stuff about boating. It must be the punishment.

Instead of preparing for my meeting tomorrow morning at the City Attorney's office, I'm now seated in a room full of ignoramuses. I know it's not nice to even think so poorly about others, but who else

156

would take this course but people as ignorant about boating as me?

When I started restoring that old Chris Craft in what was then the yard in back of where Myra and I were happily living, I had dreams of sitting on a nice boat in the Marina. My dreams never including going anywhere on the boat, they just included sitting on it. I never wanted to take our Grand Banks out with Indovine and his gang, and certainly wasn't thrilled when discovering we were going on a rescue at sea. I'm really not into boating… I just like being on a nice boat. To an adult male it's like the ultimate tree house. To be truthful, I've always been afraid of getting seasick. The stability of dry land is so nice, I can't figure out why anyone would want to intentionally get on a boat to go past the breakwater out into the open ocean, where they do nothing but bounce around, at the mercy of the elements, while impressing themselves and their guests that they can drive a boat. Please include me out.

The instructor enters the room wearing some sort of uniform. Just what I need - another officer telling me what to do. I thought that after the U.S. Army, days like this would be over. Oh well, it's only a few evenings, so I might as well make the best of serving out my sentence. I see by the Xeroxed course outline that there are two segments to be covered each night. We'll be starting out with Boat Handling and Elementary Seamanship.

I can't believe what the guy opens up with. "Ladies and gentlemen, tonight we'll be starting out with a lecture on boat handling, but I want you to know that one of my idols is sitting right here in the

157

classroom. You've probably read about it in the newspapers, or saw it on the evening news, but not too long ago, there was a collision between two sailboats about three miles out past the breakwater. One of your classmates happened to be entertaining some guests on his Grand Banks 50 that afternoon, and when he saw the collision, he devised and carried out one of the most brilliant rescues at sea that I've ever seen. I was watching it on television as it was happening, and I was fortunate to have had a blank videocassette in my machine, so I taped the whole thing and I'm going to play it for you now. Please watch it carefully, because your main goal in boating should be able to think and act as quickly as he did. Okay Walt, please get the lights."

Not only do I not know what I'm doing on the boat and couldn't turn the engines on if my life depended on it, I'm now going to be held up in front of this audience and probably asked questions about my boat handling skills. Please, shoot me now. The lights dim, the tape starts, and I sink as far down in my seat as humanly possible, looking for some loose edge of carpet on the floor that I can crawl under until this dreadful evening is over.

The tape is played and there are one or two close-ups of me behind the wheel of the boat. I watch the entire rescue and have to admit that it really was a nice job. Too bad I didn't do it. When the show ends and the lights come back up, the rest of the class recognizes me and I'm forced to stand up to a round of applause. I wish it would stop there, but the yahoo in charge drags me up to the front of the class and asks: "Mister Sharp, if you can handle a boat that

158

good, what are you doing in this class? Don't get me wrong, we're pleased to have you here, but what prompted you to enroll?

Reluctantly, I respond to his request, slowly rise and walk to the front of the room to join him at the podium. On the way there, for some strange reason, everyone I pass by feels compelled to pat me on the back. I don't enjoy being touched by strangers. I think it would be best to put an end to this nonsense once and for all, lest they wrongfully believe that I actually know something about boating.

"First of all, I have a confession to make. The afternoon of the incident that you just finished watching was the absolute first time I ever took that boat so far away from its slip. In fact it was only the second time I ever drove it. What you didn't see in the newsreel footage is my legal guardian, who was down below directing the whole operation. Thank goodness we had the extra crewmembers aboard to carry out her ingenious plan and we were able to save those sailors.

"To be quite honest, I don't remember most of what happened, and it scared the daylights out of me so much, that I realized how important a class like this would be for me to take, in case another emergency arises.

"So please, don't credit me with any extraordinary skills or knowledge, because I'm as new to boating as most of you probably are. I just happened to be unlucky enough to have been placed in a position that taught me how little I knew. So if you don't mind, I'd like to just sit down with the rest of you, and let a real pro here teach me how to do things right."

The applause was gratifying, but deep down I know what a phony I am. The teacher was kind enough to tell me how he appreciated my humility, and I am now seated, getting more pats on the back, and getting ready for the most boring evenings of my life.

It's five to ten in the morning and Patty Seymour is expecting me upstairs in her boss' office in the next couple of minutes. I check my pockets to make sure I've brought the items for my little dog and pony show. I've never met Patty's boss, but he's probably your run-of-the-mill chief trial deputy, working his way up the prosecutorial ladder. People in the City Attorney's office all share the same inferiority complex because they'll never get to try a high profile felony case like O.J. or Michael Jackson. Not because they're not competent, it's just that the City Attorney's office doesn't try felonies. All they handle are misdemeanors, and there hasn't been a high profile misdemeanor case that I can remember in the past twenty years.

I sit down in the waiting area and right on time, Patty Seymour comes out and asks me to follow her into the boss' office. Surprise number one. Her boss isn't a guy. At least I don't think she is. Her boss, Chief Trial Deputy Margaret Nash, looks like a super-macho Rosie O'Donnell, with an added swagger that indicates a condition we in the defense bar refer to as being 'badge heavy.' I hope this isn't my competition with Patty Seymour, because it if is,

It'll be the first time I ever was physically afraid of a rival.

After we're all seated, Mizz Nash proceeds to read me the riot act. "Mister Sharp, it's nice that you decided to waste your time by stopping by today, but I'm glad you're here, because I want you to know that we've been getting so many complaints about prostitution in Van Nuys on Sepulveda Boulevard that the residents and merchants in that area want to see some blood. And I'm pleased to inform you that the blood they're going to see soon will be drained from the body of none other than your client, Mister Vincent Norman, a former pornographer, whose head I will be pleased to place on a stick and parade up and down Sepulveda Boulevard with.

"Now, since I doubt if you have anything to say that I'd be interested in hearing, you can just walk out of here with your tail between your legs, because I don't intend to make any deals on this case. In fact I don't even think I'd accept your client's straight-up guilty plea to the charges, because I want this trial to let the people know we mean business.

"So thank you for coming in, and we look forward to seeing you again in court."

I usually try to be courteous and professional and show respect to others, but once in a while I run into some obnoxious bureaucrat who treats me badly and deserves to be brought down a step. Unfortunately Mizz Margaret Nash is one of those terrible people, and even though this might embarrass Patty Seymour, I gotta do what I gotta do. I graciously smile, stand up, notice Patty is avoiding eye contact with me, and start my farewell soliloquy.

161

"Mizz Nash, I want to thank you for giving me the chance to meet with you, because from what I hear, you're one hell of a prosecutor. And to show my appreciation, here's what I propose. First, taking a look at this copy of my client's property receipt, I'd like you to please tell me how a guy with only some quarters in his pocket can proposition a hooker and expect to get anything more than a refusal for a dollar or so in pocket change.

"Second, I'd like you to take notice of the fact that we have this videoCD of footage from the security system of the vehicle, which as you probably know was an armored transport truck that carried large sums of cash. The former owner had it equipped with the most sophisticated security gear, which included small hidden cameras that are automatically activated whenever a door is opened. This videoCD contains the entire four minutes that transpired, from the time that the undercover policewoman opened the door and pleaded to see the inside of the defendant's vehicle, her request for a ride down the street to save bus fare, to my client's absolute refusal to participate in any illegal activity with her – at which time, she told him to pull over and initiated his arrest.

"Never, in my more than twenty years of practice have I ever seen such a bungled attempt at entrapment. The officers involved in this miscarriage of justice should be thrown off the force, as I'm sure they will be, and I'm also sure that when they go down, they'll take with them whatever pompous prosecutor ordered them to bring in some 'johns,' whether they're guilty or not. And after the criminal case gets tossed out, the civil suit for false arrest should be a slam-dunk and bring in quite a few quarters for my client and our law firm.

"So, you have a decision to make. Do you want to accept this document that my client has executed, which relieves your office from any liability for false arrest, based on the consideration of the case being immediately dismissed, or would you like option number two, which is the filing of this case, the ultimate destruction of the careers of several hardworking sworn peace officers and one chief trial deputy, lots of terrible publicity for this office and your boss, and a big financial liability for the City?

"I don't expect you to make a snap decision that you might live to regret, so I'm just going to walk out the door now and leave behind this signed Release form. If I don't hear from your office by noon tomorrow telling me to surrender my client in open court for arraignment, I'll assume that you've come to your senses and refused to file on this case. Good afternoon."

As I slide Vinnie's Release form across the table at Mizz Nash, I see that she's sitting there red-faced, sucking air like a fish out of water. I catch a glimpse of Patty looking at me, and remember her exact words when she spoke of the possibility of the case being filed. She specifically wanted to remove the 'I' pronoun from the decision process, so it looks like she really wasn't behind this whole farce. I still hope there's a chance for me with her, because I hate to see such a nice specimen of femininity going to waste... or to Mizz Nash.

Once back in my Hummer, I take the disc allegedly containing footage of Vinnie's botched entrapment, slip it into the slot on my dashboard CD player, press the 'play' button, sit back, relax, and listen to Ella Fitzgerald and Louie Armstrong sing a duet, backed up by the Oscar Peterson Trio. Gee, I guess I must have made a mistake and brought the wrong disc.

Needless to say, the twenty-four-hour noon deadline has passed about an hour ago and I still haven't heard from the City Attorney's office with an arraignment date. I've decided to not tell this story to the good folks at StuartCorp.

Looking down the dock, I see that Laverne has just returned from her nudist vacation and has a nice tan. Maybe later this evening I'll check out the extent of it. She's carrying her small suitcase and boarding her houseboat I've been on vacations with women before, and even if it's only going to be an overnighter, a female feels compelled to bring enough outfits for any occasion. The female brain seems to think that even on a two-night camping trip up in the National Forest, there's always a chance of bumping into the President of the United States, who will invite her to join him at a black tie campfire. I'm impressed to see that Laverne traveled so lightly, but then again because she went to a place where no clothing was required, I guess all she needed to bring were her tooth-brush, lots of sunscreen, and a depilatory.

The phone's ringing and I recognize Jack B.'s cell phone number on the display.

"Yes, Jack, what have you got for me?"

"I did what you said, Mister Sharp, and Phyllis went in to the market while Beverly Luskin was shopping."

"Okay, what's she got to report?"

"Strange thing. She saw the widow Luskin shopping, and she was wearing those large sunglasses you told me about, but Phyllis noticed another bruise on her face, other than the black eye. Phyllis says that it looks like she tried to cover it up with makeup, but any woman could tell that it was there. It looked large, like she was slapped real hard, on the same side of her face as the black eye."

"Have you seen anyone else go in or out of her house?"

"Nope. Just her."

"So what you're telling me is that on one day she didn't have that bruise, and then on the next day she did have that bruise, and in between not having it and having it, she was in her house all the time, and you didn't see anyone either come in or go out?"

"That's right. If she got slapped, it must have been inside that house."

"How about the groceries Jack? What's she picking up at the market?"

"Nothing unusual, just milk, cereal, pasta, eggs, steaks, sanitary napkins, cleaning stuff, frozen dinners, you know, things like that."

"Okay, Jack. You guys are doing a good job. I'd like you to stay there another couple of days and watch her house for a while after dark too. Maybe you'll get lucky and see some shadows by a window. And Jack…"

"Yes Mister Sharp?"

"Have Phyllis keep track of Luskin's shopping list, and if you see her dump any plastic trash bags, please make sure to get them before the city's pick-up truck comes. I want her garbage brought over to Victor's lab when you return."

I know I might be getting into trouble with the office by authorizing this money for Jack's snooping, but we took a five thousand dollar retainer from Beverly Luskin, and in view of the fact that she's being beaten in her own house, I feel justified in spending her money to find out how we can protect her from further abuse.

Talking to Jack about all the groceries that Beverly Luskin is buying has made me hungry. The kid and her dog are spending the night at Myra's, so I'm on my own for dinner, and since I'm not in the mood for FatBurger, I'm going to have to forage for something to eat.

Being a friendly neighbor, I think it would be nice to invite Laverne over for a 'welcome home' dinner. She'll probably bring a large can of her favorite wine and maybe we can both cook up something to eat. I'm sure she's capable of making something better than that greasy French toast she usually leaves for me.

She accepts my gracious invitation and hurriedly starts looking through her mail for this week's TV Guide, so she can find the info necessary to Tivo tonight's episodes of those crummy reality shows she's addicted to. Before leaving the boat to

166

join me, I see her grabbing some items from her pantry to bring along for tonight's feast, which will be prepared by two people wearing towels. The anchorage where our boats are docked has the largest swimming pool in the Marina, used by the boat tenants and apartment dwellers of the eight buildings in this project. We intend to get some swimming done, soak in the Jacuzzi for a while, and then shower off the chlorine, wrap ourselves in huge hotel towels, and cook our dinner.

I now know that I'm not capable of doing as many laps in the pool as I used to be able to do. The Jacuzzi helped relax the swimming muscles a little, but I know I'm going to be stiff tomorrow. Laverne and I are now bumping into each other in my boat's galley, preparing dinner.

I start by chopping the salad and adding my favorite ingredients. Laverne has signed a release form, allowing me to add chopped garlic, onions and anchovies. I have no idea what she's working on, but it smells Italian. There's a possibility that she's planning some special recipe of ravioli, stuffed with cheese and spinach. She says she's making it from scratch, so I hope I don't find any cans of Chef Boyardee in the garbage tomorrow morning. The side dish she whipped up has something to do with eggplant. It's dark, wet, and cold, but smells good.

The phone has been turned off, and we are now sitting in the salon, feasting off of the buffet we spread out on the coffee table, while we watch the evening news on the large flat-panel plasma display television screen across the room from us. We've already gone through both cans of wine, so no pain is being felt. Our towels are barely hanging on to our bodies, and we're both in an exceptionally good mood, having eaten and drank to our hearts' content. I reach over and undo her towel and then my own. Being a typical woman, she feels compelled to interrupt the mood.

"How come you didn't come to pick me up at the airport this afternoon?"

"Laverne honey, I had no idea you were coming back until I saw you get out of that cab and walk down to the boat."

"Didn't she tell you?"

"You mean the kid?"

"Yes. I called a couple of days ago and left word that I was coming back today. I left my flight number and everything."

Before I get a chance to defend myself against her cross-examination, I hear a dog bark. I jump up and look out the window.

"Oh shit, they're back. Laverne, you better put your towel on."

Laverne does more than that. She jumps up, re-fastens her towel and beats a hasty retreat down the aft deck swim ladder to the dock. As the kid, the dog, and the ex-wife come up the boarding ladder, Laverne sneaks by and runs to her boat.

The kid doesn't say anything. She just looks around, grimaces at the mess we made cooking dinner, and heads for her stateroom. The dog lingers a little longer and does a thorough job of investigating the droppings status. Myra looks great, as usual.

"What happened? I thought she was going to stay over at your place tonight."

"She didn't want to leave you alone on the boat. Must've been afraid you'd get into trouble."

"Well, she's partly right. I was going to get into something, but I wouldn't call it trouble."

"I can tell by the empty wine containers in the trash that you've been entertaining. Where did your date go, back to her trailer?

"Hey, my love life is off limits, unless I bring it up first. Did you think I was going to go celibate when you moved me out into that back yard?"

"No Petey, but I think you'd be better off if you considered it. Your choices aren't the wisest, between a lesbian, some white trash, and a possible murder suspect."

"Hey, I don't have an application form for them to fill out. All I care about is qualified people who can perform satisfactorily. Besides, I'm not looking for anything long term, because when I hit fifty, I'm going to retire to Stuart's condo in Thailand, and spend the rest of my life surrounded by young, beautiful, cherubic Thai girls."

"Good. I wish you the best of luck. I hope they have plenty of pharmacists there, because you'll need them."

"Hey, speaking of murder suspects, how're you guys doing with that shooting out in La Verne?"

"The shell casings found in your car had some prints on them, and we came up with a match for two drug dealers from Oregon. The bullets we removed from the victim also matched some that were recovered from another case, so we've got some things to go on now. Why? Looking for some new clients?"

"No, I'm just curious. Besides, I couldn't represent those perps if I wanted to. First of all, it would be a conflict of interest because I represent the victim's widow in a civil matter. Secondly, I'll probably be called as a witness, because it was my car they stole and used for the crime."

"Wrong on both counts, counselor. You'd have no conflict, because the criminal charges won't have anything to do with her civil matters. And as for your car, our office doesn't care if they used a bicycle to shoot the victim, so you wouldn't be called as a witness. So face it, you dog, you wouldn't represent those killers for only one reason, and that's because if you did, the widow wouldn't let you into her slacks."

I have to hand it to Myra. When she's right, she's really right. But it was good to hear that the hit was by professional drug dealers, because that just about completely rules out Beverly as having put out the contract. And now that Laverne has been spooked, Myra is gone, and Beverly is too busy getting abused, I'm sleeping alone tonight. Thank you, Suzi. I might as well spend the rest of the evening doing my homework for next week's class. We'll be covering coastal navigation and using nautical charts.

If I have anything to say about it, this boat will never go out past the breakwater again, so I'm not too interested in basic navigation other than to learn enough of it to pass the test at the end of the course. If I don't pass and get a certificate so that the kid can save us three dollars on boat insurance, I'll be shamed out of the Marina.

The first chapter in this lesson is about the difference between the various 'norths,' like True and Magnetic. Does anyone really care? It took me hours to learn the difference between the various categories of life jackets. Isn't that enough?

Saved by the bell, because when everyone left the boat, I turned the phone's ringer back on, and now Jack B. is calling.

"Hello Jack, tell me something I want to hear."

"I'm sorry, Mister Sharp. We parked across the street from her house after it got dark, but never saw more than one shadow at a time in any window. It looks like she's in there alone. And she hasn't been at the market recently, so we don't know if she's added any more bruises to her collection. What should we do? You want us to stick around some more?"

I tell Jack to give it another couple of days. I've got to be back in La Verne for my traffic ticket trial, so he might as well keep an eye on her place until I get there. I don't know what I'm going to do then, but a visit to her house is definitely called for. After all, I am her attorney. Now all I've got to do is figure out some way to search the house for other life forms while I'm there. I can feel it in my bones. Someone else is in that house with her, and that someone is ruining a gorgeous face.

171

13

One of these days my love for pretty women is going to get me in trouble, but when it does, it'll probably have been worth it. Myra was gorgeous with that flowing red hair. Now that she's the District Attorney, it's dark brown and kept back in an occipital bun. Her facial features still make her attractive, but she's obviously not interested in me anymore. Patty Seymour is a more robust type of female, like the kind you'd expect to see climbing a large rock somewhere, but Myra says she's a lesbian, so I guess her macho boss has a better chance with her than I do. Beverly Luskin is a beautiful green-eyed blonde, but aside from being geographically undesirable, Myra says she may be a murder suspect.

Laverne is my fallback lady, but the way she was scared off the boat when the kid and Myra showed up during our last romantic attempt, I may have lost my standing with her too. I've already been with three of these four, so it couldn't hurt to try Patty. All she can do is say no, and my ego has been bruised so many times, another rejection shouldn't bother me too much. I may owe her an apology for the way I acted with her boss, so that can be my excuse for calling, and since she wrote what looks like her home phone number on the back of her card after that luncheon we went to, I'm going to take my best shot. My luck is running like it always does: I get her answering machine.

"Hello, this is the Seymour residence. Please leave your name and number and the purpose of your call." Beep.

"Patty, this is attorney Peter Sharp, and I just wanted to…"

"Hello, hello, I'm here. Wait a sec, I'll turn off the machine. Okay, it's off. Hi Peter, how are you doing?"

"I'm doing fine. The reason I called is to apologize. I hope that my ranting at your boss didn't put you in any embarrassing position."

"Not to worry. She can be a little pompous at times, but overall she's a good prosecutor and stands behind her people."

"I have a confession to make. I'm not really calling to apologize for my actions that day. I'm calling for a strictly social reason. To tell the truth, I find myself attracted to you, and cutting directly to the chase, I wonder if it would be possible for us to get together some evening. I mean, I know that you have other interests, but I still would like to see you."

"My goodness, this is a surprise. You mentioned other interests and I'm curious what you meant by that, because I'm not married."

"Yeah, I know you're single. It's just that, well, you know, everyone has different preferences, and I just want to sort of broaden your interests and…"

"Peter, you're babbling incoherently. Come on, spit it out. Tell me what's on your mind. Something must be bothering you, because I thought you'd call me long before this."

"Well, what do you expect a guy to think when the object of his affections belongs to a lesbian club?"

"Lesbian club? What are you talking about?"

"That luncheon, the L.L.B., the Lesbian Lawyer Branch."

"Oh my God. Peter, those initials stand for Lady Lawyers Brunch. I'm not a lesbian. Who gave you that idea?"

"I'd rather not say. It was obviously a tremendous faux pas, and I really don't want to embarrass anyone."

"Well, I think it's time for an honest exchange of information, because I was told that you were gay."

That stops me cold. A womanizing dog like me, and she believed I was gay? I may be handsome, educated, know some show tunes and the names of most of Elizabeth Taylor's husbands, but I've never even come close to being thought of as gay. Just because I'm a good dancer and can put on a convincing 'sensitive' act shouldn't give anyone that idea either. I have to ask.

"Patty, I'll make a deal with you. You tell me who told you I was gay, and I'll tell you who told me you were a lesbian."

"Okay, it's a deal. You first."

"No, I'll tell you what. I'll pick you up and we'll go out for a quick drink, yogurt, or any other thing you can think of doing quickly, and we'll exchange pieces of paper, on which each of us will write down the source of our information."

She went for it, and I'm now driving down Wilshire Boulevard towards Barrington to pick her up. Almost at Sunset Boulevard, I see her standing out by the curb waiting for me.

After our frozen yogurt sundaes have been completely devoured, it's time to do some business. We both know that it's time, so we reach into our pockets, remove the pieces of paper, and wave them in the air. Then, in an act of mutual trust, we exchange the pieces.

I read what's written on hers, she reads what's written on mine, and we start to laugh, because the same name appears on both pieces of paper: Myra.

We decide that it would be a good idea if gay guy and a lesbian girl went to her apartment, had a few drinks, got comfortable, and found out if it was possible to convert each other to the 'straight' life.

After an entire night of successful scientific research, I can now definitely state with confidence that conversion is possible, and that we should both keep this newly discovered phenomenon to ourselves. She doesn't want her boss to know about it, because she feels that Mizz Nash has designs on her, and doesn't want to antagonize her with the fact that her arch-enemy has been to places where she will never go.

I would rather not have Myra find out about this tryst, because now that I see what she's done, I'd like to think that there's still some interest there for me, and I know that the kid is staying up nights trying to design some devious plan to get Myra and I back together again.

This works, and if I can avoid screwing it up like every other relationship I've ever been in, then the loss of consortium with Laverne and Beverly won't be too hard to handle. We also agree that our meetings should not be at the boat, unless we can figure out some way to make it look completely harmless. When I explain how sharp the kid is, we both realize that the boat is out of the question. I can live with that.

It looks like something is finally going right in my life. I'm on the way back to the Marina and my cell phone is ringing with a call from Stuart.

"Hello Stu, what's up?"

"I've got bad news and good news."

It sounds like he's got at least a half hour of explaining to do, so instead of driving through Santa Monica talking on my cell phone and possibly getting arrested for it, we decide to meet for a cup of coffee.

When Stuart walks into the deli, I can tell by the happy smirk on his face that the bad news isn't really that bad.

Last year Stuart started a new business, based on a Federal law that had been passed, making people who send out unsolicited 'junk' faxes liable for their acts. Stuart started soliciting people who had received the junk faxes and had them file Small Claims Court actions. Stuart would then have those people assign the claims to him, so that he could go into Small Claims Court and win up to the statutory five hundred dollars on each one. When Stuart won in court, he shared the proceeds with each assignor. This business was going pretty good for him until someone informed the court that what Stuart was doing violated the court's own rules.

The Rules of the County of Los Angeles' Small Claims Courts allow for an individual or entity to be represented by an assignee like Stuart, but not if his compensation is derived strictly from the making of the appearances. In other words, a company can send one of its regular employees in to court, but the rules want to avoid the creation of people like Stuart, who wanted to make a living by pressing Small Claims Court actions for others.

"Stuart, I understand the court's rules, and I realize that you're now out of the small claims court business. What I don't understand is why you're not too upset by it. From what you told me, you were making many thousands of dollars a month doing that. Am I correct?"

"You are correct, my friend. But being stopped from doing one thing only gives me the opportunity to do another thing that's even better."

I've said it before, and I'll say it again. Next to a certain young Chinese multi-millionaire who runs a law practice, Stuart is the most enterprising person I've ever met. Whenever life gives him a lemon, he certainly knows how to make lemonade. He brought a copy of the Federal law with him, and highlighted the portion he's now concentrating on, which provides that the fine can be increased as high as fifteen hundred dollars, if the sender of the unsolicited fax 'willfully or knowingly' violated the law.

The law requires that mass broadcasters of fax advertising must give a toll-free telephone number

177

for fax recipients to call, be removed from the list, and not receive further faxes from that sender. By tracking the toll-free 'removal' numbers given, Stuart discovered that most of them came from the same sender, a notorious mass fax broadcaster located in the San Fernando Valley, not far from Stuart's warehouse.

I now understand why Stuart is pleased that his original Small Claims Court business has been shut down. From now on, instead of going into court with the faxes from nine or ten customer who he must split the winnings with, he can now go into court with just three of his own faxes and show the court that they were sent out by the fax broadcaster, and ask for fifteen hundred dollars damages for each one.

How he can keep track of all his enterprises baffles me. The ones that I know about include selling a weight-reduction liquid, selling Toyota Camrys that he brings in from New Jersey that were formerly stolen and recovered, introducing men to Thai girls, going to Small Claims Court, his private investigation business, and those two armored trucks that get rented out to disgruntled heirs.

That was certainly an interesting lunch meeting. While driving back to the Marina I recall how at one time or another I was dragged into each of Stuart's businesses, due to legal problems that arose. I think the most interesting was when Stuart was sued for 'negligent nymphomania,' because his weight-reduction formula allegedly increased a female customer's sexual appetite. His auto supplier in New Jersey is a gangster named Billy Z., who I had the pleasure of meeting, and I was caught with my pants down once with four young units of his Thai girl inventory. I think Stuart deserves a new title. From now on I'll refer to him as the Warren Buffet of Van Nuys.

Back at the boat there's a message waiting for me. My contact at Uniman Insurance called to let me know that they've heard from Kathy Potter, and that she's agreed to come in to their office to sign the final claim forms in person. This is going to take some planning, so I call her back.

"This is Miss Murphy, how can I help you?"

"Miss Murphy, this is attorney Peter Sharp. I'm returning your call about the Potter life insurance claim. Did you speak to Kathy Potter yourself?"

"Yes I did, Mister Sharp. She wants to come in and execute the final forms for that claim on her husband's death."

"Was an appointment set for her to come in?"

"Not yet. I knew you'd want to know about it, so I told her to call us back tomorrow to make an appointment."

"Good move. Let me ask you a couple of question. How many floors are there in your office building?"

"Let's see, we're on the twenty first floor, and there are several more floors above us, so that would mean…"

"That's okay, I get the picture. It's a big office building, probably with several levels of underground parking, right?"

"Yes, I believe there are at least four levels."

"Does Uniman Insurance have any branch offices in smaller buildings, maybe like only one floor, with parking spaces outside?"

"One of our branch supervisors has an office in Redondo Beach that's in a two-story building. I believe they have a parking lot out in back of the offices."

"Great. Would it be possible for you to have the paperwork for her claim sent out to that office? We'd like to have her come to an area where it'll be easier for us to observe her coming and going."

"No problem Mister Sharp. I'll have our courier take the paperwork over to that office and fax you the address. When Kathy Potter calls me tomorrow, what time would you like me to set her appointment for?"

"One PM, the day after tomorrow."

All right. The game's now afoot. I've just instructed our office to rent seven extra cell phones with speaker attachments and get everyone over here, including Stuart, Vinnie, Olive and at least one Thai girl who speaks English. Suzi arranged for the Asian Boys to deliver and serve us a gourmet Chinese dinner, at which time I intend to lay out our battle plan.

As usual, both the dinner and the service are exceptional, as is the fact that Suzi has decided to join us all at the expanded table. Now that everyone has finished the main course, it's time for the commercial. I clink a glass to get their attention and start with the plan.

"Boys and girls, the day after tomorrow, at one in the afternoon, Miss Kathy Potter will be appearing at an insurance office in Redondo Beach to execute the final papers required to collect on her dead husband's life insurance policy. I succeeded in requiring her to come to that location for one reason alone: after she leaves that building, I want to know where exactly where she goes.

"This is very important Stuart, and that's why we've retained your whole investigation team to help us out. Here on the table in front of me are seven new cell phones, each with the optional speakerphone feature. During the entire operation I'll be sitting here in our control center with four of these phones side-by-side on the table here. Each of the other three phones will be assigned to a surveillance team member, so we'll have continuous open lines between Stuart's car, Olive's car, and Vinnie's car. The fourth phone will be open to Jack's cell phone. He and Phyllis are still on their stakeout assignment out in La Verne.

"At twelve noon on the day of this operation, Olive will be sitting in the insurance company's office, and all of our phone calls will begin, including Olive's. As soon as Kathy Potter checks in at the insurance company's front desk, the receptionist will give Olive a signal, and from that instant, we're all in play. Olive, as soon as you get the signal you'll go over to another desk in the same office and pretend like you're signing some papers with an office staff person, but you're to constantly keep your eye on Kathy Potter. Your phone will be live, so we'll all know that you've got her covered. The important

181

thing for you to do then is make sure that you leave when she does, and follow her to the parking lot. I want us to be able to identify her vehicle.

"Everybody else, you'll be overhearing the small talk that Olive will be doing with Kathy, so you'll all know when they're about to exit the building. When they come out, Olive will walk over to her car and everyone else will keep their eye on Kathy, to see what car she goes to.

"Once Kathy's in her vehicle, I want you all to follow her in a convoy, so that if you think you've been seen, you can drop out of the tail and the team member in back of you can carry on." I see that Olive's hand is in the air. This lecture must be the closest she ever got to high school.

"What's your question Olive?"

"Why do Vinnie and I have to be in separate cars?"

"Because once Kathy sees you upstairs in the office, your cover is blown. After that time, if she happens to notice you in a car behind her, she'll know she's being followed. You will follow, but you'll be the very last car in the caravan.

"I want constant communication from the lead car at all times. I want to know every street you pass by, because I'll be here on the boat tracking you guys from page to page in my Thomas Guide, while Suzi is doing the same thing on the internet, using Mapquest.com. If these speakerphones work as good as they're supposed to, each one of you will be able to hear all of our conversations in your own earpieces.

182

"It's important that we don't lose her. Has everyone got it? Any questions? Good. Now let's finish our dessert, and Stuart, please make sure that all of your team's cell phone batteries are fully charged and that the cars are filled up with gas."

Suzi pipes in with "save all the receipts."

Olive has another question.

"How come Jack B. isn't in on this?"

"Because he did the initial interviews with her, and she already knows he's part of our team. Remember, the name of the game here is not to spook her. And Olive, please pee before she gets to the office. I'm sure that Uniman Insurance's branch office has a bathroom you can use."

Dinner is over and while the Asian Boys clean up, I call Jack B. to fill him in on the plan and tell him to sit tight out there in La Verne. He now knows that at exactly twelve noon the day after tomorrow he should call me at the cell phone reserved for his communication, and keep an open line until I call it a 'wrap.'

So far, so good. If everything goes according to plan, forty-eight hours from now we'll know where Kathy Potter is hiding, why, and from whom. Once we've got a location on her, Jack B. can take another crack at questioning her. The mere fact that she sees we know where she's hiding should loosen her up enough to answer some questions.

It's show time. We're sitting here on the boat at our 'command center' with four cell phones in front of us. It's exactly twelve noon, and they're all starting to ring. Suzi and I reach forward and press buttons on each one. Once they've all been answered, I start out. "Jack, check in."

Then one by one, each of the team members lets me know that they're on the open line, can hear me loud and clear, and can also hear incoming conversation from the other team members.

A visitor surprises me. Myra steps into the boat. No doubt the kid tipped her off about the whole operation, so she snuck out of the office early to watch us amateurs at work. I signal for her to sit down and stay out of the way.

She's a little early. At about ten minutes to one, Kathy Potter walks into the insurance company's branch office. I ask the other team members if they saw her pull into the parking lot, but none of them did. Jack suggests that she either parked on the street out in front or was dropped off out there. No problem. We'll find out for sure when Olive follows her out of the building.

We can all hear from Olive's phone that she's over at another desk signing some phony insurance papers.

After a couple of minutes Olive thanks whoever was helping her with the forms and walks towards the office door. She accidentally bumps into Kathy Potter as they walk out of the office. We hear her excuse herself and comment on what a lovely dress Kathy is wearing, and that light blue is a perfect color for her.

Smart move by Olive, letting everyone know what Kathy is wearing. I tell Vinnie to pull around in front of the office, just in case someone is picking Kathy up. We can tell from the background noise that

Olive and Kathy have walked outside. Olive is trying to be helpful, so she makes an offer to Kathy. "I have my car here, can I give you a lift?"

Kathy replies. "No, thanks, I've got someone picking me up." I hear from the team members that Olive is now walking to the parking lot and Kathy is standing outside of the building, waiting to be picked up.

In another minute or so, a mini van pulls up to the curb and Kathy gets in. The whole team is alerted and the convoy is in motion. Vinnie's is the lead car, and he gives us a description of Kathy's vehicle, along with its license plate number. He also tells us that a husky skin-headed guy with a handlebar moustache and wearing sunglasses is driving it. Suzi is already at her computer in the foreward stateroom running the minivan's license plate through her various secret databases.

The caravan pulls out onto Sepulveda Boulevard and heads south. They all follow to 190th Street, at which time the minivan turns left, going east, and everyone follows. Fortunately, there's just the right amount of traffic that time of day, so the tailing convoy doesn't stand out too much, but can still maneuver around to keep in position.

Crossing through the traffic light at Western Avenue, all the cars make the light except Olive's. She has to stop, so she's out of the game. I tell her to come back to the boat and she says that as soon as she stops somewhere to pee, she'll be on her way back. Vinnie butts in. "Honey, I told you to go first." They start to have a little argument while the other team members giggle in the background. I call it to a halt and tell everyone to shut up and concentrate on the task at hand.

Further down the road and closer to the Harbor Freeway, the minivan changes lanes without signaling, and Vinnie is trapped in a right-turn only lane. There's a cop car in back of him, so to avoid being arrested, he makes the turn, drops out of the caravan, and also is told to come back to the boat.

It's all up to Stuart now, and I can hear the two Thai girls in the car with him as they chatter in excitement. They think this is just like a movie that's a favorite in Thailand: the *French Connection*. I hear laughter on all the other cell phone speakers.

Stuart keeps up with the minivan as it gets on the freeway, and follows it north. As they get into the Los Angeles downtown area, Stuart loses it. The minivan is the same color as about five others in front of him, and there's no way to tell which is which. The game is over. It lasted less then an hour, and now everyone is on the way back to the Marina.

It's now three in the afternoon, and we're all sitting here on the boat in state of depression. We had such a good plan. We're now having the post mortem that usually follows every unsuccessful mission. Stuart knows what went wrong. "We should have hired a helicopter for you to be up there in, directing the ground team where to go." Suzi, our budgetmeister, gives him a look that goes right through him. She doesn't have to talk much: it's not hard to know what's on her mind.

After another half hour of everyone assuring everyone else that it was nobody's fault that the

186

minivan got lost, we all decide to call it a day. We never thought about the fact that the four cell phones on the table are still open. Stuart, Vinnie, and Olive had all hung theirs up when they got to the boat, but Jack's line is still open because I never told him it was a 'wrap.'

Just as everyone is getting ready to step off the boat, we hear a voice from one of the cell phones on the table, so we all walk back into the salon to see what's up, and hear Jack speaking.

"Hey, you guys still there?" I act as spokesman for the group.

"Yes, Jack, we're still here. I'm sorry, I forgot you were holding a line open. You know what happened, so you can hang up now, it's a 'wrap' for today."

"No, wait a minute. I'd like you to read me the license number of that minivan."

I have no idea of what he wants if for, but it happens to be on the table right in front of the phones, so I give him the plate number.

"Okay, Mister Sharp, now it's a wrap. I got your minivan for you."

Everyone in the room including Suzi crowds around the cell phone. I ask the question. "What are you talking about, Jack?"

"Beverly Luskin's automatic garage door just opened up and your minivan pulled into it."

14

We're all sitting here speechless, trying to figure out what is going on. How can this have happened? Why is Kathy Potter at Beverly Luskin's house? Myra stands up and looks at her watch. "It's been nice seeing you all, but since I'm the only one here who's got a real job, I really must be leaving. And Peter…"

"Yes Myra?"

"Please try listening to me once in a while." Suzi takes her hand and they step off of the boat together and walk to the parking lot. A few minutes later when the kid returns alone, she goes into her stateroom and then comes back out with a piece of paper that she hands me. It says that the minivan's plates come back as being registered to a car rental company.

This isn't much, but it's still a lead. I call Jack B. and tell him to call Suzi's private line, so she can give him the details about the rental place where the minivan was picked up today. Maybe we'll get lucky and pick up a lead on the identity of that bald guy driving the minivan. Jack has to be pulled off of the Luskin assignment anyway, because with Kathy Potter in the Luskin house, Jack's cover has now also been blown.

I'm pretty sure that these recent events have finally attracted Myra's attention. She can smell a conspiracy a mile away, and I'm glad she's finally on to one that I don't have to worry about being a suspect in. We all agree that there's no good reason on earth for Kathy Potter and Beverly Luskin to know of each other's existence, let alone be together in the same house.

My problem at this point is a possible conflict of interest. Beverly Luskin is my client. Myra wanted to know the results of our investigative efforts, but I was reluctant to give her any information that might cast my client in a bad light. I know in my heart that she's already called her office from the car and instructed them to compile a complete dossier on each of those two women in Beverly's house.

Jack didn't see any minivan pull out of Beverly's garage, and when the automatic door to that attached garage opened up twice a day for Beverly's grocery run, Jack never saw the minivan in there, so this must mean that we've got a new player in the game. I hope that he can get some info out of that car rental agency. In the meantime, I've got my traffic ticket trial coming up soon, so I better make some plan of attack if I intend to contact Beverly when I'm in La Verne on the day of my trial.

There's no shortage of suggestions. Vinnie thinks we should report the assault and battery on Beverly and let the La Verne Police investgate it. Olive suggests that I try to get into the house to visit with Beverly on a social basis, and Stuart says the whole affair is none of our business and we should let Beverly take care of her own problems.

Unfortunately, they're all good suggestions. I better make my mind up soon, because if I don't, it'll be out of my hands. Myra has access to all law enforcement assets of Los Angeles County, and I'm sure she'll have Beverly in front of a grand jury in the next week or so. But Myra's also prone to acting prematurely, and in the past she's come dangerously close to destroying her career several times by jumping to conclusions. This matter is a complicated one, and I sure hope Myra doesn't embarrass herself by acting too rashly.

As intriguing as this case is turning out to be, I have other things on my plate. Tomorrow night is my Power Squadron class, and I have to study up on what we'll be covering there: Piloting, Navigation Rules and Marine Radio-telephone Use. Along with most of the stuff I was forced to learn in high school, college and law school, these are just another three subjects that I never intend to have any use for in my life. Looking back at my education, I think the only two educational subjects I learned that had anything to do with attaining my present station in life are Reading and Typing.

Reading was not an optional subject. Everyone in our class at Chicago's Hibbard Elementary School was taught that subject. On the other hand, a high school typing course was something that not too many guys were interested in signing up for. The only reason I became interested in it was that there were only two classes where all the girls were: one was typing and the other was cooking. Having been a piano player, typing came very naturally to me and eventually became a tremendous asset in my life. Not only was I the star of the class and very popular with

190

the girls, but the skills learned there catapulted me into the much-desired position of Clerk Typist in the U.S. Army, which meant that I was needed in the commander's office, and was therefore unavailable for the more unsavory tasks like hiking and field maneuvers. It also really came in handy when I first started practicing law, because before computers became so ubiquitous, I used to be able to make that old Selectric typewriter really smoke.

My reminiscing is interrupted by the telephone. It's Jack B. calling.

"Jack. What've you got for me?"

"The minivan was rented for a week and paid for by Kathy's credit card. The clerk who waited on her didn't remember any bald guy with her, but they've got a security camera in the office there, so I've paid them to make a copy for us. It'll show all the people who came in during the half hour before and after Kathy Potter was there."

"Do you know how she got there?"

"The clerk thinks he remembers her arriving in a cab. I'm checking with the local cab companies now to see if their records show a drop-off at the car rental place. If they do, I'll try to find out where they made the pick-up."

This is a start. If the bald guy didn't come there with her, then she probably picked him up somewhere on her way to the insurance company office. I call Jack again and tell him to find out from the car rental place exactly how many miles were on that minivan when she picked it up. He's then to drive from the rental car place to the insurance company, and see if it's the same amount of mile. If it isn't, then we'll know there was some other another stop along the way. If we can't do it that way then we'll have to find some way to see how many miles are on the minivan as it sits in Beverly's garage.

I wish there was some way to pull the phone records of Beverly Luskin's house, because there's no way that this is all a coincidence, and it looks like Beverly's pulling all the strings. Damn. I can't ask Myra to pull Beverly's phone records if it might do something to incriminate her. Like it or not, she's still our client.

Last night's boating class didn't disappoint me: it was as boring as expected. There must be something wrong with the rest of the people in the class, because for some reason, they don't find it as sleep inducing as I do. Just a few minutes before the class ended I discovered that once again the kid has ambushed me. The instructor knocked his pointer on the lectern and said he had an announcement to make. "Ladies and gentlemen, we received a call from Mister Peter Sharp's office today, letting us know that the day after the final exam next week, the entire class has been invited over to his boat for a class-ending party, which will be catered. It's all on Mister Sharp, so we owe him another debt of thanks."

The freeloading dullards all gave me a standing ovation. Back at the boat, it's a different story. I decide to send a strong warning to my office staff.

Dear Ms. Braunstein:

This is to acknowledge the fact that we are having a catered party on the boat next week to celebrate my completion of the boating course – all arranged by you.

Please be informed that on the day of the party, if the engines of this boat are started up for any reason, the boat will be immediately offered up for donation to charity and a one-bedroom apartment will be rented in the adjacent building, in which I will sleep in the bedroom, and both you and the dog will sleep on floor of the unfurnished living room. This living arrangement will continue until your eighteenth birthday, or your highly anticipated emancipation, whichever occurs first.

Very truly yours, the bigger person.

Having finished this eloquent ultimatum, I can now answer the ringing telephone and find out what Jack B. has discovered.

"Hello Jack. Are we any smarter now than we were yesterday?"

"A little, Mister Sharp. I saw the security videotape that the clerk at the rental car place prepared for me and it looks like Kathy was in the office alone. I also saw some footage from their outdoor camera. She did come by cab, and was riding in it by herself. I was able to make out the name of the cab company and the cab's number and went to their dispatcher's office. The cab that dropped her off there had picked her up earlier that day on the southeast corner of Wilshire Boulevard and Sepulveda Boulevard, in West Los Angeles. Is there anything else you want me to do, Mister Sharp?"

"Yeah, find the driver and ask him if Kathy was alone all the time. And if they stopped along the way to pick the bald guy, where was the stop made?

The most interesting piece of information he gave me was where Kathy Potter was picked up, because that's the corner where the West Los Angeles Federal Building is, and confirms my suspicion that FBI Special Agent Snell is involved.

He already told me to back off of anything that concerned Kathy Potter, and now his hand has completely been tipped. I call his office and for some strange reason, have no problem getting put right through to him.

"Hello, Sharp, what do you want?"

So much for first names. It looks like today it's going to be strictly business. My, how people forget. It wasn't too long ago that I made a hero out of him by giving him all the credit for a bank robbery gang that I had discovered. And now, just a few months later, he's being snippy with me.

"Special Agent Snell, I just wanted to call and thank you for all your help with our investigation into the Kathy Potter matter."

"What are you talking about, Sharp? I told you to back off on that. You weren't supposed to talk to her at all."

"Exactly. That's the help I'm talking about, along with your even calling a cab to come and pick her up at your office the other day. Well, with your assistance, our investigation is now almost complete, and when I have my press conference I'll be sure to mention your name several times to let the media know how helpful you've been."

194

That must have pressed the right buttons, because I hear him start to growl on the other end of the line.

"Okay Sharp, what do you want?"

"Ah, I thought that would bring you around. I guess you're not looking for any extra publicity this month; on this matter, especially, right?"

"Sharp, you're in so far over you're head, that you wouldn't believe it even if I explained it to you."

"I don't think so. This is just a simple case of conspiracy, two murders, and a probable multi-million-dollar insurance scam. I'm not in over my head. This is where I always am, smack dab in the middle of a case that's already been botched by you and your Keystone Kops. Here's what I propose. You and I have a little sit-down, and if everything works out okay, I'll have some good news for my client, and you'll be a hero all over again. You know, some day when you get appointed Attorney General of the State of California, you'll look back and be thankful for all the help I gave you. No, on second thought, you probably won't look back at all. How's about an hour from now at your place?"

The meeting at his office gets off to a very discouraging start. He asks if I know where Kathy Potter is and I tell him I have a pretty good idea. From there on it's all down hill. If I don't tell him where she is right then and there, then he won't tell me anything. It winds up being a complete standoff. The only tidbit of information I give him is the fact that I'll probably be seeing his Kathy Potter in the next day or so. He is not a happy camper. I also promise to call him if I need his assistance, so that he can be in on anything that goes down.

I kept my word to him last time, so even though he's not too fond of me, he knows that I'm a person of honor and won't try to make him look bad, no matter how things turn out.

Now on the way back to the Marina, I'm getting a call from Myra.

"Yes, my dear, what can I do for you today?"

"Peter, are you aware of the fact that in La Verne, our office prosecutes misdemeanors too?"

"How nice for you. And that affects me how?"

"Oh Peter, stop playing dumb. We both know you've got a parking ticket trial out there tomorrow, and my deputy Wendy will be handling it for our office."

"I get it. You're afraid of being humiliated again when I beat your office on another case. Okay, I'll tell you what: you have my word of honor that after I win tomorrow, there'll be no press conference called. I won't tell anyone that you lost."

"You wanna know something Peter? Your stupidity is only exceeded by your arrogance. I see that after you get a couple of decent fees and finally wind up on a boat that actually floats, the real you comes out, and it's not a pretty picture. I'll never know what that adorable little girl sees in you."

This is astounding because if I understand what she's saying, it means that Suzi has confided in her that she really likes me. Wow.

"Okay I'm sorry, I was only kidding. What do you want me to do, plead guilty straight up to the charge of overstaying the twenty minutes in that

196

passenger loading zone? What's the deal here? You can't be worried about my case, it's not worth it."

"It is to Suzi. Whether you realize it or not, you're the only human being in the world that she's got, and she doesn't like to see you arrested or charged with crimes. And when you are, it reflects poorly on me, in her eyes."

"All right, I get it. I'm crazy about her too. I'll try to avoid getting into any more trouble. Are you going to come to La Verne and handle the trial personally?"

"Goodbye, Peter."

The day has arrived for my big traffic ticket trial in the nearby Pomona Courthouse, where all of La Verne's cases are sent for trial. I requested a jury, but due to budget cuts, the State Legislature discontinued allowing jury trials on misdemeanor traffic infractions, so I'll have to take my chances in front of a judge.

The trial is set on the court's afternoon calendar, so I'm taking a leisurely ride out there and practicing my two-minute final argument, while listening to Errol Garner's three-against-four piano style on a CD.

Because of the light traffic I'll probably get to Pomona at least an hour early, and since it would be poor taste to ask the prosecutor or police chief to have lunch with a defendant going on trial the same day, I've got some time to kill. I also have a suspicion that my subconscious mind arranged for me to have this spare time. I hear two voices fighting for my attention. One is telling me to be a good boy and stay away from Beverly Luskin's house. The other is my old self, telling me to go knock on her door and ask her what the hell is going on.

Fortunately the good boy voice wins out. Notwithstanding my burning curiosity to know what's happening with her, Kathy, and that bald guy, I'm trying to turn over a new leaf for the kid's sake. I'm not going to get in trouble. I'm going to keep my nose clean. However, it couldn't hurt to just drive by her place. Maybe they'll all be outside on the lawn, with some big banner explaining everything that's been going on.

Nah. I'll just sit here by the park and wait until it's time to go to court. I've always got an extra paperback in the car, so maybe I can get a little reading done, and this one looks like it's got advice I can really use. The title is *Female-to-English Dictionary: A Guide to Interpreting and Manipulating the Female Thought Process,* by Dr. Nick Shoveen, Ph.D.

When I'm on the boat, every time I decide to relax and read a while, something happens. It can be anything from a mere telephone call to a catastrophic event, like me getting arrested. I see that the same magical sequence of events happens when I'm off the boat too. Just as I open the first page of the paperback, my cell phone rings and the caller ID display shows it's coming from someone I know. Beverly Luskin.

"Hello Beverly, I was wondering if I'd ever hear from you again. How're you doing?"

"Oh, Peter, it's so nice to hear your voice. I've been pretty busy putting my late husband's affairs in

198

order, and stuff like that. You know how it goes. The paperwork never stops. The main reason I called is because I remember your mentioning that your court date was supposed to be scheduled for today, and I was wondering how it went this morning. Did you win?"

"Not yet, but thanks for asking. Because of the driving distance, I requested an afternoon trial, so the case won't go on for another hour or so. I'm here in Pomona sitting near the park and doing a little reading."

"That's wonderful. As long as you've got some time, why don't you stop by? I'd love to see you. We can catch up on things, and maybe after you win the trial, you can come back and we can get some dinner."

Oh oh. This is trouble. I know she's probably still got those people in the house, and now she wants me to stop by for a social call. Something doesn't compute here. I can feel it in my bones. If I set one foot in that house, I'll be getting into trouble. But what can I do? I really want to see her, I'm dying to find out what's going on over there, and I do have almost an hour to kill. Aw, what the hell.

"Sure, Bev, I'll see you in a little while."

I haven't felt this reluctant since the day I got married. I still don't know how I got through that day. Oh yeah, now I remember. I was drunk. But that won't help me here. First of all, there's no time to get plastered because I'm only about five or ten minutes away from her house, and I really don't think the judge would appreciate me coming to court drunk.

199

Oh well, this is going to be one of those sober experiences that I'll be forced to remember. I didn't know the Hummer could drive this slowly. I don't know why I'm doing this. I must be the biggest jerk in the world. If Suzi were here right now she'd probably reach over and pull the keys out of the ignition, to stop me from going over there.

Well, I'm here on her street, and I can see her house down the block. The driveway is empty, so I might as well just pull up there and park. I'm not worried about blocking her garage door, because if Kathy and the bald guy really want to leave they can always politely ask me to move my car, and I'll be glad to oblige. Fat chance of that happening.

After I park the car, I open the rear door, remove my suit jacket from the door hook, and put it on. My next move is to look at my reflection in the car's side window, to check that my tie is on straight and that my hair hasn't been too messed up from driving with the window open. I see a narrow window on the garage door, so under the guise of grooming, I walk over to the window and pretend to use my comb while trying to look inside the garage to see if the minivan is still there. No such luck. There's too much sunshine outside, and I can't see into the dark garage without putting my face right up against the window. That wouldn't look good, so I finish up my act, comb my hair a little, and walk to her front door.

The front door of her house is a large arched affair with a lot of molding that makes it look the whole thing was carved out of a massive tree trunk. There's a big metal doorknocker hanging just below eye level, so I gently lift it up and use it to make a few polite knocks. There's no answer. Is this some sort of game she's playing? I just spoke to her less than five minutes ago and she invited me over. How could she not be around to open the door? The last time I visited her house, she was striking a seductive pose in the open doorway. I guess the honeymoon's over.

I try the doorknocker again, this time a little harder and louder. There's still no answer. She did invite me over, and I am her civil attorney, so it wouldn't be out of line to be worried that something might have happened to her. I try the door and discover that it's not locked. This is the moment of truth. Should I go in? I slowly open the door and stick my head in, shouting her name. No response. I can't take it any longer. The suspense is killing me, so I open the door and walk in.

The sight I'm now facing is one that I'll never forget. The foyer looks like a mess, with things thrown all over, like some people were fighting here. The umbrella rack is on its side, a chair has been broken and various other things strewn around make the place look like a war zone. I hear Beverly's voice. It sounds like she's running into the room to meet me.

"Oh Peter, thank God you're here."

As she rushes toward me, I see that she's holding a gun in her hand, but not in a way that it can be fired. She's holding it by the barrel. I can see that she looks as messy as the room does. Her hair is all over the place, her dress is ripped, and her face is bruised. I even think I see a little blood dripping

201

down from the side of her mouth. As she reaches me, she blurts out. "He's here, the man who's been beating me. I was afraid to tell you about him, but he's in the other room, and I'm afraid he's going to come out here and beat me again. Here, take this. You may need it to protect us both."

I feel her grabbing my wrist and shoving the gun into my hand. She then falls back unconscious in a dead faint. I still don't know what's going on, but I do know that I'm now standing here in the middle a completely trashed room with a beaten up bruised woman out cold on the floor in front of me, and I've got a gun in my hand.

Because of the excitement I don't notice the sound of approaching sirens, but they're now quite loud. It's always strange to hear a siren wind down, because it means that whatever emergency vehicle it's on has finally arrived.

I hear someone shouting behind me.

"Freeze! Drop the gun and put your hands in the air."

At that same time, Beverly miraculously regains consciousness and shouts out to her would-be rescuers. "Thank God you're here. He's already killed one person in the other room, and if you wouldn't have gotten here in time, I'm sure he would've killed me too. I grabbed the gun barrel, trying to pull it out of his hand, but he knocked me down with his other hand." She then starts to weep hysterically and runs into the arms of the closest uniformed person she sees, sobbing hysterically.

I'm given the usual instructions. After dropping the gun, I'm told to get down on my knees and clasp my hands behind my back. I feel the cuffs being slapped on my wrist, then they stand me up and drag me outside to a waiting squad car, where I'm tossed into the back seat.

Strangely enough, instead of the elaborate frame-up I've just been successfully put right into the middle of, the only thought going through my mind now is that this may mean I'll be late for my traffic ticket trial.

15

I am now sitting in one of the La Verne Police Station's cells trying to figure out what has happened to me. I know I didn't kill anyone, and I certainly didn't lay a hand on Beverly Luskin, so I now fit into the category of every other person currently behind bars. I've been framed.

They haven't gotten around to formally booking me, because I haven't been finger-printed or photographed yet. This situation is terrible, because I know it'll be taking a toll on the kid. Now that I realize how much she relies on me as her only protector, I really feel bad about letting her down again. Wait a minute... I didn't let her down. I didn't do anything. Why should I feel guilty? Oh, what's the difference, I'm a screw-up. I've always been one. Myra knows it, and now Suzi does too.

I'm not so worried about how Myra feels, because she always thought I was a lost cause. I hope I can get to use a phone soon, so I can tell her to get over to the boat and keep an eye on the kid.

What am I talking about? She's the top law enforcement person in the whole County. She must've been informed about my arrest less than five minutes after it happened. I know she'll go to the boat and do the right thing. If I can't get this mess straightened out in the next couple of days, they'll be transferring me to County Jail. God, I hope they don't try to take Suzi away. Oh, this is terrible.

The jailer comes into the cell area and to my complete surprise, opens my cell door and leaves some things on the bunk: my cell phone and a small television set with rabbit ears. He then leaves without saying a word. This is getting interesting and must be the nicest jail in the country. I'll have to remember to arrange for all my arrests to happen in this town. I was also given a very nice meal, probably brought in from a local restaurant. What's wrong with this picture? Here I am in custody for the murder of someone, I have a fancy meal delivered, a television set to watch, and my cell phone to use. Well, they certainly named it correctly: today it definitely is a 'cell' phone.

I call Suzi's private line and Myra answers.

"It's about time you called. We've been waiting."

"Gee, I'm sorry Myra, is there any way I can get a continuance on my parking ticket trial? If I wasn't so busy getting framed for murdering someone, I'd do it myself, but…"

She cuts me off mid-sentence.

"I'm taking Suzi home with me for a couple of days."

"Then what? I don't know how long I'll be here before they send me to County Jail, and I'm sure you'll be opposing bail. Any suggestions?"

"No, I won't be opposing bail, because I'm recusing myself from prosecuting this case. In fact, I may just take off for a while. I've got some vacation time coming, so Suzi and I will just sit around the house and watch your trial on Court TV."

"That's it? No discussion about this case? How about some hint about who they think I murdered?"

"You know I can't talk to you about your case. If you want some details, maybe the jailer will turn a television set on for you."

I don't know why I even try with her.

"Please take good care of her Myra, and tell her I'm sorry I goofed up again. Can I please talk to her for a second?"

"She's locked in her room."

"Well then just tell her I didn't do it, and after this is all over, I promise to listen to her. And tell her… just tell her I didn't do this."

There's an electric socket in the cell, so I might was well take Myra's advice. I plug in the little television set. By now the press probably knows more about this case than I do.

Oh, wonderful, it's in glorious black and white. Just before the news starts, there's a sausage commercial. In black and white, their product looks like something a dog dropped. The early evening news is coming on now and of course if it bleeds it leads, so I'm once again a celebrity. Here it comes: an interview with the victim of my beating, Beverly Luskin. Beverly's house appears in back of the newscaster, who tries to be as much like Geraldo Rivera as possible by shouting into the microphone with a sense of urgency and importance.

"I am now in the City of La Verne and have gotten one of the people involved in this criminal case to grant us an exclusive interview. She is Beverly Luskin, the widow of a man who was gunned down in the streets of this very town recently. Mrs. Luskin, please, give us some background information about this terrible series of events."

The camera now pulls back to reveal a dis-sheveled Beverly standing next to the reporter. He points his hand-held microphone towards her, and being the true actress that she obviously is, she takes her cue perfectly and begins her sob story.

"I've been seeing my attorney, Mister Peter Sharp, on a strictly platonic social basis since my husband was killed, but I never realized how strongly he felt about me. He was handling all my legal affairs, and I needed his services very badly, so I didn't complain to the authorities when he flew into a rage last week and gave me a black eye. I was planning on replacing him with another attorney when he came barging into my house, and upon seeing my girlfriend's male friend, he flew into a

206

jealous rage, accused me of betraying him, and beat me again.

"He pulled out a gun and threatened to kill the man, who then ran into another room. I tried to grab the gun away from him, but he hit me hard, and I fell. The next thing I knew, there was a shot fired in the other room, so I grabbed the phone and called 911. Fortunately, the police arrived before he was able to kill me too."

The newscaster then turns his attention to another man standing there who is introduced as Beverly Luskin's 'spokesperson.' He then is allowed to make an announcement that startles me, and shows me how vicious a person Beverly really is, and how much planning she must have put into this scenario she created.

"We have several affidavits from witnesses who have sworn under penalty of perjury that the Defendant, Attorney Peter Sharp, was in attendance at a gun show more than sixty miles away from his residence, shortly before the murder he is now charged with committing. Reliable sources in the police department have informed us that the murder weapon was a sanitized gun with all identifying marks removed, so we can only assume that he purchased it at that gun show.

"It should also be noted that Mister Sharp drives a yellow Hummer, the same one that witnesses identified as having been in the parking lot at the gun show, and also exact same vehicle used in the recent fatal drive-by shooting of Beverly Luskin's husband, in broad daylight. We certainly hope that now the authorities have all this information, they will take a

207

closer look at Mister Sharp, not only for the murder he is now accused of in Mrs. Luskin's home, but also for involvement in the previous murder of her husband. It is the opinion of Mrs. Luskin that Mister Sharp was totally obsessed with her, and may have wanted any male she came into contact with put out of the way forever."

The newscaster on the scene is one of those typical blow-dried idiots who isn't even capable of asking a Barbara-Walters type of inane question, but fortunately has the presence of mind to ask who my most recent victim was. Beverly answers.

"I don't know, really. He came with my lady friend, and before we even had a chance to be introduced, Mister Sharp came into the house. He must have been stalking me, and saw them come in."

I knew it would just be a matter of time before some loonies came out of the woodwork. Just after they finish with the fantasy that Beverly and her spokesperson have created and performed, the studio's anchorperson comes up with an exclusive scoop. "This station has learned that Attorney Peter Sharp, the Defendant in that murder in La Verne, who had allegedly purchased an unmarked weapon at a gun show, was also retained to represent a high-profile client in Los Angeles, none other than renowned attorney Charles Indovine. Mister Indovine was arrested for possession of a concealed weapon. A source inside the prosecutor's office has informed us that Mister Sharp had planned to make a constitutional Second Amendment argument for his client, alleging that he was not breaking the law by carrying a concealed weapon. This commentator

208

finds it ironic that Mister Sharp, accused of using a handgun, purchased without the benefit of any background check, should be making that argument about another attorney charged with possessing a weapon.

"We have in our studio a member of the Los Angeles Group of Citizens Against Guns, who would like to offer a comment on Mister Sharp. We also asked for a representative from the National Rifle Association to join us, but they declined to send a spokesperson. And now, here is Mizz Angela Slyter.

"Thank you, Arthur. We would like your viewers to know that in one way, we support Mister Sharp's contention that his client had a right to own a gun. Every citizen in this country may have a right to own a gun, but that right isn't granted by the Second Amendment, instead it is as a result of the same rules that allow us to own other items of personal and real property, like houses and cars. We all own cars, and periodically must be tested for qualifications, and re-licensed to operate them. This licensing procedure in some states also requires that we show proof of insurance, so that if anyone is injured as a result of our operation of the asset, that everyone is covered by some financial responsibility... and all of those requirements are for items that are not designed to kill. They may do that on occasion, but not if used as designed.

"We have learned that Mister Sharp was formerly a member of the NRA, and that certainly was his right, but as a sworn officer of the Court and a member of our society, how can he, or any other reasonable citizen object to the same requirements being applied to guns as they are to cars? We certainly would have no problem with every gun being pre-tested by the manufacturer, with a fired bulled from each one saved in a database for future ballistics comparison. Also, the owners should be tested for proficiency and re-licensed periodically, with the requirement for license issuance be predicated also upon proof of insurance.

"A former president of the NRA and well-respected actor, Mister Charlton Heston, was a staunch contender of people's rights to own guns, but he certainly didn't offer to turn his lethal weapons in when he announced he had been diagnosed with Alzheimer's disease. If the purpose of keeping a weapon in your home is to protect yourself from intruders you don't recognize, don't you think that a person with Alzheimer's disease, who is expected to have difficulty in recognizing anyone, should surrender his weapons?

"We look forward to hearing Mister Sharp's response to our arguments."

Great. Just what I need, an argument about one of the most hotly debated and polarizing issues in this country, other than abortion rights, gay marriage, and prayer in school. Scotty, please beam me up.

It's very uncomfortable watching people tell these lies about me. I know that once we get to trial I'll have Jack, Phyllis, Stuart, Vinnie, and Olive, who can all testify to the fact that it was almost twenty four hours earlier when that person she wasn't introduced to actually entered her residence. That's the upside. The downside is that I have to go to trial on a murder charge in order to prove she's a liar.

Well, there are sure no interruptions here in the cell, so I might as well just sit back, relax, and try to figure out some way to get myself out of this mess. I've still got my cell phone, so first thing tomorrow I'll call Snell and let him know that Kathy Potter is the mystery friend of Beverly's. Maybe he'll get interested enough to look into this. Why wait? I might as well call him now. He should be available, unless the FBI closes at five PM.

After a few minutes on hold, I get patched through to Snell.

"Hello Sharp, what do you want now?"

"I want you to get over to Beverly Luskin's house. The girlfriend she's been talking about on television is none other than your Kathy Potter. I have no idea who the guy is that I'm supposed to have shot, but I'm sure you can get Kathy to tell you all about it."

"Do you remember me telling you to stay away from this matter? Whatever situation you're in now is your own doing. You got yourself into it, so you get yourself out of it. And that lady friend of Beverly Luskin's is not Kathy Potter. And Sharp... please don't call me anymore. This isn't a Federal matter."

That definitely tells me he knows more than he's letting on. He knows we found out about Kathy Potter taking that cab when she left his office, so he must know that we followed her. For some reason, he's backing off on that Potter dame. Is he really willing to let me fry, just to let her get away? And who is the dead bald guy, and who killed him? I

211

know it wasn't me, so it must've been one of those women. But which one did it, and why?

I hate to even think this, but there's only one person who can probably put all this stuff together, figure out what's going on, and clear me, and that's the kid. Next to Nero Wolfe, the original armchair detective, she's got the best analytical mind I've ever encountered. With her brains and Myra's connections, I'll bet they can have me out of here by tomorrow. I know that Myra wouldn't do anything to help me on her own, but she's already let me know how the kid feels about me, and I know that Myra loves the kid, so who knows what will happen?

I might as well stretch out and take a nap. For once, I know that my getting comfortable won't cause anything bad to happen, because there's nothing else left that can be done to me. I'm now at rock bottom, and that conniving Beverly caused it all. I should have listened to the kid when she gave Beverly a thumbs down.

The nap didn't work. It's almost two in the morning. Hey, wait a minute. I've still got my wristwatch, and I also realize that my money and credit cards are still in my pockets. What's going on here? Am I under arrest or not? Aren't they supposed to strip search prisoners and take everything away from them? I hear someone coming.

"Let's go, Mister Sharp." The cell door slides open. I don't know who this is or where they want me to go, but anywhere on earth where I might be able to watch a color television set will be better than this cell, so I'm following his orders.

When we walk out the rear exit of the police station I see that it's one of the cops, but in plain clothes. We both get into his unmarked vehicle, and he starts to drive. In about ten minutes he pulls into an alley and drives down to the middle of the block. He pulls over, stops, points at an open rear fence gate, and tells me to get out of the car. I follow his instructions and walk over to the open gate. I can see that I'm now in the back yard of a large house, and there's a light on in the open rear door of the house. This must be the place where they want me to be, so I walk towards the light and into the doorway.

I'm now standing in a small laundry room. There's a hallway off to my left, and I can see light coming into it from another room. Someone shouts out to me. "Over here, Mister Sharp, we've been waiting for you." I walk down the small hallway and into the room. Seated at a table are Special Agent Snell, two of his men, and Chief Stan Olshansky of the La Verne Police Department.

"What took you so long, Sharp?" Snell must be kidding. He knows exactly where I've been. I guess it's my turn now.

"Would someone please tell me what the hell is going on? Am I, or am I not under arrest for murdering someone? And if so, exactly who am I supposed to have murdered? And what about that lying broad Beverly Luskin? Oh, by the way, I haven't had a chance to wash my hands yet, so would you like to give me a GSR or paraffin test to see if I've fired a gun recently?"

The Chief finally speaks. "Oh please, give us a break. You're not under arrest, but you can't leave

213

here until we finish things up, so don't worry, everything's under control. Just relax for a couple of days and let us grown-ups handle everything. This is my house, and you're going to be my guest until we clear up this matter.

"Everyone else, including the press, thinks you're still in that cell, and we're letting no visitors in, so they'll keep thinking that. I've got a room out in back for you upstairs over the garage, and if you know what's good for you, you'll stay in it. We're taking your cell phone away from you, because we don't want anyone calling you, or you calling anyone on the outside. Your room has cable television, and my housekeeper will bring you whatever you want to eat, but she's not going to chop one of those crazy salads for you, like the one you ordered that first day we met."

Snell has the last word. "I told you to keep out of this, didn't I?. But would you listen to me? No. And now look what happened. You'd better stay here, out of our way, because if we can't straighten this thing out, you're going down for murder."

This is encouraging, because I don't think that the Chief of any police department would bring a murder suspect into his own home, and put him up in relative comfort with a maid if he thought the suspect was actually guilty. Along with everyone else in this world, they must know something that I don't know.

The afternoon news is on and I recognize Myra's house in the background. Evidently she did take off of work for a while, and a news crew is there to interview her. She comes out of the house and is

214

asked a few stupid questions. Like a true pro, she makes a statement that answers the questions that they didn't have the brains to ask.

"Due to the fact that the person charged with this crime is my ex-husband, I felt it my responsibility to turn this matter over to the Attorney General's office for prosecution, and I'll be taking some vacation time while the case progresses.

"I've been informed that they'll probably be going before a grand jury soon, so from now on I'll be out of the loop, and if you want some answers, they won't be available from me or my office. You'll have to ask the Attorney General's staff what their plans are."

The only good thing about the interview is that in the background I see the front door to her house is open and what looks like the tip of something white and furry can be seen sticking out from behind the door. Unless Myra's got a pet bear in the house, it must mean that the dog is there, and if the dog is there, then so's the kid. I also know that Myra has a broadband Internet connection in the house, so Suzi can probably do her investigative stuff from right there, and if I know her at all, she'll be using Myra's passwords for entry into the State's secure criminal databases.

In the evening I can look down toward the Chief's house and see him conducting meetings in that back room of his. Sometimes Snell is there too. They've also done a good job of not letting my true location leak out, because there's always a news crew or two staked out in front of the police station, hoping

215

to get some footage of me being transferred to another jail.

Several newscasters have quoted 'reliable sources' as having said that I'm refusing to cooperate with the authorities. One station claims that they're now negotiating with the police to get an exclusive interview with me. Film at eleven.

They were nice enough to have brought my 'grab bag' up for me. Being a single, former man-about-town, I always keep a small case with shaving stuff, extra shirt, underwear, socks, and grooming supplies in my Hummer. It just dawned on me that there's also a small flashlight in my bag, so I take it out and flash an S.O.S. down toward the house. It worked. The Chief noticed it, and sent one of his men out to my guesthouse. He escorts me down to join the rest of them in the house.

When I walk into the room, I see that Snell is there too. They don't look too happy to see me, but at least I get invited to sit down at the table and join them. I haven't had anyone to talk to for the past couple of days, so I might as well see if the vocal chords still work.

"I suppose you're wondering why I called this meeting."

They are not amused. Snell takes charge.

"Just sit there and keep your mouth shut. The only reason we allowed you to come down here is to tell you that officially, you're not under arrest. You're in protective custody."

"Does that mean you have some doubt that I killed someone in that house?"

216

Snell looks at the Chief, giving him the nod to explain it to me.

"Mister Sharp, immediately after you talked to Special Agent Snell and told him about your knowing that Kathy Potter took a cab from his office, the Feds put a tail on you. It wasn't too hard to follow you because of that huge yellow tank you drive, and also because they knew exactly where you'd be going on the day of the murder. You had a court appointment down the road, in Pomona.

"Unlike the dramas on television, the Feds are not a bunch of incompetents who always get in the way of local law enforcement. On the contrary, they work with us locals and help us out in any way they can. In this particular case, Snell called to let me know that he would be here in town on the day of your trial. One of his team followed you on the road, while he flew up here and landed at our local small plane airport. When he got to my station, we decided to ride together in my car.

"About the same time you arrived in town and decided to park and get some reading done, we received a call from your office, warning us that you might be going over to Beverly Luskin's house, and asking us to try and stop you before you made a complete fool of yourself. Knowledge about your past gave us the idea that you were perfectly capable of doing just that, so we had one of our unmarked squad cars parked down the street from the Luskin house, and we followed you from the park to her street.

"Beverly Luskin was probably watching for you from an upstairs window, and when she saw you

217

pull into her driveway, she placed a nine-eleven call about the murder. The nine-eleven dispatcher knew that we were in the area of the Luskin house, so she patched the call through to us, and while you were standing outside of her garage window, trying to peek in there while obviously pretending to combing your hair, we all listened to Luskin hysterically scream that you just beat her up and shot someone in her house. This all took place while we were watching you, and before you got to her front door." Snell takes over.

"We know you didn't beat her up or kill anyone, and we've already received the report from your office that Kathy Potter had been followed there two days earlier, so we also know that Luskin is lying about her friend coming that day to visit her and bringing a 'gentleman' with her.

"We're now in the process of trying to learn who the murder victim is. Kathy Potter is using another name and I'm keeping out of her sight, because we don't want to spook them out of their game just yet. We've got the victim at our federal morgue in Los Angeles, and we're running him through various databases. So far, his prints haven't turned up, so we know he's never been in the criminal justice system or applied for a license of any sort. The DNA tests can take up to two weeks to be completed, and in the meantime, we don't want them to know that we're on to them, so we have to keep you in the public's eye as the killer, while we give them enough rope to make a mistake." The Chief takes over.

218

"These women are clever, but they're not professional criminals, so they don't know all the angles. Career crooks aren't as smart as these dames are, but real thugs are familiar with police procedures, and these two aren't. They'll slip up, or we'll find out who the dead guy is, and when either one of those things happens, we may have what we need to nail them."

I'm pleased to hear all this, but have a suggestion or two of my own. "Listen, gentlemen, I have a person on my staff who can put all this together for you, if you'll only let me make a phone call to get that ball rolling.

Snell looks at the Chief with a slight 'no' nod, so the Chief reiterates his warning. "Sorry, Sharp, but we can't allow you to make any calls. My only suggestion to you is go back upstairs to your guest room and relax. Now that you know most of the facts already, we'll keep you posted if anything new develops."

I appreciate being let in on what's happening, but still have one more question. "Snell, what's the deal with Kathy Potter? Is she supposed to be important to you on some other case?"

Snell doesn't answer me, but his silence tells me more than he wants me to know. The Chief's deputy motions for me to follow him back to the guesthouse, so I guess my part of the meeting is over.

Back up in my room, I see that the local news is making a big deal about my Hummer being towed to some CSI lab in Los Angeles, where they expect to find more evidence linking me to the murder. Not only am I a prisoner upstairs of a garage, if I escaped, I wouldn't have a car to drive home in.

The only other news worth watching is about some upcoming trial of a crime boss with the unlikely name of Georgio 'the actor' Crescendo. Can't these mafia guys come up with any better names for themselves? About the only thing interesting about them are the nicknames they adopt. Over twenty years ago, this particular guy is supposed to have fooled some jail employees by pretending to have an appendicitis attack. His act was so good that it enabled him to escape from jail, and earned him his nickname.

I hope his trial is televised, because it would be nice to see someone who's actually guilty go to trial for a change. From what the papers have been reporting about this Georgio, he's a real piece of work. They say that compared to Crescendo, Tony Soprano is like Rebecca of Sunnybrook Farm.

I'm being brought down to the house again for another meeting. Snell's not there, so the Chief will brief me.

"Mister Sharp, we've got a slight problem. The DNA tests came back on the victim in Luskin's house, and there's a match with Kathy Potter's husband."

"So what's the problem, Chief? His body was never found, so this closes that case out."

"Not exactly. The problem is that even though the DNA is a match for Mister Potter, the fingerprints aren't, and he's got quite a record, so there are plenty of samples for comparison. This means that we've

220

either got the first successful fingerprint conversion in history, or two people with the exact same DNA. I personally don't have much hope for either of those two choices, so we're going to have to keep you under wraps for a while longer until we sort this anomaly out."

I understand their problem. Maybe they can do it in the movies, but without special effects, there's no switching of fingerprints. There is a possibility of similar DNA, but from what I understand, it can only occur with blood relatives.

This is frustrating. In my boredom, I'm going through the guesthouse inch by inch, looking for something to read. I've already finished Doctor Shoveen's treatise on how to manipulate women, and wonder if I'll ever get out of here to try it out. Eureka! There's nothing here to read, but I just found something much more interesting on a shelf behind some piled up boxes. It's a laptop computer that must be at least ten years old. Fortunately, the AC power cord is wrapped around it, so I can try it out. The battery is probably toast, but I should still be able to boot it up on 110.

Success. I see that on the back of this antique Toshiba there's a phone jack, so using the one they left up here when removing the telephone, I attach it to see if I can get online. Yes! It worked. I'm not expecting a 56k modem, but I don't care if it's only a 28, or even a 14; I'll still be happy to use it. Fortunately, before MSN came along, Bill Gates had every laptop in the world come with a pre-installed AOL program, so I use the program to get online and avail myself of their free 30-day trial program. I've

221

still got my credit card in my pocket, so after giving them all the info they need, I'm now an official member of the intelligentsia that uses AOL.

My first task is to contact the kid. I e-mail her to get back to me as soon as possible. She must have been on line, because in less than two minutes I get her response. She wants to know where I am.

I purposely don't tell her where I am, but that's for her own good. The Feds are involved in this, and I don't want her sucked into things any further than she has to be. All I want her to know is that I'm okay, and available by e-mail.

This old laptop doesn't have a built-in microphone, so I can't use any Internet telephony connections for voice contact. I'll have to settle for e-mail, so after thinking about it for a little while, I send one to Jack B., inquiring about the mileage checks he did on the minivan and distances from the insurance office where we started to tail Kathy Potter.

Jack is cool. He doesn't waste any time in asking where I am or what's going on, because he knows that information is probably available from the kid, and that if I'm contacting him, I'm already in touch with Suzi. He tells me that comparing the miles it had on it when she picked up at the car rental place, to the final mileage when it was in the garage at Beverly's house, it showed an extra twenty miles, which means that she only had to drive a maximum of about ten miles out of her way to pick up baldy. This isn't very helpful, but I want us to have every bit of information possible. This case is starting to look like a huge jigsaw puzzle, and you never can tell which piece will be a crucial one. At the end of

222

Jack's message he gives me a heads-up: just before I contacted him he received several other assignments on this case, but they have nothing to do with the minivan's mileage.

I knew it. The kid's already two steps ahead of everyone, including the Feds and me. She's got Jack checking on some things that no one has thought of yet, and probably never will, so I hope Jack does a good job.

Another day or two has passed by, and I'm still sitting here getting cabin fever. There have been no briefings from Snell or the Chief, and I haven't heard anything from the kid. I know better than to ask her what's going on, because she probably hasn't slept much over the past couple of days. She's like a bloodhound when she gets the scent of a problem case, especially one that I'm involved in. I hide the laptop whenever the maid comes with my food.. No sense in letting anyone get the idea that I'm in touch with the outside world.

I feel like the rest of the public. My only source of what's going on is the television set, and as everyone knows, if it's on television, it must be true. The only things on during the afternoon are soap operas, and this is the first time I've ever seen one. A person can get claustrophobic watching these programs because all you ever see are people in a room, usually two at a time. No one ever goes outside, and all they ever do is glare at each other with questions or accusations about infidelity, or a medical diagnosis for some disease that I've never heard of before. Cable isn't that much better, but at least MSNBC and CNN have better sets than the local guys do.

I never thought I'd be happy to see the news come on, but after two hours of watching some models that they gave speaking parts to, overacting and chewing up the scenery, and a bunch of talk shows with overweight people poring out their hearts to hosts who don't really care, the news is going to be refreshing.

Tonight's local news opens with an announcement by the Attorney General's office. Myra turned the case over to them because I'm involved in it. They show some pictures of the ugliest guys I've ever seen and say that there has been an arrest of two Oregon drug dealers in the La Verne drive-by shooting death. They go on to boast that they feel confident that these drug dealers will cooperate and further involve a well-known Marina del Rey criminal attorney in their murder conspiracy. I wonder who that might be.

After the usual items about car thefts, car accidents, car commercials, car jacking, and car chases, they have a new bulletin that 'just came in.' The newsreader drones on that District Attorney Myra Scots' office has issued an announcement, and they play a taped statement she made outside of her office.

"Our office is pleased to announce that we've made two arrests out in La Verne. The women arrested have been charged with conspiracy to commit insurance fraud and murder. Several of our investigators and myself are on my way out there now to take custody of the arrestees and bring them back to Los Angeles, where they will be processed and incarcerated. We have issued no-bail warrants for them, so they'll be guests of the County until their trial"

One of the reporters asks about me. "What about your ex-husband. Does this mean he's off the hook?"

Myra smirks at the camera. "Yes, I'm afraid he's getting away this time, but don't worry, the next time he makes a mistake I'll be there waiting, with a pair of handcuffs that have his name engraved on them."

This gets a laugh out of the crowd, as Myra dashes for her car. Boy, if they only knew how serious she was about that remark. I guess this means I'll be getting out pretty soon, so I might as well shave, shower, and get ready for my release.

The Chief has sent one of his men over to get me, probably so that I can be formally released from the police station. When we get there I'm hustled in through the back door so the press doesn't get any hint that I wasn't there all of this time.

I walk upstairs to the Chief's office and watch the news people crowding around downstairs. Off in the distance I see a sight for sore eyes. Two vehicles are approaching the station. The one in front is an unmarked police vehicle, because I can see the metal cage that separates the rear seats from the front ones. The vehicle in back of it is the Lincoln Town Car that the County assigned to Myra and her driver, but I'm sure that no one has ever seen it like this before. The Town Car's sunroof is open, and there's a huge Saint Bernard's head sticking out of it – and the beast is

225

wearing a pair of Doggles. When the press sees this, they go nuts. The cameras are all immediately focused on the car with the dog, and the arrested murderers drop to second billing. I guess everyone loves animals.

While standing upstairs in the Chief's office and watching Myra's motorcade pull up, I hear a slight noise behind me. Turning around, I see that the Chief's chair is turned around, with its back facing me.

"No reason to hide, Chief, I'll be out of your hair in just a few minutes."

The chair turns around and I see that it's not the Chief who's sitting in it, it's FBI Special Agent Snell.

"I'm not hiding, Sharp. I've been around since the first minute we spoke about the Potter murder."

"You mean you had me under surveillance? All that time?"

"Absolutely. And we also were covering your legman, Jack Bibberman."

"Why? You couldn't have suspected us of any crime."

"Well, to be quite honest, we weren't really interested that much in you. What we really wanted was your little kid."

"You suspected her of something?"

"Yes, we suspected her of having the capability to solve a case for us."

This is amazing. If I'm correct, it means that the head of the FBI's Los Angeles Office wanted the assistance of Suzi, but didn't know how to ask.

226

"But you told me to stay away from this case. Why?"

"You know why. It's because you're a rebel. We knew that the only way to suck you into this case was to tell you to stay away from it. And because there was some money involved, your kid would be interested in it too. She's quite the little business person, you know."

"Oh yeah, I know."

"Kathy Potter asked us for our help in having her husband declared dead so that she could collect on his Uniman Insurance policy with. We remembered from the last time our paths crossed that you did a good job saving that company from paying fraudulent claims, so we figured that the reason you were looking into the Potter case was because Uniman asked you to.

"The way his body disappeared with only the bloody shirt remaining, it looked too much like the type of shenanigan that our guys would pull to fake a witness' death. We didn't want our target defendant to get the idea that it was actually us playing games, so after a long discussion, we decided to bring Suzi into it, and that meant calling you with that warning to not get involved."

So I was right after all. I'm surprised to hear Snell admit it.

"I kind of thought you wanted our help on the case, otherwise you wouldn't have tried to waive me off, but I never in my wildest dreams imagined it was Suzi's brain you were after."

227

"Nothing personal Sharp, but we all know which one of you is the brains and which is the brawn in your law firm, and we opted for the brains."

"Okay, I can understand that. She's a good little armchair detective, and probably much better equipped mentally to solve a crime than the FBI, but if you were with the Chief on the day of the last murder, why the charade and my being locked up in the jail?"

"To be quite honest, that was my idea. We couldn't tip our hand too early, so you had to be kept under arrest for a while. I had no problem with your staying in the local jail the whole time, but the Chief didn't think it was fair to you, so we went along with his suggestion to move you over to his house during the end game. After we agreed to let you stay at his house, it took us another day to figure out how to hide that laptop for you to find and use. The reason it took us so long to get our plan together was that we were having difficulty in getting the right amount of dust on it, to make you believe it had been out of use for some time."

"Wow. The entire scientific efforts of the FBI put to work, just to make a laptop dusty for me. I'm glad to see our tax dollars at work so efficiently."

"Actually, it wasn't our tech department that did it. While we were talking about it, our janitor Mikhail happened to be in the room, and he suggested we give it to him, along with the small wood cabinet it sat in. He wanted to take it into his workroom and let it sit to while he emptied the vacuum cleaner bags. It only took him about five minutes to get it dusted properly, so that when you

228

lifted it off of the shelf, you'd see the dust pattern around where it was sitting. We also had to spend some time getting an older generation model, so that it would look like it had been sitting there long enough to gather that amount of dust."

"So your taking the phone instrument away and leaving the cord behind was just so I'd have a connection to plug into the laptop's modem, right?"

"Exactly. And we also wanted to wait at least a day, so that you, the press, and your kid would get the idea that you were really in a mess. When you were allowed to use that laptop, it was mainly for you to contact the kid and give her the incentive to solve the case and get you out. You know she really must care for you, because we were monitoring the activity on your ex-wife's computer, and that little girl was working almost around the clock trying to get the information she needed."

"You were spying on a computer in the residence of Los Angeles County's elected District Attorney?"

"No, we didn't have to. All the secure criminal databases keep a running log of each privileged computer that requests access. All we had to do was put out a standing request for notification every time Miss Scot's District Attorney password was being used, and we knew exactly where she was surfing.

The only problem she encountered was that the DA's password wasn't good enough to gain access to all the places she wanted to go, so by following her surfing pattern, we were able to access along with her, and grant Federal clearance for her to get in at each site she visited. Without our help, she wouldn't have been able to get all the information she needed to solve the case for us."

"So without your help, the kid wouldn't have gotten the information to solve your case?"

"That's right. Of course, we would have had to let you go soon anyway, because we all knew you were outside the house when Beverly Luskin's nine-eleven call came in, but we still wanted to know who the real murderer was, and that's where your kid came in handy.

"By getting the facts to have those two vicious widows arrested, we were able to get the information on Georgio Crescendo, and that's who we were really after all the time. Now he's going away for a long time, and as an inducement for us to send him to club Fed instead of a maximum security prison, he'll be giving us a lot of information about a lot of other people who also have names that end in a vowel."

"You really exploited that little girl didn't you? Don't you feel a little guilty about that?"

"Not really. After the drive-by shooting your car was used in, Mrs. Luskin authorized the Chief to advertise a fifty thousand dollar reward for information leading to the arrest and conviction of whoever killed her husband. Standard reward procedure is for the authorities to demand that anyone making an offer like that must place the entire reward amount in an escrow account in some local bank. That way, if someone actually performs in a way to earn the reward, there can be no hesitation on the part of the person offering it, like 'I'm out of money,' or 'I changed my mind.'

"Following proper procedure, the Chief had Mrs. Luskin deposit the money, and it was still sitting there up until yesterday, because everyone was under the impression that Michael Luskin was dead, with no suspects to arrest other than some drug dealers up in Oregon.

"That last day you visited Luskin's house was the day that he actually was killed, and we now know that it was Crescendo that did it."

"Wait a minute. You said that the reward money was sitting there until yesterday. What happened to it? Did Beverly want the money back?"

Snell starts to laugh. I didn't think he was capable of it, and I'm really curious now as to what could have possibly caused it.

"No, she didn't want the money back, and she wouldn't have gotten it even if she tried. The reward was paid out."

"Don't tell me. Let me guess."

"That's right counselor. The bank issued a certified check for the entire fifty thousand dollars one Suzi Braunstein."

"Wait a minute, you mean the check wasn't made payable to our law firm?"

"No. We asked her about that, but she told us this was a job she did on her own, and it definitely was not the firm's fee. You look perplexed. Is there a problem?"

"No, there's no problem. She's a typical female. What's hers is hers and what's mine is ours.

"And while I've got you here, what's this business about that mafia guy, and how does he figure into everything?"

231

Snell has just returned to his brick wall persona, saying that he can't comment on any file currently open, and that maybe I'll get my answers some time in the future.

I look down below as Myra makes a statement for the press. I see that the dog is still in the car, so I've got a pretty good idea of who else is in there behind the tinted glass. Now it's my turn, so I walk down the steps and enter into the sunlight, which is a nice change for me. Myra acknowledges my presence with a nod, and only has four words for me. "Get in the car." The press ignores me. They're not interested in innocent people.

The dog is happy to see me. The kid is asleep in the back seat, so I slide in next to her. We sit there and wait while Myra is inside signing receipts for the prisoners and making sure they're loaded into the other vehicle. She then walks over and gets into the back seat of the Town Car on the other side of the kid, and the driver turns toward the freeway for our ride back to Los Angeles.

There aren't too many words exchanged on the ride back, other than Myra's comments about the kid sleeping and that someone else from her office will be bringing my Hummer back for me. She tells me that this may be the first time she's closed her eyes in the past few days, since receiving my e-mail message. I'm informed that the kid worked around the clock doing internet research, meeting with Jack B., hacking into the criminal law enforcement databases, and generally working herself like a little slave until she cracked the case. I guess they were

232

both up all the time, because the dog is lying across my feet, out like a log.

I look down at Suzi and see that while asleep, her hands are holding on to both Myra and me.

16

Now that things are getting back to normal, I should get my paperwork in order, so I send a message to Beverly Luskin's new post office box address, notifying here that our office is no longer representing her on any civil matters and is disinclined to represent her on her current criminal case. I also inform her that as to the five thousand dollar retainer she paid us, while I was sitting in jail, the meter was running. She was the direct cause of my being arrested, so that means that my several days of confinement were added to her account at the rate of over two thousand a day. This means that not only does she not have a refund coming, but if and when she gets released some day, she may be getting an invoice from us for the overage. I have feeling that if I'm not around fifty years from now when Beverly might get out, the kid will remember that there's still some money due to our firm. But of course she won't be a kid any more, either.

For a grand finale to my recent efforts, I prepare an invoice for Mister Uniman and send it out to him. Due to the fact that he now has no responsibility to pay out that three million to Beverly Luskin, and two hundred grand to Kathy Potter, the sum total I saved him was three point two million, and he therefore should make his check for three hundred twenty thousand dollars payable to Peter Sharp, Attorney at Law. Uniman's a pretty fair guy, so I feel confident that even in the absence of a written retainer, he'll honor his promise of a ten-

234

percent reward on whatever my work saves him from paying. The thing I really enjoy about this fee is that it's all mine. It's about time that I arranged to avoid the kid's glomming onto a nice fat fee and turning into a 'house' account deposit. Not this time. No sharing with the firm. Fee at last, fee at last.

During my confinement the City Attorney's office notified us that they are not filing any complaint against Charles Indovine. It seems that they felt his expired 'carry permit' was the type that could have been renewed by mail, so there wasn't a strong enough legal ground to work with to make it worth their time to prosecute.

The dismissal is nice to learn about, but then there's still the matter of that huge fifty thousand dollar retainer that Indovine paid me. I call his number and once again get put right through to him.

"Yes, Peter, what can I do for you today?"

This is good: he's using my first name. I don't feel comfortable being on a first name basis with him this time, so I play it right out of the lawyer-client instruction manual. "Mister Indovine, I've got good news and bad news, and in this case, what's good news to me is probably going to be bad news for you."

"Yes Peter, I know. You've succeeded in convincing the City Attorney's office that if they went ahead with that weapons charge against me, that you'd fight it all the way to this nation's Supreme Court. You backed them up against the wall Peter, and you did a wonderful job. They caved, like I knew you would force them to do. And as a result of the strong showing you made on my behalf, we did land that big client I told you about, and he insisted on reimbursing us for your retainer check, so it's all yours Peter. Good work."

That's nice to hear. With the Peter Sharp checking account now looking a lot fatter, it might be time to consider a little vacation. Stuart's offered me the use of his condo in Thailand, and on the way there I can stop off on Maui and hang out at my yacht club in Lahaina. If things work out right, I can get caught up on my reading. Maybe I'll get a house in Thailand too. From what Stuart tells me, a non-Thai person can't own real estate there, but like Stuart's uncle did, you can get a beautiful condo or two bedroom home within walking distance to the beach, on a thirty year lease for only about thirty thousand dollars total. Full maintenance and grounds keeping fees are only a couple of hundred dollars a year, so for not too much money, I could have a retirement home in paradise. The only loose end now is the case that just concluded, and there are plenty of questions still unanswered there.

The kid's had plenty of rest for the last day or so, and I'm really curious to know how she did it, but I also know better than to ask her because that never seems to work for me. I'll find out when she's good and ready to let me find out. Myra's been pretty busy putting her case against the women together, so I haven't gotten any info from her either. I'm not going to waste my time calling Snell, so that leaves only one other person. I know that Jack B. did some work for her, so I make arrangements to get together with him for details. He tells me that he only has part of

236

the puzzle and that Suzi's report will have all the answers I need.

Getting used to freedom again, I take a stroll over to the Marina del Rey Junior Market and Liquor store for a six-pack and a can of Laverne's favorite wine. Now that Beverly's out of the picture and Patty seems to be avoiding me simply because of a mere past accusation of murder, it wouldn't hurt to be prepared in the event of my getting a wink and clink some evening soon from Laverne.

Back at the boat, I see that while I was out, the kid put a folder on my desk. I open it and remove a four-page report on everything that everyone did wrong on the case. Of course this is a negative pregnant. That's a funny sounding phrase, but it's a descriptive term I learned once in a law school course on Code Pleading. It means that by the elimination of some words, the phrase is pregnant with another meaning. The classic example is 'he used to be nervous and jerky, but he's not nervous anymore.' She probably means that all of us, including the police and FBI, were totally incompetent and her report will prove it. I'll have to forward copies to both Snell and Chief Olshansky: I'm sure they'll enjoy reading it.

Sometimes I wonder how such a big ego can fit inside such a little girl. The fact that it does is quite evident in her report, which amazes me several times on each page. She points out such obvious clues that we must have been idiots to miss them. It also mentions several things that she discovered by doing a great job of investigation.

237

I know that Jack wants all the answers, and I also owe some explanations to Stuart, Vinnie, and Olive, and the other members of our team, so I invite them all come over to the boat tonight. Suzi makes arrangements for the Asian Boys to deliver the dinner.

It's time for our evening dinner meeting, and I'm not surprised to see that Myra has decided to join us. I don't waste my time anymore wondering how she knows exactly when to show up at the boat, because I know she's got her own permanent little spy embedded here. She probably hasn't seen the kid's report, so she's here to get more ammo for her prosecutions... or because she wants to see me. No, it's for the prosecutions. No sense kidding myself.

Once we're all assembled, we agree that I should give out details from the report, and if anyone's got questions, comments, or observations they'd like to share with us, then they should just jump into the conversation. I love this part of our case because it reminds me of those classic 'showdown' scenes at the end of the old black-and-white detective films. Nero Wolfe used to have one at the end of every one of his cases too, where he would reveal how he solved the mystery and then name the guilty person.

Jack is the one who worked closely with Suzi during the crucial last few days of the investigation, so he starts out by telling us that from what he understood, Suzi was intrigued by the fact that my alleged murder victim's DNA matched Kathy Potter's husband Paul, but his prints didn't match

238

with Paul Potter's. She sensed the same two options that the Chief and I discussed, and like me, she ruled out the fingerprint change and instead went with the identical DNA theory. To go deeper into the blood-relative requirement, she must have had a photographic memory, because way back in the beginning of this case in one of my reports I mentioned the fact that the Chief had told me Beverly Luskin's husband worked his way up from orphan to successful businessman. The fact that Michael Luskin was an orphan opened up a door to the possibility that if there was one orphaned child from a family, there may have been another one too.

While I was incarcerated, Suzi was staying at Myra's house, using her broadband Internet connection and District Attorney passwords to access all of the databases available to law enforcement, so the search field was widened. She read the crime report on Luskin's first death in the street shooting and got his date of birth. With that small piece of information she was then able to search birth records throughout the states for that particular date and came up with a certain amount of paternal and identical births. By following through on those births, she was able to eliminate almost all of them except one pair of twins that was separated, each being sent to a different foster home. The philosophy behind doing things that way was to avoid the necessity of forcing one family to accept two children when there may only have been an opening for one. They also didn't want the twins to bond and then be separated, so the two different homes were used right from the beginning.

Continuing with her research, Suzi was able to track the placement for one of the twins and then found the couple that adopted and raised Michael Luskin.

Working backwards from the couple that had the boy that they named Michael, Suzi and Jack located the agency that placed Michael Luskin and his twin brother.

Knowing that that twins were involved, both being placed with different families, Suzi had the answer as to how there could be a match with the DNA, but not with the fingerprints. She then reasoned that if the most recent victim's prints weren't in any criminal database, then the person killed in Beverly Luskin's house was not Kathy Potter's husband. By a process of elimination, there was only one other person in the world who it could be: Michael Luskin.

That answered a big question. We now know who was shot in Beverly Luskin's house that day. But if Michael Luskin was the person who was killed the day that I was framed, then who was it that got shot down in the street by the guys who stole my Hummer?

By further reasoning about the blood relative requirement, Suzi deduced that the first victim was actually Paul Potter, Kathy Potter's husband, who was Michael Luskin's twin brother. At the time of the murder, his prints weren't taken because everyone in town recognized him. As a formality, they compared his DNA with some blood that had been previously stored for emergency purposes by Michael Luskin, but being twins, the DNA matched, so that was the end of it. Beverly arranged to have the body cremated, so there would be no opportunity for an autopsy to show that the victim's limp was caused by an old prison-fight wound, instead of a recent trip-and-fall accident.

At this point, everyone in the room is still at a loss to understand how those dames could get one twin to kill another, but from what Suzi's report theorizes they didn't have to. The kid figured that Michael Luskin didn't know that his twin was being set up, because up until that point in time, he didn't know that he had a twin brother. All he thought he was participating in was just a plot with his wife to scam the insurance company out of a couple of million dollars, by setting up a drug dealer to get assassinated.

Their miniscule consciences didn't bother them much for that, because it would mean less dope being sold to kids. In their minds they weren't causing a death: they were saving lives of kids and other people who might die of overdoses in the future.

Now that we know the identities of the murder victims, the question still remains as to how these two women got together to begin with, and was it before or after they discovered they were married to twins?

Once again, the answer was be found in one of my reports, because that first day in La Verne when the Chief was telling me how wonderful Beverly Luskin was, he also mentioned that she volunteered on a suicide hotline. At this point I see a light bulb go off over Jack B.'s head, because he now remembers that in one of his reports he mentioned that Kathy Potter mentioned she contemplated committing suicide, and one of the outgoing numbers on her cell phone billing showed that she did call to a Suicide Prevention Center. At the time, we didn't know that is was the one where Beverly Luskin was a volunteer.

This was the first hint of a connection between the two women. By some strange coincidence, that particular incoming call from Kathy Potter was routed to Beverly Luskin. Of course at first they didn't know that they were sisters-in-law, or related at all, but after several conversations on the suicide hotline, they must have exchanged stories about their both being abused. This probably caused them to bond, and in violation of the hotline's rules, they decided to get together.

It's not uncommon for women to show pictures to each other of their family or children, so it was no doubt a shock to both of them when they first noticed the similarities between the appearances of their husbands. They probably also discovered that both men shared the same birthday, and that final fact may have clinched their suspicions about the men being twins with neither one knowing about the other's existence.

Our information told us that Kathy was married to a bad guy, but no one knew that Beverly Luskin was also married to an abuser. For many years television magazine shows have always had good rating successes with stories about identical twins separated at birth, raised by different families, and then reunited as adults. I've seen several of them myself, and it always amazes me how often their

242

lives follow almost identical paths. There was one instance where both twins married women who had the same first name, and the twins both became firemen. The stories and coincidences abound, and in this particular case it was obvious that both twins shared the genetic trait that caused them to abuse their wives, and both women probably exchanged horror stories about the similar types of abuse that they suffered.

In 1951, famous mystery writer Raymond Chandler's story was turned into a movie directed by Alfred Hitchcock. The title was *Strangers on a Train*, and it became a cult classic, featuring Farley Granger, Ruth Roman and Robert Walker. The story was about two men who met on a train and made a pact. They both wanted their wives disposed of, so they agreed that each would kill the other's wife.

We don't know if Beverly or Kathy had ever seen that old movie, but nevertheless, they obviously decided that a similar pact was in order between them. Not having any experience as killers, they brilliantly put together a plan by which they could get others to do the jobs for them.

First of all, there were some obstacles to overcome. Kathy's husband was injured in a prison fight many years before, and he walked with a limp. He also had a full, but short beard.

When Beverly first got her husband to agree to go along with the insurance scam, they both knew that in order for it to work, Michael Luskin would have to make some changes in his appearance, in order to look like the 'double' that his wife found, to be the sacrificial lamb in their insurance fraud scam.

Over the next few months, he grew a beard and Beverly advised him exactly how to trim it. About a week before the first murder, Michael faked a trip and fall in a place where there were plenty of witnesses. He now completed the makeover by having both the requisite beard and limp.

Beverly and Kathy both knew that Paul Potter was dealing drugs, so they decided to let others do their dirty work. They would arrange for Paul's main drug supplier to have a reason to kill him. Kathy used Paul's cell phone to arrange a large buy from his dealer. By using Paul's phone, the supplier would see a familiar number on his caller ID display. Drug deals rarely go down in bright afternoon sunlight, so it wasn't too difficult to have Michael Luskin successfully masquerade as Kathy's husband to pick up the drugs. Because of their many past dealings, the drug supplier extended the usual two days of credit, so that Paul could sell the merchandise and earn the money to pay his supplier. They gave the drugs to Kathy, so that she could sell them to her trailer-park cottage neighbors and build up a little nest egg for future travel expenses.

Of course the real Paul knew nothing about the purchase, so he made no effort to pay his debt. After the deadline for payment to the supplier had gone by, Michael Luskin, pretending to be Paul, called the supplier and told him that he had no intention of paying him, and that he was moving to La Verne, where he was quitting the drug business and using the supplier's money to open up a coffee shop. He was even brash enough to invite the guy to stop by for a free cup of coffee on the day of their grand opening, which happened to coincide with the day that I visited La Verne for the first time.

Not having ever been involved in the drug trade, I'm not sure what the proper etiquette is between a dealer and his supplier, but I'm pretty sure that Luskin, pretending to be Paul, didn't follow the usual protocol when he told the guy that he was intentionally stiffing him out of almost fifty thousand dollars. This is definitely not a good career move if you want to move up the ladder of success in that business.

The next step in the plan was for Kathy to convince her no-good husband to drive to the coffee shop in La Verne, where he could be in place for the assassination. She set up a phony appointment for him with an alleged La Verne millionaire who wanted to spend a lot of money on drugs. Paul Potter believed the story, and drove to La Verne, followed instructions and stood outside the coffee shop, where the local townspeople would think he was Michael Luskin, but the drug dealers would recognize him as their deadbeat dealer.

Shortly after Paul left the Potter cottage, Kathy called Michael Luskin and told him exactly what Paul was wearing when he left the house, and also gave him a description of Paul's vehicle. Michael and Beverly knew that Paul would be arriving in La Verne, so they watched for his truck to arrive, and shortly after the shooting, using the spare keys that Kathy provided them with, they waited until Beverly could get the blood-stained shirt that Paul was wearing when he was shot. Once it was released to her, they bought a matching shirt, Michael put it

245

on, and then he drove Paul's vehicle back to Kathy's trailer park in Oregon, so that he could pretend to be Paul, slap Kathy around, and drive off in a huff. This was the scene that witnesses testified to, and also established Kathy's alibi.

As expected, Paul's drug suppliers didn't turn down the invitation for that free cup of coffee. They drove to La Verne, borrowed a nice yellow Hummer, and cruised down the street looking for Paul Potter. When they saw him on the street in front of the coffee shop, they tooted the horn. Potter recognized them, but had no idea why they were in town, because he was completely unaware of the fact that he had stolen their drug money. He probably thought they were in on the big deal he was supposed to be in town working on, so it must have been a big surprise to him when they greeted him with that barrage of lead.

The rest of that afternoon is history. One of the husbands was now dead, and we now know why Beverly Luskin pleaded for the release of that bloody shirt, as a morbid remembrance of her husband. There was no reason to take fingerprints off of Michael Luskin's body, because everyone including the coroner knew him personally. The DNA test was only performed as a formality to satisfy the insurance company and compared to Michael Luskin's stored blood. The test was done as a matter of course, and not for any criminal investigation, so it became just another non-publicized procedure of the coroner. Michael didn't know that he helped have his long lost twin brother killed.

After they planted the bloody shirt in Paul's vehicle, one of Snell's people helped Kathy have Paul declared legally dead, so she could collect on his Uniman Insurance policy. They were tricked into helping her because she contacted them and offered information on past drug deals and other crimes.

The first time I spoke to Snell about this case, he told me to back off. That warning, along with a complete lack of publicity about Paul's supposed murder in Oregon, gave me a feeling that Snell was trying to protect a witnesses. Evidently, my hunch was correct. And I now know that Snell didn't completely believe Kathy Potter, so he decided to use us to flush out whether or not she was legit.

The next step in the wives' plan was to finish off Beverly's husband, but for real this time.

After his supposed murder in La Verne, Michael Luskin had to immediately go into hiding because there were millions of dollars involved in everyone believing that he was dead. To avoid being recognized, he shaved his head and beard, lost the limp, and grew a handlebar moustache. He never realized that he was the next target of these two women, instead thinking he was still part of the insurance fraud plan. After changing his appearance he hid out in a motel a few miles west of La Verne.

Now that Kathy was able to get around unrestricted by her husband, it was time to finish off the plan by helping Beverly in finishing off Michael. The women both continued to feel that they weren't conspiring to commit any crimes, because other people are pulling the triggers. They were completely innocent and merely enabling others to do their dirty work for them.

These women also both knew that their luck couldn't hold up forever, because sooner or later someone might figure out that there were twins involved. They just wanted to get rid or their abusive husbands, divvy up a couple of million dollars in insurance money, and head for greener pastures. They were both still in their thirties and not bad to look at, so they would have no problem in starting over again somewhere else.

It wasn't too hard for Beverly to convince Michael to meet with Kathy because she helped make their insurance scam possible, and with the loss of only one drug dealer. Kathy wouldn't have to suffer any more abuse, and everyone was a winner. As the women knew, Michael would soon tire of the motel. He thought that with his new appearance it would be less of a risk for him to be in his own house with his wife. It was tricky business trying to sneak in and out of the house at night, and Michael soon got tired of that routine too.

Beverly played me like a jukebox. The only snag was probably when her husband unexpectedly snuck back into the house one night and found her coming in after she had been in bed at the motel with me. This didn't set too well with him, and because abuse was an inborn trait in his family, he took it out on Beverly, resulting in that shiner. And she couldn't complain to anyone, because that would blow their whole plan.

248

Beverly knew that I was coming to town for my big parking ticket trial, so the girls put together the last part of their plan. The finale was supposed to include getting rid of Michael Luskin and pinning it on me. Beverly knew that she couldn't keep up a relationship with me, because she feared I was smart enough to find out the truth about their plans. She also knew that if she disappeared with the money I would sense something wasn't kosher, so there was only one alternative: kill her husband and frame me for murder. Two birds with one stone.

Beverly thought that after refusing me some sexual favors for a while, I would probably not be able to resist her invitation to stop by before the trial. Being the dog that I am, she was right. The only thing left to do at that point was arrange to have someone kill her husband, because they realized there was no way they could trick me into doing it. Here's where Kathy Potter's knowledge really came in handy.

I finally got Snell to admit that Kathy's husband Paul was in the Federal Witness Protection Program. This was a result of a deal he made to testify against Georgio the actor Crescendo, a mobster that the government had been going after for a long time. Paul worked for him a couple of years and knew enough to put him away. Unfortunately, Paul got a little greedy. When his boss found out about it, Paul logically reasoned that testifying for the feds would be a better option then being fired by Crescendo, because the mob's severance package is a little different than those offered by other large organizations.

249

When Georgio heard about the alleged disappearance of Paul Potter and the bullet-ridden bloody shirt that was found, he suspected that it had to be some of the feds' shenanigans, designed to make him call off the contract on Paul's life. Even Snell was suspicious of that phony death when he heard about it and admitted to me that it was the type of trick that the feds might pull.

The girls figured out that Georgio would be the perfect candidate to do their next murder, so they arranged to have Kathy call him and pretend to offer up Paul. At that point, Georgio's suspicions about Snell faking Paul's death were confirmed, so he was very receptive when Kathy acted hysterical on the phone, telling him that she can't stand Paul beating her any more, and that she doesn't care about being a protected witness. She went on to tell him that no amount of money can make her want to stay with Paul, but she has nowhere to go.

Georgio then used a technique he learned from the feds: he made her a deal she couldn't refuse. All she had to do was tell him where he could find his former employee, and the rest would be taken care of. He had no interest in harming her, because she had no first-hand knowledge about any of his business affairs. Once Paul was dead, Georgio knew that anything Kathy would say about him was hearsay, so unless she tried to hold him up for information about where he could find Paul, he had no beef with her. What finalized the deal was when Kathy went so far at to tell Georgio that she didn't even want any of his money for fingering her husband, because the insurance money would help her disappear and go

250

back home to somewhere in the Ozarks. Kathy also gave Georgio a description of how Paul had changed his appearance, complete with shaved head and moustache. All she wanted was for him to use a throwaway untraceable gun and leave it on the floor, so that they could frame someone else for the hit. Georgio especially went for that part of the deal, and the plan was put in motion.

Because my trial was set for the afternoon, they arranged for Georgio and his men to show up in the morning, telling them that the target would be there at ten AM promptly, waiting for some cable repairmen, and the front door would be left open. They told Michael that they were going to take the minivan to the market to load up on groceries for the week, and that while they were gone, the front door should be left open for the cable repair guys. Instead of going to the market, they drove around the block and then parked down the street, waiting for Georgio's men to show up. The front door of Beverly's house was wide open.

Michael Luskin was seated exactly where they arranged for him to sit, looking over the insurance papers that Beverly had conveniently spread out on a table in the room where she wanted Michael to be sitting. She knew that he would be busy reading about all the money they were going to receive and wouldn't pay too much attention to the mafia's cable company crew.

Georgio's car pulled up at the house right on time, and at that point, Georgio decided to do the job himself. Why not? He could save the couple of thousand it would cost to have one of his boys do it, and he wouldn't even have to worry about getting rid of the murder weapon or creating some phony alibi… someone else was all set to take the fall for this one.

Georgio went inside and shot Michael Luskin, thinking it was Paul Potter. He dropped the throwaway gun on the floor and left, completely unaware that the girls were watching from the minivan and Kathy was snapping pictures.

After Georgio completed their work for them and drove away, they went inside the house, messed things up a little, and got ready for their prize sucker Peter Sharp to show up.

That's when they finally did what all criminals usually do in time… they made the one fatal mistake that was their undoing - the poorly timed nine-eleven call that Beverly made, saying that I had just killed someone, not knowing that at the exact time of the call I was standing outside being watched by a Federal Agent and a Chief of Police.

The thing that really bothers me most about this is that they waited so long to tell me that they knew I was innocent. I guess that was their little bit of enjoyment, making a criminal defense lawyer twist in the wind for while. But that also answered the question as to why I was never strip-searched, photographed, or fingerprinted, why my jailhouse meals were catered, and I was allowed to keep my belongings and watch television in the cell.

The exact details of the plan that Suzi couldn't have known were provided by Kathy Potter and Beverly Luskin, because Myra tells us that after she had them brought in for questioning, just like experienced criminals, they both started pointing

252

fingers at each other. True loyalty among friends is a wonderful thing. Beverly, being the faithful person that she is, claimed that she had nothing to do with those murderers who shot Paul, Georgio was an acquaintance of Kathy, and that there was no way that a housewife in La Verne could ever know people like that and get them to commit murders.

We were all sure that Kathy had as convincing a story, but Myra told us differently. Kathy must have made some deal with Snell and the FBI, because she didn't hesitate revealing her total involvement in the schemes. She sounded too confident of the government's protection to lie, so Myra's people believed her.

There's no doubt in my mind that the case would never have been solved without Suzi's efforts. Because I was in plain sight when Beverly made that call, I never was in any danger of being railroaded for the murder of Michael Luskin, but without her investigation, the authorities might not have been able to put together a case against the two women.

After all, who could blame them for a drug dealer making a mistake and killing someone who they thought was the guy who tried to stiff them out of fifty thousand dollars? And why should they be responsible for some mafia kingpin making a mistake and killing a guy that he thought was going to testify against him? Without the kid's discovery of the fact that there were twins involved, the authorities probably would never have been able to figure out who was killed in Beverly's house.

Even after the cops knew that she tried to frame me, Beverly's only liabilities would have been a civil suit from me, and a small fine for the filing of a false police report, neither of which would put her behind bars. At the point of the second killing, Beverly was still home free on the insurance claims, because no one would have dreamed that the guy killed in her house was her husband.

I guess there really is no such thing as the perfect crime, especially when Inspector Suzi is on the case.

There were both good and bad results from this whole case. Getting together with Beverly for that brief time was definitely a good thing. In fact, up until the time that she started shouting about me killing someone, I thought I really had a chance with her.

Unfortunately, I won't be waiting around to give her a second chance, because even if she succeeds in getting a jury to believe about her conspiracy in the murders being one of innocence, her attempts to bilk Uniman Insurance out of three million will definitely put her behind bars. Ordinarily the insurance fraud alone wouldn't necessarily bring too much of a prison sentence, but taken along with the deaths that surrounded it, she wound up with a five year stint at the women's penitentiary, but that sentence will probably be lengthened as a result of a statement that Myra is making on the evening news right now.

"Originally, the two female defendants we arrested contended that they could not be held responsible for the deaths of their husbands because one was killed in a shooting by drug dealers, and the other was killed by a known Mafia hit-man. However, these two ladies did conspire to defraud an insurance company out of money, because they made untrue statements in their claims as to the dates of death of their loved ones.

"Because they did conspire to commit the felony of insurance fraud, and two deaths were caused as a direct result of that conspiracy, we have been successful in obtaining an indictment against them both for first degree murder, under this state's Felony Murder Rule, which states that if a killing occurs during the course of a commission of a felony, all accomplices in the felony are chargeable with murder. Our office is aware of the fact that there have been rulings holding that the underlying subject felony of the conspiracy must be an inherently dangerous one, but we also feel that the recent expansion of the legal doctrine to include crimes such as second degree burglary should support our indictment on the felony murder rule basis."

As expected, there was absolutely no mention of the fact that co-conspirator Kathy Potter has disappeared into the wind. Myra tells me that Snell's people came and took her into Federal custody. I have a feeling that those photographs she snapped of Georgio whacking Michael Luskin have moved her up the food chain of protected witnesses, so she'll probably never be heard from again around these parts. I wouldn't be surprised if she's living in a new trailer and the proud owner of a nail salon in Jerkwater, Arkansas.

Another good thing that I discovered was how good an investigator Jack B. is, and best of all, how much the kid cares for me. She'll never admit to it, but I know the emotions are there. Myra can't figure out what the kid sees in me, but over time maybe the kid will educate her too. Hope springs eternal.

I hear the pitter-patter of large paws, so there must be a dog mail coming in. I see that there are several messages tucked into his collar, so after tipping him with a generous few pats on the head, I start to go through them in order, hoping to find my reward check from Uniman Insurance. It should have arrived last week.

First, there's a Certificate of Completion from my boating class. I can't figure out how this could've happened, because I was in jail during the final exam. A letter attached explains how since I was teaching everything I learned in the class to my legal ward Suzi, when she came in and passed the final exam with flying colors, they assumed that I must have taught her well from my own understanding, so they decided to give me the Certificate. They also thank me for the wonderful party I threw for them, and express their regrets that I wasn't able to attend. They also offer congratulations on my complete vindication in the murder case.

Next is a notice from the Court in Pomona, informing me that when I was unavoidably detained on the day of my trial no bench warrant was issued because the judge was also out that afternoon having emergency root canal work done. They also acknowledge receipt of the legal brief submitted by my office, which showed them the weakness of their case in not being able to prove exactly when my car was stolen, and whether or not it was before or after the allowed twenty minutes of parking had lapsed. A notice of Dismissal of the Charges is attached. And from Uniman:

Dear Mister Sharp:

We have received your personal services invoice for saving us three point two million dollars on the Luskin and Potter policies, but our records indicate that those rewards had already been paid in full before your invoice arrived, per a previous invoice from your law firm.

She did it to me again.

———◈———

The Peter Sharp Legal Mystery Series

#1: *Single Jeopardy*

Attorney Peter Sharp has been wrongfully suspended from the practice of law and thrown out of the house by his soon-to-be ex-wife, a newly appointed deputy district attorney. As a result of the eviction, he's forced to live in their back yard on an old, poorly wired, 40-foot Chris Craft cabin cruiser he's restoring, that is in danger of burning up at any time.

To make matters worse, as the result of trying to help someone fill out some claim forms, he gets arrested for conspiracy to defraud an insurance company. His alleged co-conspirator, a man charged with murdering his own wife to be with a beautiful flight attendant, is about to discover that Peter is also sleeping with her while the man is out of town. As Peter fights to get his law license reinstated, he discovers the secrets behind two murders, a fatal plane crash, and who framed him with the State Bar - all with the help of his legal ward Suzi, an adorable, quiet (at least to Peter) ten-year-old Chinese girl and her huge Saint Bernard.

Peter also gets involved in matters concerning sexual harassment, vexatious litigation, double jeopardy, and a groundbreaking case of *Negligent Nymphomania.*

#2: *...By Reason of Sanity*

In his second Adventure, Attorney Peter Sharp gets retained to defend a man accused of capital murder. The only things making this case a little harder to defend than most others are that the client's acts were captured on videotape, he confessed to the police, and he wants to plead guilty. To make matters worse, the District Attorney's office has brought in a special prosecutor for the trial: Peter's ex-wife Myra.

While he's preparing for trial on the murder case, Peter is also hired to represent an insurance company, to defend it against a man who slipped and fell while inside a bank that was coincidentally robbed later that same day. Peter thinks the case would have died when the claimant was murdered, but at usual, he's wrong.

In this adventure, while Peter is involved representing Vinnie, the prolific, peeing pornographer, he also helps solve several bank robberies by catching the entire gang, and makes the acquaintance of a new friend who runs an autopsy store - all with the help of his legal ward, the adorable ten-year-old Suzi and her huge Saint Bernard.

#3: *A Class Action*

In his third Adventure, Attorney Peter Sharp is retained to represent a man accused of murder, by the planting of bombs in vehicles. The client is also suspected of being part of a conspiracy to assassinate the President of the United States in an upcoming Fourth of July parade.

With the assistance of his legal ward Suzi, Peter cracks the case, identifies the real murderer, and at the same time solves the mystery of a dead body found in his friend Stuart's automobile trunk... all while falling for a lesbian lawyer, winning a Will contest, breaking up a stolen car ring 4,000 miles away, and battling with his ex-wife, who has been elected to the office of District Attorney.

In the adventure's finale, Suzi miraculously manages to get 'Bernie,' her huge Saint Bernard into a courtroom, where she makes her first official court appearance, holds her first press conference, and becomes a local television hero.

#4: *"Conspiracy of Innocence"*

Suzi once again saves Peter's case by finding the connection between two crimes that allegedly took place in different parts of the State, one of which Peter was arrested for. And once again, Peter falls for a woman who he thinks could really 'be the one' this time.

Peter's ex-wife Myra must make the decision as to whether or not she should resign from prosecution of a case in which she may have a conflict of interest – Peter's murder charge.

Everyone including Peter is sitting on the edge of their chairs as this double murder mystery comes to a shocking conclusion that involves a mafia hit man, revengeful drug dealers, a local police chief, and the ever-popular FBI.

#5: ...Until Proven Innocent

Tony Edwards, A dock neighbor of Peter's, is charged with murder. Unfortunately, he is a suspended police officer with a known dislike for people who are the color of his alleged victim. He's also the subject of many citizen complaints for using excessive force in the minority community.

At Suzi's request, Tony has taught her how to help him re-load his target practice ammunition, also giving the little girl a basic course in ballistics.

When a local black movie producer who Tony was working for gets killed, Suzi and talks Peter into handling Tony's defense... which doesn't look too good because he was arrested at the scene of the murder with his gun still smoking.

Along the way, Peter once again gets involved with who he thinks might be 'Miss Right,' represents a 500-pound woman who is being discriminated against, uncovers a white supremist militant organization, and also stumbles onto a group of people who are pirating DVD copies of recently released major motion pictures.

Peter's ex-wife, District Attorney Myra Scot, makes a mistake when she subpoenas little Suzi to come and testify as a prosecution witness against the defendant, Suzi's friend Tony.

After what Suzi does to solve the mystery and destroy Myra's case in court, everyone knows that the District Attorney's office will never subpoena Suzi again.

#6: *The Common Law*

Peter Sharp represents a client with amnesia, who not only can't tell Peter what his own name is, but who also has absolutely no recollection of the crime he is charged with committing. In lieu of his memory, Peter's obtains video surveillance footage that establishes his client's guilt beyond a reasonable doubt.

The usual crew also gets involved, including Peter's close friend Stuart, Jack Bibberman the investigator, Laverne the 'amorous houseboat lady', and Stuart's employees Vinnie and Olive – who are having some disagreement as to whether or not they're legally married; and last but not least, little Suzi B. and her big Saint Bernard.

The law firm is still operating from their 50-foot Grand Banks trawler yacht in Marina del Rey, California… the vessel that Peter still doesn't know

263

how to drive. As in past adventures, all involved continue to visit the local haunts.

One way or another each of Peter's cases winds up being a conflict with his ex-wife Myra, who is the county's chief prosecutor. He also may be more closely involved with FBI Special Agent in Charge Bob Snell than before, as they share a dangerous high-speed situation on a winding road. Suzi's new friend Lotus and her mother also play an interesting part in this adventure as Peter finds that he is fighting a ring of credit-card fraud and identity-theft experts.

#7: *The Magician's Legacy*

Little Suzi has decided that she wants to study magic in this eighth legal adventure she participates in. Unfortunately, her teacher is the main suspect in what appears to be an 'impossible' crime... the shooting of a man in his completely locked 'safe room.'

In order for Suzi to clear her magic teacher of liability for this crime, she must convince Peter to handle the case, which he does under one condition: Suzi must help him by solving the mystery of this locked-room murder.

Her task is made difficult because all events took place in a secure 'panic room,' with steel doors in place, and no windows. Somehow, the alleged murderer is believed to have committed the crime and successfully escaped from a room that could only later be opened by a crew using blowtorches.

Suzi is especially motivated to solve this enigma when she learns that an attorney who she dislikes may be involved.

#8: *The Reluctant Jurist*

There's a mini flu epidemic going around in Los Angeles and it has especially taken its toll among Superior Court Judges in Santa Monica, who all seem to have been infected at the same conference they attended.

Peter has been 'drafted' to fill in as a temporary judge for some civil matters, but winds up getting stuck hearing a big criminal trial involving a devious attorney as the defendant… the same attorney who Peter crossed swords with in a previous situation.

Suspense enters the picture when Peter's legal ward Suzi fails to appear as guest of honor at her own birthday party, and every local state and Federal peace officer in California wants to locate her.

This is the second adventure that Peter and Suzi B. have been involved where Suzi's Saint Bernard may be partly responsible for a successful conclusion.

#9: *The Final Case*

Suzi dislikes a certain devious attorney who Peter keeps coming up against. She feels that he has no business being licensed to practice law in the State of California.

When Peter's new romantic interest invites him to a cocktail party, Suzi and the other guests are shocked by a loud noise down the hall, coming from their host's study.

Other guests at the party include the chief of police, mayor, and district attorney, who unanimously conclude that the dead body they discover is the result of a suicide.

Even Suzi is inclined to go along with their conclusion… until she learns that the devious attorney she dislikes may be involved in handling some legal matters for the deceased.

Suzi won't let go of this one. Against everyone's advice, she keeps working to prove her suspicions about that devious attorney and his connections to what Suzi believes must have been murder.

The conclusion to this mystery is a complete surprise to everyone.

#10: *an Element of Peril*

In this tenth and newest Peter Sharp Legal Mystery, Peter faces a double task: defending a person who is charged with murder, and also trying to locate the missing victim, who was allegedly killed in a completely locked room.

Somewhere behind the tangled mess of a down-ward-spiraling celebrity starlet, a battling married couple, a missing currency trader and a disappearing corpse, attorney Peter Sharp and his legal ward Suzi must find where the truth lies.

As in the past, while Peter's client's trial nears, Suzi has failed to come up with any workable solution that can save Peter from certain defeat and humiliation in court.

#11: *a Good Alibi*

In Latin, the word "alibi" literally means "somewhere else," and to any person charged with a crime, it is an extremely valuable asset to have, because it can mean the difference between an acquittal and a conviction.

However, just having an alibi isn't enough: it has to stand up to scrutiny, because any good prosecutor knows that breaking an alibi and proving it was fraudulently concocted can lead a sure-thing conviction.

In this eleventh adventure of the Peter Sharp Legal Mysteries, Peter is forced into a role he never thought he'd be playing: that of a prosecutor.

#12*: Legally Dead*

Nobody likes a killer, but sometimes you have to put your personal feelings on hold when you're a trained professional called upon to do a job.

When attorney Peter Sharp's former wife Myra calls to ask a favor, he finds it difficult to refuse her, because any occasion to work with her is always a pleasure for him.

The favor that District Attorney Myra asks is for Peter to represent a client in court who wants to plead guilty to a crime. A plea bargain the defendant agreed to is already in place.

Peter agrees to the contemplated one-hour of work as a court-appointed defense attorney and makes the court appearance. But when the case is called, the surprises start, and don't stop until the unexpected end of this twelfth of the Legal Mystery series, during which time Peter gets his first opportunity to defend a dead person charged with murder.

All twelve of the Peter Sharp Legal Mysteries are available at bookstores and can easily be ordered from Amazon.com

To order at your local bookseller or online, simply provide the title's ISBN (International Standard Book Number), or insert it into the online seller's search block.

Single Jeopardy_____ISBN 1-882629-19-1
By Reason of Sanity_____ISBN 1-882629-13-2
A Class Action ISBN 1-882629-66-3
Conspiracy of Innocence ISBN 1-882629-09-4
Until Proven Innocent _____ISBN 1-882629-51-5
The Common Law ISBN 1-882629-39-6
The Magician's Legacy_____ISBN 1-882629-15-9
The Reluctant Jurist ISBN 1-882629-72-8
The Final Case ISBN 1-882629-81-7
An Element of Peril_____ISBN 1-882629-76-0
A Good Alibi_____ISBN 1-882629-84-1
Legally Dead ISBN 1-882629-75-2
The Series is also now available in eBook form. See
http://www.magiclampdigital.com for details

Editor's Note:

If you notice anything you think is a blatant 'typo' or other error, please don't hesitate to contact the author: I don't want to take the blame, because he was the last person to sign off on this book.
Reach him at:
gene_grossman@yahoo.com

About the Author

Gene Grossman worked his way through high school, college and evening law school as a shoe salesman, welder, process server, bail bondsman, tire changer, saloon piano player and 'extra,' appearing in seven major motion pictures.

He then spent 20 years as a trial lawyer, during which time he served as Dean of a small local law school, where he also taught several classes.

His film & video company produced over fifty special interest DVD titles on various subjects that included everything from boating, to bankruptcy. Now retired from the practice of law, Gene writes aboard his yacht in Marina del Rey, California.

You can see pictures of Peter Sharp's boats, yellow Hummer, Suzi's e-cart, and Laverne's houseboat at:
www.petersharpbooks.com

On the next page are some pictures of the author, hard at work on his next Peter Sharp Legal Mystery.

Sometimes he prefers to be alone at sea in his dinghy, and other times he like to work on Catalina Island, in the small city of Avalon.

C.S. Champe

Other books from **MAGIC LAMP PRESS**:

By **EDWIN H. SINCLAIR, Jr.**

SECRETS TO PERSONAL SUCCESS
PUBLISH & PERISH
BUYING FORECLOSED PROPERTIES

By **Dr. NICK SHOVEEN, Ph.D.**

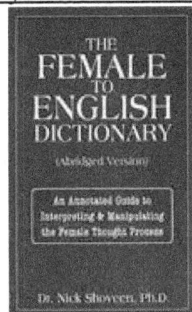  

The FEMALE-to-ENGLISH DICTIONARY
A GUIDE To MEETING WOMEN
HOW TO BE A PORNO PRODUCER

By **BARRY NEAL**
Get Started & Manage Your Comedy Career

Magic Lamp Press also offers several classic books that are now available for your pleasure.

Full details for all of these books, as well as the entire 10-book set of Peter Sharp Legal Mysteries are at:
www.magiclampdigital.com

273